Dear Reader,

I loved writing *Gone in a Flash* for you. Aunt Edie's old photo collections took me back to when my sisters and I went through an album our grandfather had made in 1917. He was a young farmer from Maine, and he went to work for a while on a farm in Massachusetts. We also had a box of his pocket diaries, and in one of them he described going to town to get his new camera before leaving for Massachusetts. Imagine our delight when we realized we had the photographs he took with that camera while he was at World's End Farm in Hingham.

The whole farm at World's End is now part of a park, and part of it is on an island joined to the mainland by a causeway. Later, my three sisters and I were able to visit the site of the farm, and we took copies of the best photos and that portion of the diary to the trustees.

Grandpa usually kept his journal entries very short, like this one from October 22, 1917:

Oct. 22. I helped shingle. I took a picture of the flagpole.

We found a photo of a flagpole in the middle of a cornfield. The trustees were thrilled to see our pictures, especially of corn growing on the island. They said they had suspected it was grown there at one time, but had no proof.

I hope you enjoy Anne's story and Edie's photography adventures as much as I have enjoyed my grandpa Page's.

Blessings as you read,
Susan Page Davis
writing as Emily Thomas

Secrets of the Blue Hill Library

Nowhere to Be Found

Shadows of the Past

Unlocking the Truth

Theft and Thanksgiving

The Christmas Key

Off the Shelf

Gone in a Flash

EMILY THOMAS

Guideposts
New York

Secrets of the Blue Hill Library is a trademark of Guideposts.

Published by Guideposts
110 William Street
New York, New York 10038
Guideposts.org

The characters and events in this book are fictional, and any resemblance to actual persons or events is coincidental.

Every attempt has been made to credit the sources of copyrighted material used in this book. If any such acknowledgment has been inadvertently omitted or miscredited, receipt of such information would be appreciated.

Cover and interior design by Müllerhaus
Cover illustration by Rob Fiore, represented by Artworks Illustration
Typeset by Aptara, Inc.

Printed and bound in the United States of America
10 9 8 7 6 5 4 3 2 1

Gone in a Flash

Chapter One

Anne Gibson drove into the bustling school yard and looked toward the row of vendor booths along one side of the parking lot. She spotted her friend Wendy Pyle spreading a checked tablecloth over a long folding table. At a dozen other tables, people were setting up to sell things. Anne eased her car as close as she could to their spot and got out.

"How's it going?" she greeted Wendy.

"Great," Wendy called. "I unloaded the boxes of costumes you gave me and most of our decorations."

"Feel like carrying more stuff?" Anne opened the trunk of her silver Impala, revealing six cartons of used books and two clear trash bags full of clothes.

Wendy came over to peer at them. "Wow, you sure collected a lot of books at the library."

"People were very generous," Anne said. She pointed to the plastic bags. "I also brought those costumes we made back when you had the library day camp."

"Terrific! I'd almost forgotten about those. Let's put the boxes of books on the table," Wendy suggested. "Then I'll set up the character dress-up station for the kids while you move your car." She glanced around the area. "Oh, and put it way over on the far side of the parking lot, beyond the petting zoo and the rides. They want to keep the whole front area clear for the customers."

"Will do." Anne hefted the first carton and lugged it to the table. By the time she and Wendy had carried all the boxes over and hauled the bags of clothes to the dress-up station, Anne was puffing a little. She peeled off her zippered sweatshirt, welcoming the warm May sunshine. "At least we have great weather today."

"*Mm-hm.* It's supposed to get even warmer later on." Wendy brushed back a strand of her dark hair and looked at her watch. "Better get that car out of here. The gates open in half an hour, and you need to fix the book display."

Anne jumped into the car and complied, trying not to let Wendy's take-charge attitude ruffle her. Wendy had become a very good friend since Anne moved back to her hometown. Even so, their personalities occasionally clashed. Wendy was an outspoken, outgoing go-getter, while Anne was more reserved, but together they made a dynamite team for a project like this. Anne was certain they would raise a lot of money for the library today at the Blue Hill Spring Festival and Street Carnival.

She parked the car in the approved area and sauntered back toward their booth, taking in the varied attractions and wide assortment of vendors' wares. The entire community seemed to have come out to celebrate spring and raise money for their favorite causes. The PTA was preparing for a pie-eating contest, and the Daughters of the American Revolution women arranged handmade quilts on racks in their booth. Other tables held knitted baby clothes and locally made jewelry, and several art students from the high school were selling original paintings, drawings, sculpture, and pottery to fund a trip to visit the large art museums in New York.

As tempted as she was to stop and talk to some of the other vendors, Anne knew she should get back and help Wendy. Her friend was right—they needed to have their booth ready when the gates officially opened and the customers poured in.

When Anne came in sight of their table, she saw that Wendy had finished setting out the signs indicating that all proceeds would benefit the new Blue Hill Library. She hadn't stopped there. She had already unpacked two of Anne's boxes, leaving the books in piles on the table to be sorted.

Anne picked up her pace and hurried behind the table.

"Oh, good, you're back," Wendy said. "Do you want me to take the rest of these books out of the boxes?"

Anne considered that. "All right, but please keep the ones from each box together. I had roughly sorted them at home. One box is all children's, and one is mysteries, and so on."

She plunged into the work, trying to make their table as attractive and buyer friendly as possible. When she had finished setting out all the books, she pushed her glasses up on her nose. They had ten minutes to spare.

"Mind if I spruce things up a little?" Wendy held up a little bag of tiny plastic star confetti. "I promise not to make a big mess or mix up the collections."

Anne smiled. "Go for it. I want to lay out some of the dress-up items and entice those kids in."

A couple of the event volunteers had strung tape across the driveway to keep customers from driving into the area where the booths were set up. People were beginning to congregate outside the festival area, waiting for the gate to open.

"Looks like we'll have a good crowd," Anne said.

She went to the spot where Wendy had left two large cardboard boxes and an old wooden trunk from Anne's attic. All held vintage clothing and accessories, mostly from the collection of Anne's great-aunt Edie. Wendy had come up with the idea of inviting children at the festival to dress up in the old clothes, wigs, hats, and shoes, so that they could pretend to be their favorite book characters and act out scenes from stories they loved.

"This was a brilliant idea," Anne called to Wendy, as she draped a lacy crocheted shawl over the open lid of the trunk.

"Are you sure we don't want to charge anything for the dress-up activity? "

"I'm pretty sure. I'm hoping that while the kids are busy playing dress-up, their parents will be browsing the books."

"True." Wendy came over and opened one of the bags of costumes. "I called Chad and asked him to bring me something to hang clothes on. He'll rig something for us."

"Great. And I brought my digital camera to take pictures of the kids. I'll put them on my computer afterward, and if the parents want, I'll e-mail copies to them."

"Better suggest they make a donation," Wendy said. "That could be time-consuming, and the library ought to get something out of it."

Anne didn't comment. She couldn't see charging outright for something that wouldn't cost her any money, though she understood Wendy's logic. Her time was precious, and, after all, the whole point of their participation in the event was to raise money for the library. If parents asked, she might mention that donations would be appreciated.

She hooked a cane over the edge of the trunk, so that it stood up beside the chest, and pulled out a black dress. She spread out the folds of the skirt, enjoying the feel of the old, crinkly fabric.

"Is that a mourning dress?" Wendy asked.

Anne looked over her shoulder. "That's what I was thinking. I didn't go through all of these things. Do you think I should remove it?"

Wendy laughed. "No, one of the kids might want to dress like the Wicked Witch of the West."

"Yeah, or Old Mother Hubbard. Not." Anne chuckled and laid the dress to one side. She pulled up the next item, a striped cardigan with a shawl collar. It smelled a little of mothballs, but that was probably a good thing—the wool sweater was intact.

The next item was a short blue bolero-style jacket.

"This is kind of cute."

Wendy came over and opened one of the cartons. "Oh, you brought scarves and handbags too. The girls will love this stuff."

"Yes, and I threw in a couple of neckties and Ben's cowboy hat and holster belt, to make sure the boys had something."

"What about this?" Wendy held up a white safety helmet.

"Alex brought that in when I told him what we were doing."

Anne's friend Alex Ochs had helped her with a lot of things, including repairs to the house she had inherited.

"Great addition," Wendy said with a grin. "I'll try to convince my twins to get gussied up. Will you take pictures if they do?"

"Of course." Anne straightened and checked her watch. "Almost time." She and Wendy moved behind the table and sat down in their folding chairs. Anne got out the metal cashbox she had stocked with change.

"You know, this may be the last chance we have all day to sit," Wendy said.

Anne smiled. "You may be right. One of us will need to stay near the cashbox all the time though." She set her camera on the table among the books.

Wendy looked toward the gate. "Well, here we go! You ready?"

"I sure am." Anne needed no prompting to put on her best smile. One of the first people to hurry across the parking lot was Alex, with his nephew, Ryan Slater, and Anne's son, Ben, in tow. Ryan was Ben's best friend in Blue Hill. Ryan lived with Alex, since his parents had died, and Alex's house was not far from Anne's, which meant they saw each other often. So far, she hadn't let the fact that she and Alex had been high school sweethearts nearly two decades ago affect their current friendship.

The boys were eager to get to the games and rides, so they didn't want to stop long at the library booth.

"We'll be back later," Alex promised.

"Have fun." Anne smiled as the tall, handsome builder strolled off with the boys. Alex was comfortable with himself and the man he had become. Hard to believe this was the same boy whose heart she had broken when she'd moved away to New York to pursue her dreams.

The next hour passed in a blur. Wendy supervised the dress-up station, while Anne tended the cashbox and helped the people who were browsing the books. The mysteries and romance novels were going fast.

"Mommy!"

Anne looked up to see her five-year-old, Liddie, running toward the booth with a paper cone of cotton candy in one hand and a small stuffed animal clutched to her chest with the other.

"Hi, honey!" Anne had dropped Liddie off at her "bestest" friends' house that morning, after she delivered Ben to Alex's home. Mrs. Jacobs and her two little girls, Cindy and Becca, were only a step behind Liddie.

Stopping before the table, Liddie turned to Mrs. Jacobs. "Could you hold my candy, please?"

"Sure." Becca and Cindy's mother took the pink confection.

Anne gasped as Liddie ducked down, and then Anne laughed as she realized the little girl had lifted the edge of the tablecloth and was wriggling toward her beneath the table. "You little scamp."

Liddie popped up next to her and hugged her around the waist. "Mommy, look what I got at the beanbag toss!" She held up the toy—a diminutive plush tiger.

"Oh, how cute." Anne admired the little stuffed animal.

"He's very fierce, except when I pet him," Liddie explained.

Anne laughed and looked at Mrs. Jacobs. "Thanks so much for watching Liddie today."

"The girls are having a blast," Yvette Jacobs said.

Liddie tugged on Anne's arm. "When do we get to dress up?"

"Anytime. The clothes are right over there, where Mrs. Pyle is." Anne turned Liddie toward the dress-up station. A little boy was already trying on a vest and Ben's cowboy hat.

Yvette chuckled as her girls scampered toward Wendy. "They're all very excited."

Wendy welcomed the three girls with enthusiasm, and they started picking out items to try on.

"We'll hit the petting zoo after this," Yvette told Anne, "and then the carousel."

Anne nodded. "I figure that by noon, Liddie, at least, will be tuckered out and ready to go home and nap."

"That's what I'm hoping for Cindy and Becca too. I know I'll be tired when we're done here, but it's great seeing them have so much fun together." Yvette scanned the children's books on the table.

"We've sold a lot," Anne said. "I hope you find something you like."

Yvette browsed for a few minutes more and then picked up a couple of books. "I'll take these two," she said as she handed some money to Anne.

"Mommy!" Liddie called. "Help me. I want to be Pippi Longstocking." The last part was muffled, as Liddie's head was immersed in the trunk.

Anne laughed. "I need to stay here with the books, sweetie." Two other mothers were drifting toward the dress-up station with small children, and several people were browsing the used books on the table.

"I'll go help Wendy," Yvette said. "And I'll make sure Liddie comes to show you her Pippi outfit."

"Thanks." Anne glimpsed Liddie pulling on a floppy sun hat. She turned with a smile to help a woman who had selected an armful of books. "Here. Let me give you a bag for those."

She collected payment from three customers and took a deep breath. Their small allotment of history books was gone. Overall, she had sold about a third of the books already.

"Look, Mommy!" Liddie ran toward her, wearing the old striped cardigan, a feathered hat, and a tiered challis skirt. With both hands, she held a camera out to Anne.

"Where did you get that?" Anne took the heavy object from her and held it up close. The Pentax single-lens reflex camera appeared to be a good model, probably fifty years old but in near-pristine condition.

"It was in that attic trunk you took down in the elevator yesterday."

Anne glanced toward the trunk. "I knew I should have sorted to the bottom of that trunk. This must have belonged to Aunt Edie."

"Can I have it?" Liddie asked.

Anne frowned, looking at the top of the camera. "No, honey. It's breakable—and besides, I think it still has film in it." She held the camera down where Liddie could see the top. "See these tiny numbers?"

"Uh-huh."

"That tells how many pictures have been taken on this roll of film. It's on eighteen. There's probably room for at least twenty-four on the roll. But that means somebody took eighteen pictures that are still in there."

"Can you put them on your computer?" Liddie asked.

How times had changed, Anne thought. Liddie probably had no idea what she meant when she spoke about the photographic film. "This is an old camera. Very old." At Liddie's quizzical look, Anne smiled. "Older than me, even. So I think we need to take it to someone who knows how to take out the film and develop it for us. This isn't the kind of camera with a little chip that plugs into your computer."

"Oh." Liddie's face fell but then lit up in a grin as her attention shifted. "Do you like my costume?"

"I love it." Anne stooped to kiss her. "As soon as a few of these people are finished buying books, I'll take your picture, okay?"

Wendy walked over to her. "I just wanted to tell you—after Liddie pulled that camera out of the trunk, I checked to see if there were any more surprises."

"Find anything good?"

"Just this." Wendy handed her a small box.

Anne opened it and gazed down at a jumble of brooches and rings. "Costume jewelry."

"You'd better set it aside with the cashbox," Wendy said. "Find out if any of it's valuable before you let the kids play with it."

"I'll do that. Did you notice that this camera has film in it?"

Wendy shook her head. "She found it and ran straight to you with it."

Anne looked down at the Pentax and smiled. "I wonder what's on the film? There could be some family pictures that I've never seen before."

"Or some pictures of Blue Hill from the past," Wendy suggested. "I remember your aunt taking pictures at a church picnic." She returned to the dress-up area, and Anne got caught up in a deluge of book buyers for the rest of the festival.

That night, even though she was exhausted, it took Anne a long time to fall asleep. The day had been successful, for which she was thankful, but her mind veered away from the new library books she could purchase with the money from the sale. Instead, she wondered what fascinating images were on the undeveloped film in the old camera that she assumed had belonged to Aunt Edie. It was one more in a string of unexpected discoveries since she had inherited Aunt Edie's house and moved back to Blue Hill. As she drifted off to sleep, a smile played at her lips. Aunt Edie certainly had been good at keeping secrets.

Chapter Two

Anne found that breakfast was always a good time to chat with her children, and she tried to make sure it wasn't rushed or stressful before they went to school. On Monday morning, she prepared muffins, scrambled eggs, and a fresh fruit medley while Ben and Liddie got dressed.

Ben zoomed into the kitchen first and set his backpack in the corner near the door.

"Is it okay if I take that library book on airplanes to school? I want to show Mr. Layton the drawings of jet engines."

"Sure," Anne said. "Just make sure it doesn't get mixed in with your school library books."

"I'll bring it home tonight."

"That's fine." She smiled as she set his plate in front of him. Ben read voraciously, and his latest interests were Antarctica and engines of all types. "Did you comb your hair?" His brown mop was getting a little shaggy, and this morning it was in disarray.

"Mom!" he protested as Anne reached out to smooth down a lock. "I'll comb it after I eat."

"All right. And don't forget to feed Hershey."

"I never forget that."

Anne smiled. It was true. Ben and his dog were practically inseparable since they'd adopted Hershey from the pound. The young chocolate Labrador retriever was a terrific companion for Ben, and the boy had taken on the responsibility of his care. Anne had tried to draw the line at letting the dog sleep in Ben's room upstairs, and he had a fenced run near the back porch, where he spent nights in a cozy cloth dog bed.

Liddie came in next, carrying her backpack and a hairbrush. "Mommy, I've got a tangle."

"Sorry, sweetie. Why don't you sit down and eat your eggs while they're still warm, and I'll fix it afterward?"

Liddie set her orange backpack next to Ben's gray one and handed Anne the brush, then wriggled into her chair.

"Let's tuck a napkin into your collar," Anne said, unfolding a paper one. "You don't want to get that cute shirt dirty."

She asked the blessing and then fixed herself a cup of tea while the children began to eat.

After a few minutes, Ben asked, "Mom, are we going to see Grandpa and Grandma Summers again anytime soon?"

"I'm not sure," Anne said. She missed her parents, but she knew they loved living in the balmy climes of the South. "They're getting older, honey, and they prefer to live in Florida now because it's warm and sunny down there, even when it's wintertime here."

"I know," Ben said, "but I wish they were closer. I keep finding things I'd like to talk to Grandpa about."

"Me too."

Ben's words tugged at Anne's heart. She would love to have her family close by, but it seemed God had other plans for her parents. They loved Florida, and living there made oversight of her grandparents easy for her father. His parents, Marvin and Arlene Summers, lived nearby in a senior home.

Since Aunt Edie's bequest had designated Anne to organize and run the new Blue Hill Library in the Victorian house she'd willed to Anne, living anywhere other than Blue Hill, Pennsylvania, was out of the question for Anne and her children right now. Her parents planned to visit several times a year, but that wasn't like having them nearby. They had only managed one visit to Blue Hill since Anne and the children had moved in.

"We should go see them," Liddie said.

Ben scowled at her. "We can't."

"Why not? We could just get in the car and surprise them."

Anne smiled. "It's not that simple, honey. We have school and the library to think about. Florida is a long way from here. But maybe they'll come see us this summer, while it's hot down there."

"Phooey," Liddie said, picking a blueberry out of her muffin. "Are these raisins?"

"No, they're blueberries. You like blueberries."

"Whew." Liddie popped the berry into her mouth and licked her stained fingers.

Anne went to the sink and wet a clean cloth to wash Liddie's hands. "You know, you two could do something after school for Grandpa and Grandma."

"Like what?" Ben asked.

"How about if we make some greeting cards to mail them to tell them how much we all miss them? Wildflowers are starting to come out. We could dry some to decorate the cards. Grandma would love that."

"Yeah," Liddie said. "She *loves* flowers."

"She sure does." Anne took her daughter's hand and gently cleaned each finger. Most of the blueberry stain came off, she was happy to see. "I'm hoping when she visits again that she'll help us add more plants to the flower garden. The cards would be a wonderful way to tell her we're thinking of her and Grandpa."

"Okay," Ben said. "Maybe I can draw a picture of a jet engine for Grandpa." He took a bite of scrambled eggs and chewed thoughtfully. "Mom, did you know there aren't any flowers in Antarctica?"

"No, not really, but I might have guessed that."

Ben nodded solemnly. "They've found some moss and lichen, though, in the summer."

"What's lichen?" Liddie asked.

"It's that scaly stuff that grows on rocks," Ben said. "I'll bet there's a book about it in the Children's Room."

"I'll look today, after I open the library," Anne said. "I know there are books on plants, and Ben is probably right—we're likely to have at least one with pictures of lichen in it. But you two could probably find the real thing outside. It grows on a lot of big rocks."

"Maybe we can look when we pick the flowers," Ben suggested.

"Let's do that." Anne looked at the clock. "Let me work on your hair, Liddie. It's almost time to go." Another blessing since they'd moved to Blue Hill was that the children were now comfortable with walking the short distance to school. Anne had gotten over her initial fears as well, though she still drove them occasionally.

"I need to take care of Hershey!" Ben jumped up and quickly took his dishes to the counter, then dashed out the door that led down to their private back entrance.

A few minutes later, both children were ready and out the door together, bound for the elementary school. Anne cleaned up the kitchen and went downstairs to the library's front desk. She caught up on a few routine chores and had time to locate and set aside a simple book on moss and lichens for Liddie.

When Anne checked her e-mail, she found three requests from mothers who wanted copies of the pictures she had taken of their children at the festival on Saturday. She answered each one, attaching photos of the children in their storybook costumes. She'd fulfilled two other requests the previous evening. The costume station had turned out to be very successful. Maybe next year, she and Wendy could make some simple dress-up accessories to sell. Hats, maybe, and crowns. Definitely crowns.

At nine-thirty, she unlocked the front door and turned the sign to Open. Coraline Watson was coming up the walk with a tote bag of books, and right behind her was Remi Miller, one of Anne's part-time assistants.

"Good morning," Anne called, and the older woman smiled and waved.

"Hello, Anne!" Coraline's green eyes twinkled behind her glasses as she came up the steps. She followed Remi to the checkout desk and dumped out her tote bag, spilling library books, a half-finished knitting project, and a shopping list.

"I can check these books in for you," Anne said, handing her the list.

Coraline stuffed it into the tote bag, along with her knitting and ball of yarn. "Thanks. I hope you got some new romantic suspense."

"Check the new-book display. I think you'll find something you'll like."

Anne had a busy morning, not uncommon on Mondays. Remi and her twin sister, Bella, swapped off to help every Monday, Wednesday, and Friday. Remi was especially good at helping people use the computerized catalog, and Anne turned over a patron to her for a short lesson.

After lunch, traffic slowed in the library, and Anne left Remi in charge while she paid a visit to the *Blue Hill Gazette's* newspaper office, housed in a red, two-story Victorian on Main Street. She loved the old house, which blended perfectly with the architecture of the other downtown businesses.

Grace Hawkins, the editor of the newspaper, had become a good friend, and she stood near the front desk talking to her young receptionist when Anne entered the office. The lovely blonde smiled and came to meet her.

"Hello, Anne. Great to see you."

"Thanks. Are you super busy today? I thought maybe you could give me some advice."

"I'd be happy to," Grace said. "What's up?"

They walked through an archway to Grace's desk, and Anne set down her tote bag.

"It's this." She took out the camera Liddie had found in the trunk of vintage clothing.

"That's a nice old Pentax." Grace took it and examined the camera appreciatively. "A classic 35 millimeter, and it probably still works great. Was it your aunt's?"

"Yes, I think so. We just found it Saturday, in a trunk from the attic. And it has exposed film in it."

Grace nodded. "So you want to get it out and see what's on it."

"Exactly. That film may have been in there for forty or fifty years—I just don't know. But I want to salvage the images if it's possible."

Grace smiled. "I'll have the photographer take a look at it. Even though it's old, if it's been undisturbed all this time, you may have something there. And if it's black and white, Jay can develop it for you right here in our darkroom. He still does that—he likes the quality of the images. If it's color, you'll have to send it out, but at least we can get it out of the camera safely for you."

"Terrific," Anne said.

"The photographer's out on assignment right now, but I can take the film out if you want."

"Sure. I was afraid I'd mess something up if I tried."

"This is actually a lot like a camera I used to own. Old, but very dependable. They take great pictures. But I just use digital now." Grace lifted a small crank on top of the camera and wound it carefully, watching the numbered dial as she did so. "There. It's all wound back into the canister."

She popped the back of the camera open. A roll of film with a yellow, white, and black label sat inside.

"Tri-X black and white." Grace smiled. "Boy, it's been a while since I've seen that. If you don't mind leaving it..."

"That's fine," Anne said. "Let me know when he's had a chance to work on it, and I'll come pick it up. Thanks so much."

Grace closed the camera and handed it to her. "I'll tell Jay to be extra careful."

"Great. I can't wait to see what's on that film!"

Anne went outside and walked toward Kepple's Jewelry Store. When she got there, she stopped on the sidewalk and gave Remi a quick call to make sure she wasn't overrun with patrons at the library.

"Take your time and run your errands," Remi said. "There are only a couple of people here right now."

Anne went inside, enjoying the warmth of the old building. Heidi Kepple greeted her from behind the counter.

"Hi, Anne! What can I do for you today?"

Anne took out a small box containing the items of jewelry Wendy had found in the trunk at the fair. "I wondered if you could take a look at these. They were in Aunt Edie's things. I think they're just old costume jewelry, but I wanted to be sure."

Heidi picked up each piece, exclaiming over the quaint designs of the three brooches and two rings. Her husband, Hank, who had been one of Anne's classmates, came from the workshop area in the back and walked over to stand by Heidi.

"Hi, Anne. What have you got there?"

Heidi showed him the pieces while Anne explained how they'd been found.

"This ring is nice, but I don't think it's a real emerald. You don't usually see them that big." Hank picked up a ring with a large, square-cut green stone and looked at it through a jeweler's loupe. When he lowered it, he shrugged, smiling. "Yeah, it's a fake, but it's a good one. With that art nouveau setting, you might get a couple of hundred dollars for it retail."

"How old do you think it is?" Heidi asked.

"Probably 1940s." He picked up a brooch in the shape of a turtle. "Cute, but made from glass and pot metal. You could probably sell it for fifty or sixty dollars. The ring is definitely the most valuable of these."

"Thanks. That's about what I figured." Anne didn't wear a lot of jewelry herself, and she couldn't imagine wearing the flashy ring. She might put on one of the small pins for a special occasion though. "I like having some of Aunt Edie's things, so I'll probably keep them. Maybe someday Liddie would like to wear them."

"We do buy vintage jewelry, if you decide to sell them," Heidi said, "but I know what you mean. Sentimental gems are the best kind."

Anne put the box back in her bag and headed over to the market for her next task. As she wandered through the grocery store, her mind drifted back to the film in the old camera. She wondered if Jay would have time to develop it today.

After a few minutes, she made herself concentrate and pick out the items she needed. She paid for her groceries and drove home. When she turned in at her driveway, a few cars sat in the gravel parking area. She rolled past a couple of the parked vehicles, recognizing Wendy's and one other. But at the end of the row was a white sedan that looked vaguely familiar. She glanced at the license plate and gasped.

Chapter Three

Anne parked next to the sedan and jumped out of the car. The doors on the visitors' car opened as she ran toward it.

"Mom! Dad!" Laughing, she fell into her mother's embrace. "What are you doing here?"

"What does it look like?" Her father held out his arms, and Anne went to him for a big hug and a kiss.

"I didn't expect you," Anne said, "but I'm so glad you're here!"

"We were purposely vague about our next visit," her mother admitted. "We wanted to surprise you and the kids."

Her father nodded. "That's right, but it was hard to keep the secret. We've missed you."

"You did a great job of it," Anne said. "Have you been here long?"

"Just pulled in," her father said. "We stayed over at Aunt Joanna's last night."

Joanna was his sister, who lived about an hour and a half away from Blue Hill.

"And you didn't call me from there?"

"It was tempting," her mom admitted.

Anne laughed. "Come on in. I was running a couple of errands, but the kids will be home from school soon. They were just telling me how much they wanted to see you!"

Her dad popped the trunk of the sedan. "Where to?"

"The guest room, where you stayed before. We'll all be on the third floor." Anne smiled. "I'm so glad you're here! Use the elevator for the luggage."

"I sure will," her dad said.

Anne looked toward her car. "I'd offer to help with the luggage, but I've got two bags of groceries in my car. I was planning to make tacos for supper."

"Sounds good," her mother said. "I brought a coffee ring for breakfast and an apple pie."

"*Mmm!* I can tell we're going to be spoiled while you're here—and we'll love it!"

Anne hurried back to her car to get the groceries, then followed her parents as they took their suitcases in.

Remi came from behind the checkout desk, eyeing Anne. "Either you have guests, or the library patrons have started bringing their luggage with them."

Anne laughed. "Remi, I think you've met my mom and dad, Charlene and Dale Summers. The kids and I were just talking this morning about when we might see Grandpa and Grandma again, and here they are. They drove up from Florida."

"Nice to see you again." Remi stepped forward with a big smile. "Let me take that for you." She rescued the pie container that Anne's father was balancing on top of a wheeled suitcase.

"Just set it on the table here, and I'll get it later," Anne said.

"Now, don't you have a sister?" her mother asked Remi.

"Yes, Bella, my twin."

"Remi and Bella help me out three days a week," Anne said.

"How nice." Anne's mother gazed around the foyer. "This looks wonderful, Anne!"

"Thanks. I haven't done much since you were last here, except for the exhibits, but you can take a look around after you're settled."

A patron approached the desk with a couple of books, and Remi excused herself. Anne's parents headed for the old-fashioned cage elevator that would take them upstairs. Anne figured it would be quicker for her to go up the stairs to the family kitchen on the second floor than to wait for her father to send the elevator back down for her.

Just as she reached the top of the stairs, Wendy came out of the Children's Room with her four-year-old twins, Ethan and Jacob.

"Hi, Wendy," Anne called.

Wendy rushed toward her. "Let me help you!"

"Thanks. Did you hear? My parents just arrived."

"No! That's wonderful." Wendy grabbed one sack of groceries and carried it for Anne, with the little boys trailing behind. Anne unlocked the door that separated the family quarters from the public areas of the library.

"Normally I'd have gone up the back stairs, but I brought Mom and Dad in through the foyer," Anne said as they entered the family kitchen.

"Well, you're going to be busy, so unless I can help you, I'll get these little guys out of your way. I think we're ready to check out our new supply of storybooks."

"Thanks a lot," Anne said. "Remi will help you. Boys, I hope you enjoy your books!"

Wendy herded her sons out, and Anne quickly unpacked her groceries. She put the hamburger meat and fresh vegetables for the tacos in the refrigerator. She made a trip back down to the foyer for the pie and coffee ring her father had left there and carried them up. Leaving the containers on the kitchen table, she hurried up to the third level to see how her parents were doing.

"I've always loved the view from this room," her father said, turning away from the window that looked out over the hillside and the town below. "I remember when I was a kid, standing here and imagining what was going on in town and where the people were going."

"I love being way up here," her mother said as she hung a blouse in the closet, "but I'm also glad for the elevator."

"It's been a lifesaver with all the cartons of books we've had to haul around in this house," Anne told her. "Do you need anything? I think there are clean towels in the bath."

Her mother smiled. "Everything's lovely. We'll come down in a few minutes. I want a full tour of the library."

"Great. I'll go down and see if Remi needs anything."

As Anne stepped into the hall, her cell phone rang, and she pulled it out to answer it as she walked. "Hello?"

"Anne, it's Grace. Jay's back, and he's working on your film right now. You can pick it up this afternoon if you want."

"Thanks! If I can't make it today, I'll come in the morning."

She continued down the grand staircase, her hand brushing over the mahogany rail. Remi was heading for the Nonfiction

Room with a loaded book cart, so Anne knew the checkout desk wasn't too busy at the moment.

Ben and Liddie arrived about a half hour later, when Anne's parents had just finished touring all of the library rooms.

"Stay here for a minute," Anne told her mom and dad, and she went out to meet the children on the driveway.

"Hey, how was your day?" she asked them.

"Great," Liddie said.

"Pretty good," was Ben's verdict.

"Just pretty good?"

Ben scowled. "We're learning verbs. Verbs are boring."

"What do you mean?" Anne teased. "Verbs are full of action!"

Ben rolled his eyes but cracked a smile.

"I have a surprise for you inside," Anne said. "Guess who's here."

Ben shrugged, but Liddie said, "Mrs. Pyle?"

"No, she was here earlier with the twins, but she's gone now."

"Reverend Tom?"

"No, it's your grandpa and grandma Summers."

"Woo-hoo!" Liddie dashed up the walkway, her curls bouncing.

"Yay!" Ben shouted. He ran after Liddie and soon overtook her. When Anne got inside, she found them engulfed in their grandparents' arms in the foyer.

"How long are you here for?" Ben demanded.

"Oh, we thought we'd stay a couple of weeks," his grandfather said. "If you can put up with us that long." He glanced at Anne.

"Of course we can," she said. "We'll love every minute."

"Where are you sleeping?" Liddie asked.

"They're in the guest room," Anne said. "Same as before."

Her mother smiled and grasped Liddie's hand. "Would you like to go up there with us? I brought you a little something."

"Me too?" Ben asked.

"You betcha," Anne's father said, reaching for Liddie's backpack. "Let me carry that, young lady."

A few minutes later, they had all crowded into the guest room. Liddie sat on the bed, bouncing up and down with excitement while her grandmother opened a suitcase and took out two small packages. She handed one to Liddie and one to Ben.

Liddie ripped the paper off hers and squealed. "Look, Mommy! A seahorse family!" She held up the box of colorful plastic toys.

"Oh, cute," Anne said.

Ben took his time removing his wrapping paper but smiled when he saw his gift. "Thanks, Grandma and Grandpa." He held out his gift to Anne—a small bag of real seashells and a nature guide to help him identify them.

"You probably have a book like that in the library," her father said.

"I don't think so. That looks very interesting, Ben."

"Yeah. I don't get to the shore much. Since we moved here, I don't think I've even seen one seashell." He opened the bag and took out one of the shells and ran his fingers across the smooth spiral, nodding. "This is cool."

"We brought you something too, Anne." Her mother pulled out a packaged set of tropical fruit jellies. "There's a family business that makes these a couple of blocks from our condo."

"Oh, yum." Anne read the labels. "Mango, pineapple, star fruit, and papaya."

"The mango is to die for," her mother said.

"Thank you."

"What is it?" Liddie asked, eyeing the package doubtfully.

"It's jelly made from tropical fruit."

"Do I like it?"

"Probably. It's sweet." Anne smiled at her parents. "Listen, I forgot to get milk when I was out earlier, and I wanted to stop by the newspaper office this afternoon. I left some film there for the photographer to develop. It was in an old camera that I think was Aunt Edie's."

"Yeah, and *I* found it," Liddie said, tugging at her grandfather's sleeve.

"You did? Wow, that's very interesting," Anne's father leaned down to look into Liddie's eyes.

"Yup, I did."

"I can't wait to see what's on the film," Anne told him. "The editor offered to run it through the darkroom at the *Gazette*. Would you mind if I made a quick run? Maybe you'd like to go with me, Dad."

"You go on," her father said. "We'll be fine here with the kids."

"All right. Liddie can tell you all about how she found the camera," Anne said, ruffling Liddie's curls.

"I want Grandpa to play catch with Hershey and me," Ben said.

"And I want to show off my room." Liddie looked up at her grandmother. "I got a new bedspread. It's very pretty."

"I'll bet it is," Anne's mother said. "I can't wait to see it. You can tell us about the camera afterward."

After a reminder to the children to change into their play clothes, Anne drove first to the newspaper office.

"Hi," Grace called as she walked through the door.

"I can't stay long," Anne said. "My folks arrived unannounced this afternoon, and I need to get right home and start supper."

"Well, you're in luck. Jay not only finished with your film, he even made a few prints. I've got them right here." Grace picked up a folder and held it out.

"That was fast!" Anne opened it. On top lay a small envelope marked "negatives" and a glossy sheet of thumbnail views.

"He made you a contact sheet of all the exposed frames, and he did up prints of the ones he thought looked the best."

"How nice of him!" Anne couldn't wait to look at the photos, and she began to flip through them.

"Yeah, he'll do things like that if he's not too busy. He was interested in this, too, since it was your aunt's film, and she used to talk photography with him sometimes."

Anne's excitement grew as she looked at the black-and-white photos. Two were views of the Queen Anne house she now owned, but the rest on the roll seemed to have been taken on a trip. One showed Edie with the Washington Monument pointing skyward in the background. She must have gotten someone on the National Mall in Washington, DC, to snap her picture. The next one featured a sign to an exhibit at the 1976 bicentennial celebration, which Anne vaguely remembered her great-aunt talking about. She was grateful for this evidence that would help her date the photos but disappointed that nobody she knew was in the picture. With any luck, she'd find more with Aunt Edie in them. She turned to the next one and studied the photo, puzzled by what the camera had captured.

"Something wrong?" Grace asked.

"I don't know. Maybe." Anne stepped closer to her and pointed to the picture. "That's Aunt Edie on the left, and this roll seems to have been taken in 1976. She went to Washington during the nation's bicentennial hoopla."

"What fun," Grace said. "That's a real slice of history. But who's that with her?"

"I'm not sure," Anne said, frowning down at the likeness of a tall, smiling young man in military uniform, standing close to Aunt Edie. "At first I thought it was my dad, but on second glance, I can tell it's not him."

"They both look happy," Grace said.

"Yes, and he has his arm around her, so I assume they know each other fairly well. He sure does look familiar." Anne glanced up and smiled at Grace. "I know. I'll ask Dad. He may be able to enlighten me." She closed the folder and tucked it under her arm. "Thanks again!"

Anne dashed out to her car and drove to the market. She made a quick stop for milk and added a half gallon of ice cream to her cart, as well as a container of her father's favorite fresh mushrooms and flavored coffee to help make the welcome dinner more special.

The library had closed by the time Anne got home, and she pulled up in front of the garage to find the overhead door open. Just inside, her father was bent over the old riding lawn mower that had been moldering at the back of the garage since Anne had arrived. She'd been paying to have the yard work done, but now her dad, with a little help from Ben, seemed determined to get Aunt Edie's old mower going. Hershey paced around the garage, alternately going to Ben for a pat and sniffing about the area where Anne kept her garden tools.

She shut off the engine and gathered her purse, grocery sack, and folder of pictures.

"What are you guys up to?" she asked as she approached the open doorway.

"We're fixing the lawn mower." Ben said it with such confidence that Anne smiled.

"Trying, anyway," her father said. "Have you run this thing lately?"

"Afraid not. I tried starting it once, and it didn't run, so I've left it alone ever since. I've been so busy, it wasn't high on my list to get it looked at."

"Will it upset your routine if I get it going and cut the grass?" Her father stood and wiped his hands on a rag.

"No. The young man who does it for me has to bring his mower in a truck, and I know he has lots of other customers. That's why the grass is so long right now—he's really busy."

"Maybe you can cancel him for this week, if I get this thing going. I don't think there's much wrong with it." Dad looked down at her son. "Right, Ben?"

"Right! And Grandpa will teach me to drive it if it works."

Anne frowned. Ben was young to be driving a lawn mower, but she decided to have that discussion with her father later.

The door to the house opened, and Hershey barked. Anne's mother stood on the step. "Anne, you're just in time."

Liddie squeezed past her and ran to Anne. "Mommy, we're making sugar cookies! You can help decorate them."

"Sounds like fun." Anne stooped to kiss her forehead. "You go in with Grandma, and I'll be right there." Anne handed off the bag with the ice cream in it to her mom. As soon as Liddie and her mother had disappeared into the kitchen, she opened the folder of photos. "Dad, could you take a look at this, please?"

Her father stepped closer and looked down at the photo she had placed on top of the stack—the one that showed Aunt Edie and the young man at the bicentennial celebration.

"Do you know who this is with Aunt Edie?" Anne asked.

Her father leaned in and looked closely at the picture. His expression softened. "Huh. That's my cousin Carl. I've never seen that one before."

"I don't think anyone has. It was on the exposed film in the old camera I was telling you about. Carl was Uncle David's son, right?"

"Yes. We were good friends, almost like brothers."

Anne knew that Uncle David was a brother to her grandfather, Marvin. Now she saw the resemblance the young man in the picture bore to him.

"Carl and I were really close when we were teenagers." Her dad shook his head. "I still miss him."

"He died early, didn't he?" Anne asked, trying to put together things her family had told her about Carl in the past.

"Yes. Killed in action in Vietnam. What else is on the film?" He wiped his hands on the rag but refrained from touching the photographs. "I'm greasy."

"Look at this one. It was the frame before the one with Carl." Anne held up the one of the sign.

"Bicentennial?" Her father eyed the photo keenly, his eyebrows drawing together in a frown. "How can that be?"

"These pictures were taken in Washington, DC. Aunt Edie went there during the 1976 celebration."

"But that's impossible! I mean, Carl…" Her father shook his head. "Let me see that first one again."

Anne held it up. "I've seen him in other family pictures, but it's been a long time, and I never knew him. But you're sure it's Cousin Carl, right?"

"It can't be," her father said slowly.

"What?" Anne glanced at Ben, who stood impatiently near the lawn mower, watching his grandfather and then her. "Why do you say that?"

Her father let out a deep breath. "Because Carl died in 1970."

Chapter Four

Anne stood very still, holding the picture so her father could continue to examine it without touching it.

"Are you sure it's him, Dad?"

Her father nodded slowly. "There's nobody else in the family who's the right age and could look that much like him. Are you certain this was taken in 1976?"

Anne nodded. "There were photos from the bicentennial exhibits before and after it on the roll."

"Okay. Let me think about it."

"I don't think he's in any of the other photos. The photographer only printed six—and there were eighteen on the film, so I'm not sure." Anne tucked the picture into the folder and closed it.

"I'll look at them all after I've washed up," her father said.

"Grandpa," Ben said as he eyed him anxiously, "are we going to finish fixing the lawn mower?"

"You bet we are." He turned back to Ben and the balky mower. "We'll get it running, and then we'll get cleaned up for supper."

Anne turned away, disappointed that they couldn't immediately get to the bottom of the photo mystery. She told herself to practice patience and went into the kitchen. Her mother had put the food items away, and Anne joined her and Liddie for a riotous half hour of cookie decorating while the meat for the taco filling simmered on the stove.

The roar of the lawn mower engine caught their full attention.

"Well!" Her mother grinned. "Sounds like the men have succeeded in their mission. We'd better clean up here and set the table."

Anne went downstairs and opened the door to the garage. Hazy smoke filled the air, so she paused just long enough to give her father and Ben a thumbs-up, then shut the door again. She went back to the kitchen and quickly chopped tomatoes and lettuce, while her mother got out cheese, salsa, and other taco toppings. Liddie helped set the table.

Over dinner they discussed the mysterious photograph, and when they had finished, Anne's mother asked to see it. "That certainly looks like Carl," she said. "I don't know who else it could be."

"It's him," Anne's dad said with more certainty than ever. "Growing up, we were more like brothers than cousins."

"That's why he looked so familiar," Anne said. "I saw a lot of pictures of him in your albums. That, and he looks a lot like Uncle David."

"Yes, he does," her father said, flipping through the other pictures Jay had printed. "These do all seem to be from that one trip—except the two of this house."

"They were at the beginning of the roll," Anne said. "She must have snapped them before she left for Washington."

"It's a puzzle," Mom agreed, "but right now I think we should have dessert."

"Yay," Liddie said. "Can we have some of the cookies?"

"Yes."

Ben's face lit up. "Grandma, can we use some of the jelly you brought and make sandwich cookies?"

Anne's mother arched her eyebrows at Anne. "What do you say?"

"Why not?"

The children ran to the counter with their grandmother to prepare a selection of cookies. Anne got up and poured milk for Ben and Liddie, and coffee for herself and her parents. A few minutes later, they all agreed that the cookie experiment was a good one.

"But I think you'd better stop after two," she told the children.

"Maybe you can take some to school tomorrow," Anne's mother said, and Liddie's frown disappeared.

Anne sat back in her chair and sipped her coffee. "Thanks, Mom. I know you're tired, but you're great with the kids."

"No problem." She picked up one of the jelly jars. "I think it's nice that these jellies were made by a family business, with all the family members working together."

"That would be a fun way to make your living," Anne said. "Assuming the family members get along well, of course."

"They seemed like nice people," her mother said. "It makes me glad we could take this trip and be with our family for a little while. We'll make the most of our time here." She looked fondly at the children and sighed. "Isn't it great having three generations of the family under one roof?"

"It sure is." Dad reached toward the plate of cookies and then drew his hand back. "Guess I should quit now too."

"I just had an idea." Anne sat up and glanced at her mother and then her dad. "What if I invited everyone in the family to come for a Summers family reunion?"

"When? Now?" her father asked.

"Yes, while you're visiting."

"It would be rather short notice, wouldn't it?" her mom said.

Her dad pursed his lips. "I'm not sure how many of them could come, but we could try. Your grandparents can't be here, of course."

"They're too frail to fly up here on their own," Anne's mother agreed.

Her dad shook his head. "Not this time. But we could invite anyone else who's close enough."

"We could at least make some calls and see if anyone's interested," Anne's mother said. "I'm sure Joanna and Philip would come, and maybe some of their children. You've got cousins within a couple of hours' drive too, haven't you, Dale?"

He nodded. "A few. And some of them I haven't seen in ages."

"I think it's a wonderful idea," Mom said.

Anne smiled. "All right, then. Dad, you'll have to help me with the guest list, so we don't miss anyone."

"Oh dear, I wish I'd brought my address book." Her mother glanced around. "But I suppose I can find some of them online."

"You can use my computer," Anne told her. "When should we have it? How about Sunday afternoon?"

"Better allow them at least a week to get their plans together," her father said.

"A week from Sunday, then." Anne walked over to the calendar and wrote a note on the second Sunday to come. "That's Memorial Day weekend. Do you think that's okay?"

"It'll have to be," her father said. "If people have other plans, they just won't come."

"All right. Now for the menu…" Her mother held out her hand for the pen. "Of course we'll want Aunt Edie's dill potato salad?"

"I love that." Anne sat down and made some suggestions for the menu.

"Don't forget sandwich cookies," Liddie said.

"I wonder if I could finish the deck by then," Anne's father mused.

Anne looked up at him. "Deck? What deck?"

"Exactly, dear," her mother put in. "We were saying this afternoon that you need one. It would be perfect for a family barbecue, don't you think? It would make the backyard so much more inviting."

Her father nodded. "Benches, flower boxes, a picnic table. I can picture it now. Two levels, maybe."

Anne held up one hand. "Let's not get too carried away, now. That sounds pretty elaborate."

"All right, one level. But next summer I can come back and add onto it." Her father pulled out a pocket notebook and settled happily in his chair to make a few sketches. "Redwood, do you think?"

"Sure. But I keep thinking about those pictures." Anne reached over and flipped open the folder. "It's so weird." She took out the contact sheet and held it close. "There are others that Jay didn't print, but most of them don't have people in them, or at least, not up close. Some have tourists out in front of the exhibits."

Her dad nodded. "Have you found any of Edie's other pictures? I remember her taking a lot."

"Some. There was an album in one of the bookcases, but it was full of more recent pictures than this. Maybe there are more in the attic. I haven't had time to go through even a tenth of the stuff up there."

"Maybe you should look," her dad said. "You might find some others from the '70s."

Anne smiled. "Want to go exploring after the kids are in bed?"

"That sounds like fun."

Her mother stood and gathered up cups and glasses. "You go ahead and get the kids to bed, Anne. I'll start the dishwasher."

The bell for the back-door intercom rang, and Anne frowned. "Excuse me. I have no idea who that is." She went over to the side wall and pressed the button on the intercom. "Hello?"

"Hi," came Alex's voice. "It's me and Ryan."

"Oh, hi. Come on in." Anne pressed the remote button to unlock the door for them and hurried around to meet them at the top of the stairs. Alex and Ryan climbed up to her level. Both were dressed casually in jeans and sweatshirts.

"Hello, Ryan," Anne said. "Ben's in the kitchen. My parents are here, and we had a late supper."

"I heard they'd arrived and thought I'd stop in to say hi," Alex told her as Ryan dashed away to see Ben. "I hope it's not too late."

"They'd love to see you," Anne assured him. "Come on. I think there are some cookies and coffee left."

Anne's parents greeted Alex warmly.

"What are you up to these days?" her father asked.

"I'm putting an addition on a house on Hill Road," Alex said. "How long are you folks going to be able to stay?"

Anne's mother smiled. "We just started planning a family reunion, so it looks like we'll be here a couple of weeks."

"Great." Alex accepted coffee, and he chatted for a few minutes with Anne's father while she helped her mother clear the table and clean up the kitchen. When he heard about Dale's proposed project of building a deck on the back of the house, Alex offered to help.

Her father grinned. "If you've got some free time, I won't say no."

"I should be done with the job I'm on now in a couple of days," Alex said.

"If you're going to work with Dad during business hours, I'll pay you," Anne said.

"In that case, I'll come in my off hours."

"*Hmm*. We'll talk about that later," Anne said. She didn't want to take advantage of Alex's professional skills, but she didn't want to fuss about money in front of her parents either.

Half an hour later, when Alex and Ryan had left and Anne had tucked Liddie and Ben in bed, she and her dad climbed the narrow attic stairs. The room didn't cover the entire house—the foyer that was now the main room of the library soared all three stories high. But over the other rooms, there was enough space for an attic that could hold the wares of a department store.

"Aunt Edie apparently never threw anything away," Anne said apologetically as she switched on the bare overhead lightbulbs.

"That's the best way to stock an attic," he said with a grin. "Any ideas on where to start?"

"Over here, maybe?" She turned to one side, where stacked cartons and odd bits of furniture vied for floor space. "We have to be careful not to get sidetracked though. We're looking for photos."

"I'll keep it in mind." Even as he spoke, her father picked an old Bakelite radio out of a pasteboard box of odds and ends. He held it up toward the light and examined it.

"Dad, that is not a photo album."

"Huh? Oh, right." He placed the Philco radio back in its nest.

Anne laughed. "You can have that if you want it."

"No, no. Just interesting. Maybe Ben and I can take it apart sometime. We might even be able to get it working. Wouldn't that be great?"

"Ben would love it."

He lifted the flaps of a carton. "This looks like old copies of the *Saturday Evening Post.*"

"That will make interesting reading sometime," Anne said, "but not tonight." She spotted a small leather case, smaller than a piece of luggage. "Hey, this looks like it could be an old camera case." She picked it up and carried it over to her father.

"I think you're right." He set it on top of an antique cherry end table and undid the clasp. Peering inside, he let out a low whistle. "That's an oldie."

"I'll say. Older than the one Liddie found." Carefully, Anne lifted out the bulky camera. "It looks like it took rolled film," she noted.

"I'm thinking it's from the '40s, or maybe even the '30s," her father said. "It's a Kodak. I'll look it up on the computer later."

They set the case aside. A little more browsing turned up several albums and two small boxes of loose photographs and envelopes of negatives. They put those with the camera case. Anne was just about to call it quits for the night when her father found another, older camera.

"Oh man, this is one that used glass plates."

She hurried between the boxes and bric-a-brac to his side. He was looking into a sturdy old wooden crate at a large antique camera, flash pan, and tripod.

"Wow! I wonder if Aunt Edie used this."

"I'd say it was before her time—unless she tried it as a hobby."

"I just had a thought," Anne said. "I could do a photography display in the library and show off some of these old cameras, along with some of Aunt Edie's photos."

"The people in town would love that." Her father gestured toward the albums and boxes they had stacked near the stairs. "I saw some great pictures of Blue Hill, and I'll bet you'll find more as you go through all that stuff. You could do an exhibit of her work through the decades."

"Great idea. And maybe we can figure out which photos were taken by which camera and show them together."

It took them two trips to carry all of their finds down to the family living room.

"I'm beat," Anne said.

"Me too. Maybe we can dive into this stuff tomorrow, while the kids are at school."

"Right. Oh, and Dad, I meant to ask if you'll give Ben a haircut while you're here."

"Sure. Any special time?"

"No. Well, before the reunion."

Her dad laughed and bent to kiss her on the cheek. "Good night, Anne."

"'Night, Dad." She tiptoed to her room.

When Anne crawled into bed, she was exhausted, but she began to thank God for the many blessings the day had brought. As she reached to turn out the lamp, her gaze fell on the photo of Aunt Edie and Carl, which she had placed on her nightstand.

She looked at it for a long time. Nothing in the picture gave her any clues to the mystery of its origin. Carl had been a soldier, and he appeared to be wearing his dress uniform. Maybe that would tell them something. The idea that the snapshot was taken several years after the young man had been declared dead intrigued her. There was definitely more to this story.

She put the picture down carefully and snapped off the light. If Anne had anything to say about it, she would uncover the truth behind the unexpected image and this missing family member's appearance at the wrong place and time—or at least the wrong time.

Chapter Five

Tuesday morning was a flurry of motion in the family kitchen, as Anne and her mother fixed breakfast for the children and helped them get ready for school.

"I thought I'd take your mother to the diner for breakfast, for old times' sake," Dad announced when he came down from upstairs.

Anne looked around at the messy kitchen. "I don't blame you."

He chuckled. "We don't have to..."

"No, you go ahead. I'll have a little time before the library opens to work on the guest list for the reunion."

"Oh yes," her mother said. "We need to get the invitations out soon—today if possible."

"Liddie, don't forget your sweater," Anne said as her daughter got up from the table.

"Would it help you if we dropped them off at the school?" Dad asked.

"Oh boy!" Ben said. "Can we ride with Grandpa, Mom?"

"I guess so," Anne said, knowing she would actually be more at ease if the children weren't walking today. "Just don't expect him to take you every day."

Her mother quickly loaded the dishes into the dishwasher while Anne cleaned the table and counter. By the time her parents and the kids headed down the stairs, the room was fairly presentable, and Anne felt justified in going to her computer.

Her first task was to type a list of people they would invite. She wrote down Grandpa Marvin and Grandma Arlene Summers, though she knew they couldn't come; her father's sisters, Joanna and Faith, and their families; and Carl's sister, Pauline Stowe, as well as a distant cousin, Madeline. As nearly as she could tell from her father's explanation, Madeline was actually the granddaughter of great-grandpa John Summers's brother.

A little disappointed, Anne perused her list. Surely there were more members of the Summers family she could include. Unfortunately, her mother's kin lived too far away to drive to Blue Hill for the reunion. This would be Dad's family, and it had shrunk over the years to a fairly small bunch.

She had been envisioning a grand event for this party, but now it was beginning to look like a small get-together. She felt like a pressure cooker with the valve removed, and her steam was rapidly escaping.

The front doorbell rang, and she glanced at the time in the corner of her screen. Only five minutes until opening time. She hadn't realized how late it was getting, and now a patron had come a little early.

She dashed down the stairs and across the foyer to unlock the big front door. Mildred Farley stood on the steps, clad in an eggplant-hued pantsuit, smiling as always and carrying the hardcover mystery she'd borrowed last week.

"Hello, Anne. Am I early?"

"Not really. Come right in." Anne hung the Open sign and led Mildred into the side room, where the checkout desk stood.

"I heard from Grace that your parents were here, and I really came by to say hello to Dale and Charlene."

"They'll love it, but you'll have to wait a little while. They went to the Keystone Cafe for breakfast." Anne reached for her book. "You're welcome to keep me company until they come back."

"Sounds like fun. I'll let you check that book back in."

"Did you enjoy it?" Anne asked as she went through the routine to clear Mildred's account.

"Yes, it was cleverly written. I'd try another by the same author."

"Great. We have several of hers."

When they had located the next mystery, no other patrons had arrived, and Anne invited Mildred to sit down with her in the History Room.

"What are you up to while they're here?" the older woman asked.

Anne smiled. "We've decided to throw a Summers family reunion of sorts, and Dad sees that as an excuse to build me a deck out back."

"Oh, nice. You'll enjoy that."

"Yes, we will. But I'm finding that the family is smaller than I'd realized. I'm not sure I'll be able to get enough folks together to make a party."

"Dale will be glad to see anyone who can make it."

Anne sighed. "I'm sure there are more relatives out there, but I don't know how to find them. Dad couldn't even remember

Cousin Madeline's last name, and he doesn't remember very many of Grandpa's cousins. I wish I could invite any who are still living."

"Is your grandfather Marvin coming?" Mildred asked.

"I'm afraid not. He and Grandma have some health issues, and Mom and Dad agreed we couldn't ask them to fly up here."

"Maybe you could call him and your grandmother for ideas on the extended family. They might be in touch with some of the cousins' children."

"You could be right."

"And you could always check an online ancestry site."

"That's a good idea," Anne said. She had used a family history Web site before, to find information on one of Blue Hill's older families.

Mildred told her the name of the site she liked best for working on her family tree. "You can post on a message board there, under your family name. Ask anyone who might be able to provide information on other undiscovered family members to contact you."

"That sounds like a good way to do it. I can ask for information on descendants of...*hmm*...I think Grandpa Marvin's father was John Summers. I'll double-check with Dad on that."

"There you go. Search for his descendants. You may even discover someone who has done a family tree or a Summers family history."

"That would be something, wouldn't it?" Anne thought of the photos she and her father had puzzled over. "Mildred, can I show you something? I found one of Aunt Edie's cameras with some film still in it, and I had it developed. One of the pictures really has me puzzled."

"I'd love to take a look."

A few minutes later, Anne placed the photograph of Edie and Carl in Mildred's hands.

"Oh my. Isn't that one of her nephews?"

"Yes. We believe it's Uncle David's son, Carl," Anne said.

"When was this taken?"

Anne told her about the strange timing and the mystery behind the photograph.

"That certainly is odd," Mildred said. "I don't know a lot about Carl, but I do recall Edie saying the young man feuded with his father."

"Uncle David?"

"That's right. After Carl's mother died."

"That would be Aunt Natalie," Anne said, reaching into her memory for anything about a fight within the family.

"It seemed as though David wanted his son to become a partner in the family business, and Carl didn't want to. David couldn't forgive him for refusing."

"They had a furniture store," Anne said.

"That's right. I remember your aunt Natalie. She worked in the store a lot, and Edie said that David wanted Carl to take over her responsibilities. I guess he felt it was his son's duty, but Carl wanted to live his own life."

"I never heard about any of that." Anne frowned. "Did Edie tell you anything else about Carl?"

"Not really. She mentioned him now and then, especially while he was overseas, but I wouldn't say she really told me much."

"My dad said he was killed in action."

"Yes, but..."

"But what?" Anne asked.

Mildred shrugged. "I always wondered. From the way Edie acted, it seemed there was more to it than that. She never said right out, but I wondered if the army was wrong."

"Wrong about what?" Anne stared at her.

"Oh, please. I didn't mean to start a rumor or to upset you. There were just one or two little things she said that made me think maybe Carl wasn't killed when the army said he was. Maybe they made a mistake, or maybe...I don't know, maybe they had deliberately misled the family."

"You mean...maybe he died on a secret mission or something? Wouldn't they tell his folks?"

"Probably."

"And if it was a mistake, and he was still alive, I should think he would have told his family, even if the army didn't."

"One would think so, wouldn't one? Unless he didn't want his father to know." Mildred smiled. "There, I've got you all in a tizzy, and I didn't intend to do that. But this picture at the bicentennial...well, it does give one pause."

"Yes, it does," Anne said.

"I wonder where exactly they were when this picture was snapped?"

"I'm not sure," Anne said. "I thought it was somewhere along the Mall."

Mildred peered closely through her glasses at the photo. "Maybe, but I don't see the Washington Monument or anything like that. To the side here, there's a building, but you can't see much of it. I wonder if you could find out what it is."

Anne leaned over and looked where she pointed. "I can try. It has white columns, but a lot of buildings in Washington do." She looked up suddenly as an idea struck her. "What's that building they use in movies because it looks like the White House?"

"I'm not sure." Mildred gazed down at the glossy picture. "It can't be the White House, but, yes, I see what you mean."

"I'll check online," Anne said. "Several other well-known buildings are in her pictures. Maybe I can find this one."

Mildred stood. "Where did you say your folks went to eat? The Keystone Café?"

"That's right."

"Maybe I can catch them there."

Anne was about to protest when they heard the front door open. She jumped up. "Sounds like someone else is here."

"I'm going in search of Dale and Charlene. Thank you, Anne—and don't put too much stock in what I said about Carl. I was only speculating."

"Of course." But Anne knew it would bother her until she knew the truth.

In the foyer, she found two homeschooling mothers with a total of five children, ages two to eight, headed for the Children's Room.

"Hello," Anne said. "Can I help you with anything?"

"We're starting a new unit on birds," one of the mothers said.

"We have some beautiful books on birds," Anne assured her. "Some are in the Children's Room, but there are also a couple of very nice ones in the Nonfiction Room. One was recently donated by Coraline Watson. You might want to use one of those as a reference for your unit."

The other mother smiled. "My family is just here for storybooks and a biography of George Washington, if you have a simple one."

"I think we do. Go on in and look around," Anne said. "I'll be right with you, after I help our friends find the bird books."

After a busy hour, Anne had another lull, when the only two patrons in the library were quietly browsing the shelves. She sat down at her computer and went to the ancestry site Mildred had told her about. At least she could put out feelers for distant relatives.

By the time she was needed to check out books, she had posted information about the upcoming reunion and asked for help in locating family members.

She turned to greet the patrons with a smile and scanned their books to check them out. They chatted for a few minutes. When the women had left, Anne realized she was once again alone. She picked up the photograph and gazed at Carl's face. The picture intrigued her more than ever, now that she knew about the rift in the family. Was that what had led Carl to enlist in the army? Or had he been drafted?

Since her parents had not yet returned, she assumed they had connected with Mildred. She might have time to do some more investigating via computer. Anne smiled to herself. Might as well start at the top.

Chapter Six

With a triumphant smile, Anne clicked on the contact form on the US Army's Web site. "Submit your question about veterans here," the banner read, so she carefully typed in her request for information about Carl Summers's military service. Finding the right place to inquire had taken her a while, but she was confident she had found the right page and that someone out there would read her message and help her.

With that done, she began a search for phone numbers of men named Carl Summers. However, the name turned out to be so common that she felt overwhelmed by the hundreds of listings. She decided to narrow the search to Pennsylvania. Perhaps he had lived near Washington at the time of the bicentennial though. He'd been near enough to meet Aunt Edie there. Of course, if he'd been stationed on a military base at the time, he probably was no longer there. But in that case, the army wouldn't have said he was dead, or at least would have corrected their mistake—wouldn't they? Anne didn't find it hard to believe there had been a mistake, but one that hadn't been corrected for more than forty years?

A little confused and slightly discouraged, she printed out lists of the Carl Summerses and C. Summerses in Pennsylvania; Washington, DC; Maryland; and Virginia. Even that was more than she could comfortably handle.

She punched in the first number on the list and got a busy signal. Anne considered what she would've said if someone had answered, and decided that she needed to work that out before she made any more calls.

The entire thing was a bit daunting. Maybe Mom and Dad would help her tackle the list this evening. The front door opened, and she peered out into the foyer, expecting to see her parents returning, but it was a regular library patron.

Time to get back to work, she told herself. She took a last glance at her e-mail server and saw a message from an address she didn't recognize. Probably another mom wanting pictures of her child in costume.

"I'll be right with you," she called to the patron.

"No rush," the man replied.

Anne opened the e-mail message.

Hi. I saw your post on the ancestry site. My name is Heather Dailey, and I live in Ohio. As nearly as I can tell from the info you posted, we're third cousins. Or something like that.

Anne laughed in delight. It had worked! Just wait until Mildred heard about this.

Quickly, she typed in a reply: *Fantastic! I'm at work right now but would love to chat later. We're planning a family get-together soon, and you're welcome to come.*

Anne shoved back her chair, avoiding the temptation to see if Heather replied right away. About ten minutes later, her parents came in.

"Hi, honey," her mother said cheerfully. "Sorry we were gone so long. Mildred came to the diner and we had a nice long chat, and then we stopped at the Thrifty Drugstore. That place has hardly changed at all."

"I know," Anne said. "We love it."

"We'll get out of your hair," her father said, looking around at the handful of patrons now using the library.

Her mother lowered her voice and said, "I'll fix lunch. Do you take a lunch hour?"

"My friend Wendy is going to come in at noon and spell me for a couple of hours," Anne said, looking at the old pendulum clock on a shelf between the windows. "Wow, that's less than an hour from now."

"The morning just flew," her mom agreed.

"Well, I have stuff to tell you—about the reunion. And Dad, I made a list of people I thought we might try to call later. People named Carl Summers."

Her father's face went sober. "You think he's still alive, then?"

"I don't know," Anne said. "Do you?"

The front door opened, and three women came into the foyer.

"We can discuss it over lunch, I guess," Anne said.

"Okay," her dad said, "Do you think it would be too noisy if I mowed the lawn now? I'd rather not wait until tonight."

"You have to do it sometime."

"I'll start out, and if the folks using the library complain, you come tell me, and I'll stop."

"It's a deal." Anne knew Ben would be disappointed if he didn't get to run the mower, but she'd feel better if the job was done while he was at school.

Her parents went off up the grand staircase, and Anne went to greet the newcomers.

To her surprise, the women represented the local chapter of the Daughters of the American Revolution.

"I'm Elizabeth Wayland, the chapter regent," said the leader. "We heard you have a small collection of local history books."

"Yes, we do. It's smaller than I'd like." Anne wondered if she had anything these women would find specific enough for their research needs.

"We love libraries," one of them said.

Mrs. Wayland nodded. "Yes, and if we find a library is trying hard to serve the community, we sometimes donate historical and genealogical books for their collection."

Anne caught her breath. "That's wonderful. Let me show you to the History Room."

She ended up giving them a complete tour of the library. When they ended at the checkout desk, she took a moment to tell them about Aunt Edie's bequest to the town so that Blue Hill could have its own library.

"Oh, isn't that a picture of Miss Summers?" One of the women pointed to the photograph Anne had left lying beside her computer.

"Yes, it is."

"I knew Miss Summers," the woman said. "She was very civic minded."

Anne picked up the photo. "We think this is a nephew of hers with her in Washington."

"Look, Elizabeth," the woman said.

Mrs. Wayland sidled close to her. "What?"

The other woman pointed to the photograph. "Isn't that Constitution Hall?"

"It certainly is."

Anne's pulse raced. "That's it! I was trying to think what it was called. Aunt Edie traveled to Washington in 1976 to see the bicentennial celebration. So, you recognize the spot?"

"Oh yes, that's the DAR's national headquarters," Mrs. Wayland said. "I go every year for National Convention."

"Are you certain?" Anne asked.

"Absolutely."

The third woman scrutinized the photo and agreed.

"Thank you very much," Anne said.

"Perhaps we could take a closer look at your county histories," one of the women said.

"Of course. We only have two so far, but I'm watching estate sales and online auctions for more."

"It would be nice if you could build a local genealogical collection too," Mrs. Wayland said as they walked toward the History Room.

Wendy arrived ten minutes later with her four-year-old twins in tow. Anne quickly filled her in on the patrons currently in the building.

"There are three women from the DAR in the History Room," was her final announcement. "I talked to them and showed them what we have so far. They said their chapter would consider donating some history and genealogy books to help us build our collection. Right now they're browsing in there."

"Wow, that's great," Wendy said. "I'd go in and say hello, but I need to keep the boys with me for a few minutes. A friend is coming by to pick them up for a playdate. I'll make sure they stay in this room until she comes."

"That's fine," Anne said.

"I've been wondering about that camera Liddie found. Did you do anything with it yet?" Wendy asked.

"I did. You won't believe it. Jay McAllister, over at the *Gazette*, developed the film for me, and one of the pictures has Aunt Edie in it with a man."

"A man?" Wendy stared at her. "What man?"

"That's what we're trying to figure out. He looks awfully like my dad's cousin Carl, but Carl died before the picture was taken." Anne showed her the mystifying picture of Edie and Carl.

"Unbelievable," Wendy said. She collected the twins' jackets and settled them in a corner of the room with a backpack containing a few of their toys. "Mrs. Drane and Parker will be here any minute," she assured them. "And you guys remember other people are here too. Use your library manners."

"I have so much to tell you," Anne said to Wendy. "My dad and I went up in the attic last night, and we found some other, even older cameras. I'm thinking of doing a display here in the library of Aunt Edie's cameras and some of her best photos."

"That woman was amazing." Wendy put her boys' jackets on an empty chair and tucked her purse into a desk drawer. "I'll do anything I can to help you with that."

"Thanks. I'm also planning a family get-together. Something tells me I'm going to be busy every minute Mom and Dad are here."

"Where are they now?" Wendy asked.

"Mom's upstairs fixing lunch. Dad was going to mow the lawn, but I haven't heard the engine." She frowned and listened for a moment, but she was certain no lawn mower was running within a quarter mile of the library.

"You'd better go on up and eat," Wendy said. "And take your time. I'm here until two o'clock, and if you need extra time, just tell me."

Anne smiled. "Thanks, but I know you have tons of stuff to do at home too. I really appreciate your giving me the middle of your day." She went upstairs, eager to tell her parents all the news. She now knew precisely where Aunt Edie and the young man they thought was Carl had posed for the mysterious picture. But would that do any good in her search for the truth about what had happened to Carl?

Her mother had made good on her promise and was just taking a bacon quiche from the oven when Anne arrived in the kitchen.

"Oh, that smells divine," Anne said. "All the library patrons will want to be invited to have lunch with us."

Her father was already seated at the table.

"Didn't the mower start?" Anne asked.

"I never got that far. Got sidetracked. Come sit down and tell us what you found out this morning."

Anne took a seat, and her mother joined them. After her father asked the blessing, she unfolded her napkin.

"I e-mailed the army's public site. They had a place where you could ask questions, so I put in a query about Carl's military career. I haven't heard back yet on that."

"That may be helpful," her mom said.

"Or not." Her father held out his plate for a serving of the quiche.

"Why do you say that?" Anne asked.

"You just never know with government agencies. Maybe they'll surprise me and be extremely helpful." He smiled. "Now, what are all these calls you want us to make?"

"Just listings of people named Carl Summers. Dad, there were tons of them, so I only printed off the ones in Pennsylvania and the Washington area. I thought we could run through some of them tonight."

"I guess we could."

"I tried a number already, and I learned one thing: We need to work out ahead of time what to say to people and their answering machines." Anne put salad on her plate and let her mom serve her some quiche. "Oh, there's something else. I posted online, on an ancestry site, and I heard back from a woman in Ohio who thinks she's related to us."

"Really?" Mom said. "What's her name?"

"Heather." Anne frowned, racking her brain for the last name. "I told her we could chat later. Do you have any cousins named Heather, Dad?"

"*Hmm*, sounds familiar. You know my grandfather had brothers and sisters. Maybe she's descended from one of them."

"That's another thing we should work on—a detailed family tree."

"Sure, we can do that. Start with what we know and fill it out as we learn more."

Anne smiled. "I'm really excited about meeting Heather. And then three women from the DAR came in. I showed them the picture of Aunt Edie and the man we think is Carl."

"You did?" Her father paused with his fork in midair. "Why would you do that?"

"It was an accident but a lucky one. I'd had a hunch about the building behind Carl in the picture. I felt as though I should know what it was. The DAR women recognized it right away. It's Constitution Hall. The DAR owns it."

"So Edie met Carl—or whoever that man was—in front of Constitution Hall," her dad said.

"You did great this morning, honey," her mother told her with a smile.

Her father nodded. "I agree. We haven't been here twenty-four hours, and already you've discovered a relative you didn't know existed and found out exactly where the mystery picture was taken. I call that good work."

Chapter Seven

When they had finished lunch, Anne still had more than an hour left before she needed to be back in the library.

"Let's work on that family tree right now," her father said.

The three of them cleared the table, and Anne got out some paper and pens. Her father sketched out a rough ancestry chart, beginning with himself at the bottom. He put in his parents, Marvin and Arlene. They were followed by Uncle David and his wife, Natalie, and Aunt Edie, who was a sister to Marvin and David. Above the three siblings, he put in his paternal grandparents, John and Elizabeth Summers. Beside his own name, he wrote in his two sisters, Faith and Joanna.

"Now what?" Anne asked.

"I wish my memory was better," her father said, frowning down at the paper. "I know one of Grandpa's brothers was Frederick. I saw quite a lot of Uncle Fred when I was a kid." He wrote *Frederick* to one side of his grandfather's name.

"And wasn't he married to Sally?" Mom asked.

"That's right. Aunt Sally. Probably her real name was Sarah, but I'm not sure." Dad jotted *md. Sally* next to Frederick's name.

"How does Uncle Henry fit in?" Mom asked. "Wasn't there an Uncle Henry?"

"You're right. He was Aunt Olivia's husband, and Aunt Olivia was Grandpa and Uncle Fred's sister." Dad added to his chart as he spoke. "Now, if I remember right, they had several children, but don't ask me to pull their names out of thin air. I haven't seen any of them in years."

"Don't forget Cousin Carl," Anne said.

"Oh, right. And his sister."

Under *David* and *Natalie*, he wrote in *Carl* and *Pauline*. He sat back and surveyed his work.

"That's a big help," Anne said. "I can look for these people on the ancestry site. Do you remember Uncle Henry's last name?"

"*Hmm*, not right off the bat, but it will probably come to me in the middle of the night."

"Yes, and you'll wake me up to tell me," Mom said, rolling her eyes. "Seriously, I think you're doing a good job. If we were home, I could help more. I'm pretty sure I could find Uncle Henry and Aunt Olivia's last name in my old address book, though they're both dead now. When we were first married, we used to send them Christmas cards."

"I should have kept up with the family better." Dad shook his head regretfully. "Well, Charlene, how about some more coffee? Anything left in that pot?"

She stood and took his mug. "I think so."

Anne looked over the chart again. "Why don't I take this to my computer and see if Heather sent me any more information? Maybe we can figure out where she fits into all this."

She left her parents in the kitchen and hurried up to her bedroom, where she had left her laptop, carrying her father's family tree. A message from Heather was waiting for her, giving her ancestry for four generations on the Summers line. Anne printed it out and sent back a joyful reply. She gave Heather the few names on her chart that weren't in Heather's message, including hers and her dad's.

With the printout in hand, she hurried to rejoin her parents and found them in the family living room. "Dad! You were right. Heather's grandmother was Aunt Olivia. Look!" She showed him the message.

"That's really something. Let's add her family to our little chart."

"Aunt Olivia and Uncle Henry's son Robert O'Brien was Heather's father," Anne said.

"O'Brien! That's it." Her father wrote the names *Robert O'Brien* and *Heather* on the chart, and also put *O'Brien* after Uncle Henry's name.

"It's starting to look like a real family pedigree, or whatever they call them," her mother said.

"That gives me an idea." Anne could already picture it in her mind. "That ancestry site has a place where you can download blank charts. We can make a really nice one for the reunion."

Her dad grinned. "I'll bet we can order a big, fancy one to hang on the wall—bigger than you could print out."

"Now you're talking." Anne plopped down on the couch, smiling. "It's so neat to find all of this. And Heather said she'll talk to her husband about the reunion. She said that since it's on a Sunday, they might be able to drive over. Their kids are grown, but she said she might be able to bring a couple of their grandchildren along."

"Wouldn't that be fun?" Her mother's eyes danced. "It would give Ben and Liddie someone to play with. I've been jotting down more ideas for the menu and decorations."

"Good," Anne said, "because I haven't had a minute to think about that yet."

"What we need is a great theme," Mom said, gazing dreamily toward the window.

"Since when does a family reunion need a theme?" Dad asked.

"Days of Summers," Anne said quickly.

"Oh, I like it," Mom said, and they both ignored her father's groan.

He held up both hands. "Okay, I give in. We have a theme and some newly discovered relatives for honored guests. I'm sure by the time the day comes, we'll have gorgeous decorations and the finest food in town."

"And a deck," Anne said. "Don't forget the deck."

"That's right. I should take some measurements and go over to the lumber store this afternoon. But first I want to get that grass mowed." Her dad stood and stretched.

Anne glanced at her watch. "And I need to get back to work downstairs. Thanks, Mom and Dad." As she hurried down to relieve Wendy, she felt more confident that the reunion would be a success and that she would find out if the man in the photo was really Carl. She wasn't so sure about the deck being finished.

* * *

By suppertime, Anne's father had mowed the lawn, decided on plans for the deck, ordered the lumber, and connected through Alex with a contractor to set the footings. He went down to the foyer just as Anne was closing up the library for the night.

"Wow," she said when she'd heard his accomplishments. "When you get a bee in your bonnet, you don't let the grass grow under your feet."

"Oh, Anne." Dad laughed. "You're mixing metaphors, but that's the way I like to work. It gets things done."

"Are you too tired to make some calls tonight and maybe go through some of Aunt Edie's old pictures?"

"As soon as I get something in my stomach, I'll be ready to roll."

"Great." Anne turned out the overhead lights in the foyer.

"Of course, I want to spend some time with the kids too," her father added as they mounted the stairs together.

"I wouldn't have it any other way."

Liddie and Ben both had ideas about what they wanted to do with their grandparents. Anne's mother coaxed them into showing her their schoolwork. Liddie happily displayed her latest worksheets, and after a while Ben brought out his math and the paragraph he had written for his language class the next day.

"Jet engines, huh?" his grandfather said. "I'm impressed."

"It sounds like a science paper to me, not a language assignment," Anne's mother added.

Ben sighed. "Mr. Layton said we could write about anything we wanted to, Grandma. Besides, if it was for science class, I'd have put in a lot more technical stuff."

"I see." Anne's mother hid a smile.

"Ben's really interested in engines right now," Anne said.

Her dad nodded. "So I saw, when we were working on the lawn mower. Maybe you can write a story about that, Ben."

"Yeah, maybe."

"Can we play a game now?" Liddie asked.

"I don't see why not," Anne replied. "Why don't you and Ben go choose one? And, Ben," she added, giving her son a meaningful look, "make sure it's one Liddie will enjoy too." Although Ben was beginning to enjoy more complicated games designed for adults, he was usually pretty good about playing with Liddie. Anne knew that with their grandparents involved, even the simplest activity would take on a new dimension of fun.

The whole family wound up playing a noisy game of Chutes and Ladders around the kitchen table. Hershey lay nearby, content to be close to Ben, but occasionally, when their voices rose, he lifted his head and gave a little bark.

"Was this your game when you were little?" Mom asked, examining one of the old wooden tokens.

Anne shook her head. "It was Aunt Edie's. We used to play sometimes when I was visiting."

"Yeah, I remember playing this with her too," Dad said.

"I keep some games in the Children's Room. In fact, I've picked up a few at yard sales to supplement what Aunt Edie had. I put a few new stuffed animals in there for the toddlers too."

"Mom lets Ryan and me go in there and play games sometimes," Ben said.

Anne smiled. Usually the boys wanted to play outside, but on rainy evenings, the game stash came in handy. Ryan and Ben had felt very grown-up to be allowed the run of the library when it was officially closed.

They played until it was nearly Liddie and Ben's bedtime, and then Anne shooed them off to brush their teeth and put on their pajamas.

"You go ahead," her mom said. "I'll pick up the game. I know you and your father are dying to get into the family stuff."

Anne chuckled. "You read us pretty well."

"Aren't you going to help us?" her father asked. "If we use the house phone and a couple of cell phones, we can tear down that list pretty fast."

"All right," her mother said, "but if Anne doesn't mind, I think first I'll get on her laptop and check my e-mail. Maybe I can look for one of those big family tree charts too."

"Oh yes! If you find a good one, order it," Anne said.

While Liddie got ready for bed, Ben took Hershey out for a final run in the backyard and then settled him for the night. Anne left him to take his shower upstairs and promised to come up and say good night after a while. Liddie had brushed her teeth and put on her pajamas, so Anne let her go down to the family living room to kiss her grandparents good night. Then she went upstairs with Liddie and tucked her in under the pretty bedspread covered with romping ponies. When Anne returned to the living room, her dad was talking to someone on his phone.

"I guess you're not related to us, then," he said. "Thanks for chatting—and sorry I bothered you." He hung up and shrugged at Anne. "I'm checking off the ones I've done."

"I ordered the chart. Now give me part of the list," her mother said, and soon all three were at it.

An hour later, Anne looked over the results.

"Okay, we actually talked to thirty-seven people, and we left messages for twenty-two more. Fifteen numbers were either out of service or not answered."

"That's pretty good," her father said. "Of course, it would be even better if we'd found someone who knew something about *our* Carl Summers."

"What next?" her mother asked.

"I think we should look through Aunt Edie's old albums and the boxes of loose pictures we found in the attic. If that really was Carl in the Washington picture…"

"Then that would mean he was still alive in 1976," her mother finished.

"Yes. And maybe Aunt Edie saw him other times."

"That's a thought," her dad said eagerly. "We might find some other pictures of him."

"Now, that would be a real find." Anne stacked the telephone lists together and put them on the bottom shelf of the coffee table. "I'll leave these here, so later we can try some of the numbers we didn't reach if we want to. And now I'll go up and get the photos I left in my room."

"Need some help?" her dad asked.

"No, I'm good. But pull those albums out of the bookcase, would you, please?" Anne pointed to the bottom shelf of the bookcase in the living room, where she had stashed a couple of albums that were in the house when she took possession, along with those from the attic. She hadn't wanted to leave something that personal in the library and had brought Aunt Edie's current album up here to enjoy at her leisure.

When she got upstairs, Ben's bedroom door was closed and a soft light glowed from under it. She knocked softly.

"Come in," Ben called.

She walked in as he turned out the lamp, and she used the light spilling in from the hallway to get to his bedside.

"Hi," he said sleepily, and he promptly yawned.

"Sorry I took so long." Anne leaned down to straighten his quilt and kiss his forehead.

"Can I take Hershey over to Ryan's tomorrow after school?" Ben asked, tucking the book he'd been reading under his pillow.

"We'll see. You might have homework, and besides, Grandpa may have some project for you to work on."

"Yeah." Ben looked up hopefully. "Maybe Ryan could come here."

Anne smiled. "Maybe so. Let's wait and see how much schoolwork you have. If things work out, I'll call Alex."

That seemed to satisfy Ben, and he snuggled down under his covers.

"I was hoping you might get a haircut sometime soon too," Anne added. "Grandpa said he'll do it. We just need to remember at the right time, I guess."

Ben sat up. "He can do it now." He seemed perfectly ready to get out of bed for the adventure, but it was already later than Anne liked for his bedtime.

She tousled his hair. "Not tonight."

"I'll ask him tomorrow if I don't forget," Ben said.

"Thanks." It would save both time and money if her father gave Ben a haircut after school.

"I already said my prayers, because I wasn't sure you were coming," Ben said.

"All right. Sleep tight."

Anne stopped at Liddie's room and looked in, certain the little girl would be fast asleep. Instead, Liddie said drowsily, "Mommy, did you and Grandpa find that guy yet?"

"What guy?"

"The one who's missing. Carl."

"He's not exactly missing, honey." Anne sat down on the edge of Liddie's bed. "We've thought for a long time that we'd never see Grandpa's cousin Carl again. And we probably won't. The army told the family that he died a long time ago. But that picture sure makes us wonder, doesn't it? It makes us think maybe he didn't die when we thought he did. But that doesn't mean he's still alive. Anyway, it's something for us to think about."

Liddie's eyelids drooped. "I'll pray for Cousin Carl from now on."

"That's nice," Anne said. "I think I will too, and that we'll be able to find out what that odd picture means."

Anne sat for another minute, until she was sure Liddie was finally asleep. Silently, she thanked God for the years she had shared with Eric and for giving her such wonderful children and a close, loving family.

Poor Carl, she thought. *He's missed all of this. But he might be out there somewhere, going through his life without a family to love and support him.* She hoped that if he was alive he had found someone to love and had a family of his own.

She tiptoed to her bedroom and picked up the two small boxes of photos and negatives she and her father had come across in the attic, along with three more albums they had found.

When she got back to the living room, both her parents had a photo album open on their laps.

"This one isn't old enough for what you want," her mother said, "but there are some beautiful pictures in it. Edie was a wonderful photographer." She held the album out so that Anne could see a two-page spread of details of the house. "Aren't these great?"

"They sure are," Anne replied. "Especially the ones of the town. You can see the changes on Main Street through her pictures, and she photographed lots of the lovely old houses."

"The album isn't full," her mom said, turning to a few blank pages in the back, "and one of the last pictures is of Edie and Mildred together." She pointed to it.

"Oh, that's at Mildred's house. It looks fairly recent too."

"Maybe this is her most recent album," her mom said.

"And I think this one's older." Anne's father held out the one he was perusing. "In fact, this picture of the church says 'June 1993' under it."

"Well, if Carl really did live beyond 1970, we don't know when he might pop up again in a picture, so we'll have to look closely at everything, I guess." Anne set down her load and took the albums they'd rescued from the attic to the sofa. "These are probably older than either of the ones you're looking at." She opened the top one. "Oh, wow. This one is really ancient."

Her father leaned over to look. "All black and white."

"Yes, and look at this." Anne pointed to a view of a young woman sitting in a chair swing. She was dressed in a flowing white dress and a broad-brimmed picture hat. "It says 'Edie 1947.' What do you think of that?"

"She must have been a teenager." Her mother came over to look over Anne's shoulder. "Oh, how pretty. She was a lovely girl."

They went on browsing through the albums, stopping often to show each other an interesting picture.

"Is this your father or David?" Anne's mother asked at one point, showing a page to her husband.

"I think that's Dad, but I'm really not a hundred percent sure. Is there a date?"

"You know, all of the Summers relatives seem to share a strong family resemblance," Anne said. "I noticed it in that picture of you and Carl on the fishing trip. He looked a lot like you."

"Or I looked like him," her father said with a chuckle.

"Are you sure that's not you with Aunt Edie at the bicentennial celebration?" Anne asked, half serious.

"Not a chance. I'd remember."

"Anne has a point." Her mother sat back with a smile. "This whole Cousin Carl mystery could be nothing but a case of mistaken identity."

"That's why we're doing this. To see if there are any more pictures of him, or if there are some of another man who looks like him at about that time." Anne's father stretched his arms and yawned. "How about some coffee, honey, if you expect me to stay awake much longer?"

"Sure." Anne put aside the album she was holding.

"I'll get it." Her mother stood. "Want anything with it?"

"No, thanks," Dad said.

"Don't forget that apple pie we brought. We should use that soon."

"Oh, now you're tempting me."

"I'd have a small piece," Anne said.

"I'll get it."

As her mother left the room, Anne's father smiled at her sympathetically. "If we're honest, I guess we have to admit she could be right. But I still think that's Carl."

"Me too." Anne picked up an old, tattered album, the last of the stack. The leather binding was ragged and the spine in shreds. She carefully turned back the front cover. A faded photograph slipped out from between the pages and slid to the floor.

"What's that?" her dad asked.

Anne bent over to pick it up. The back faced up, and it bore the unmistakable lines and notation of an old postcard. She lifted it and turned it over. "Looks like a picture glued to a postcard backing."

"They used to do that a lot," her father said.

Anne smiled. "It's Aunt Edie on one of her trips."

"In Washington?"

"No, the other side of the country. She's standing in front of Grauman's Chinese Theater." Anne turned back to the postcard side and read the message. Her heart began to pound. "Dad, Aunt Edie wrote a message on this, but I don't think she ever mailed it. There's no postmark or anything. And it just might be a clue to this mystery we're trying to solve!"

Chapter Eight

"Let me see." Anne's father scooted over onto the couch beside her. She handed him the postcard, picture side up. "That's Aunt Edie, all right."

"I wonder whose footprints she wanted most to see at Grauman's," Anne mused.

"I don't know, but she always liked Cary Grant. Maybe we'll find other photos from this trip."

"That's right!"

Her father turned the card over and sat still for a moment, reading the message. "Oh, wow! I see what you mean. *'Dear C., Maybe we should meet here next time? Having a wonderful time with your cousins. Aunt E.'*"

"Do you think *C* is an abbreviation for Carl?" Anne asked.

He frowned. "It could be, but she wrote 6/20/77 up here. If that's the date, it was written in 1977. It's even later than the Washington photo."

"True. I wonder who was behind the camera."

"Good thought. Aunt Edie wasn't, obviously, unless she did it with a timer, which is doubtful in a busy spot like that."

"She probably grabbed some other tourist and asked them to take it," Anne suggested.

"No, she says, '*Having a wonderful time with your cousins.*' Someone else was with her. They probably took the picture."

"Were you with her?" Anne stared at him. "I mean, Carl's cousins…That would be you and who else? I didn't know that Carl had any first cousins besides you."

Anne's mother came back into the room carrying a tray with mugs of coffee and slices of apple pie. "What are you talking about?" She set the mug down on a coaster near her husband.

"Take a look at this." He showed her the postcard and explained their dilemma. "There were only three siblings in my father's generation—him, Aunt Edie, and Carl's father, David. Aunt Edie didn't have any kids."

"Did either of your sisters go to California with Aunt Edie?" Anne's mom asked.

"If they did, I must have forgotten. But hey, Carl must have had cousins on his mother's side."

"Yes, but why would Aunt Edie take them with her?" Anne asked. "They wouldn't be any relation to her."

"What if they weren't first cousins?" her mom said. "We know there were more family members if we go back one more generation. Anne, your great-grandfather John Summers had siblings, and they had children."

"That's right," Anne's father said. "I suppose Edie could be talking about Madeline, or even our newfound relative Heather's people."

"Madeline! How could I have forgotten about her?" Mom said with a little laugh. "Anne, we have to invite her to the reunion. Although she might be too frail to come."

"She's got to be at least eighty," Anne's father said. "But she always had a flair for adventure. She might surprise us and get on a plane."

"If she could come, I'll bet she'd love it. She'd be thrilled to see all of us, and she'd be tickled to see what you've done with this house, Anne." As she spoke, Anne's mother distributed the coffee and pie.

"Well, as soon as we find her phone number, we can contact her," Anne said.

"Maybe you should talk to Carl's sister." Her mom sat down and picked up her own dessert plate. "She probably knows more than anyone else about this."

"You're absolutely right." Anne looked to her father. "Dad? What do you think?"

"I'd hate to upset Pauline. We'd have to be careful not to suggest that Carl isn't dead or anything like that—nothing to do with any irregularities concerning his death."

"I agree," her mother said. "But maybe Anne could call and tell her she found a photo of him with Aunt Edie. Pauline might recall something that would help."

Anne shook her head. "No, then she'd ask when it was taken. We can't lie to her."

Her dad's brow furrowed. "Let me think about this." He sipped his coffee.

"Your sisters probably don't know anything about it, do they?" Anne asked. "We could call Aunt Faith and Aunt Joanna."

"If they knew something about Carl, they'd have told me," her father said. "Let's just let this simmer overnight. Maybe something will come to me."

"All right." Anne frowned. "Mom, you're a C. Charlene. You don't think she wrote this postcard to you, do you?"

"Why ever would she? And what cousins of mine would she mean?" Her mom shook her head. "Too far-fetched."

"I guess you're right." Anne took a bite of her pie, then laid down her fork and absently turned a page in the old album.

"Dale, I do think your cousin Madeline is a good one to ask about this," Mom said. "She lives in Southern California. Maybe Aunt Edie was visiting her when she went to Grauman's Chinese Theater."

"That's a thought. Have you remembered her last name?" Dad asked. "It used to be Hendricks."

"That was before she remarried." Anne's mother sighed. "I guess we're getting older, when we can't remember something like that."

Anne's father had no comment, he just sipped his coffee as he ruffled through the photographs in one of the boxes.

"Mom, this pie is really good." Anne cut off another bite. "And how does Madeline fit into the family again?"

"She's Uncle Fred's granddaughter," her dad said. "She lived not far from here when she was young."

"I'd better write it down on that family tree, or I'll forget." Anne reached under the coffee table and pulled out the chart her father had begun. "Don't worry, Mom. You'll remember her new husband's name in due time."

Her mother laughed ruefully. "He's not exactly new. It's been fifteen or twenty years since Madeline married him. But we see her so seldom." She shook her head. "Well, anyway, it looks like we're going to have plenty of people to invite to the reunion. I'll call Joanna tomorrow, and she can help me with the addresses."

"Great," Anne said. Her dad's sister was tech savvy, she knew. "Tell her that e-mail addresses would be even better if she has them. Time is getting short."

As glad as she would be to reconnect with the rest of the family, Anne would be even happier if they could find out something about Carl.

"Hey, look," her dad said. "I found an envelope full of California pictures. Here's one taken at the entrance to the MGM Studio."

Anne took it eagerly. "Who's that with Aunt Edie?"

"That's Madeline."

Her mom leaned in. "Sure enough."

"Aha!" Anne smiled. "We're making progress. At least now we know she connected with Madeline on that trip."

"That's right," her father said, "if it was the same trip."

And maybe, Anne thought, just maybe Cousin Madeline would know something about Cousin Carl and how his service in Vietnam ended and how he died. She would just have to be patient until one of her parents remembered Madeline's married name, or until either Aunt Joanna or Aunt Faith, her dad's sisters, helped her out.

She sifted through all the photos in the envelope. Though she found several poses of Aunt Edie at Hollywood attractions and at the beach, she didn't find any more photographs depicting Madeline, or any hints to indicate Carl was alive at that time. Even so, she felt the unsent postcard was a strong clue, and she set it aside so it wouldn't get lost in the avalanche of old photographs. She wasn't about to give up. Somewhere there must be more evidence that would lead her to the truth, and they would learn what had really happened to Carl Summers.

Anne's mother stood and began gathering up cups and newspapers.

"I'm heading for bed, honey."

"Okay." Anne walked over and kissed her on the cheek. "I think I'll check my e-mail one more time."

"I'm good for a little while longer," her father said. "Do you want me to look through this other box of pictures?"

"Thanks, that would be a help," Anne said. "You recognize the older generations so much easier than I do."

She went to her computer and logged in to her e-mail account. Her heart pounded when she saw a message from an address beginning "chsummers." She clicked it open and read through it quickly.

Hi. My name is Carl H. Summers Jr., and I live outside Washington, in Fairfax, Virginia. I saw your posting on the family ancestry site, and I wondered if we're related.

The e-mail included a telephone number, and Anne glanced at the time. It was far too late to call anyone now.

"Dad, take a look at this." She rose and carried the laptop to him.

He looked up at her, his eyebrows arched. "What have you got?"

Anne handed him the laptop and sat down on the arm of his recliner. "This message. Tell me what you think." She put her arm around his shoulders and waited for him to read the e-mail.

"That could be a real lead," he said after a moment.

"Do you think it's him?"

"Impossible to say."

"It could be his son," Anne said eagerly.

"Maybe. But there's one thing against him."

"What?"

He looked up at her through his tortoiseshell-framed glasses. "Cousin Carl's middle name was John, after his grandfather. This fellow is a junior, and his middle initial is *H*. I'd say, don't get your hopes up."

Anne felt as though someone had pricked her with a pin and let all the air out of her. "Guess you're right. But he could still be related."

"That's true," her dad said, "and he could know something about the Carl we're looking for."

"Well, it's late. I'll call him first thing in the morning."

Her father passed the laptop to her and stood, and Anne closed the program.

"Thanks, Dad. Did you find anything in that box?"

"Sure. Plenty of great pictures. I'm struck again by Edie's great talent for photography."

"Any good ones of Blue Hill?" Anne asked as she took the laptop over to the desk and closed it down for the night.

"Lots of them." Her father picked up a photo from the coffee table. "Have you ever seen this?"

Anne stepped closer and looked down at the black-and-white snapshot.

"No! Is that one of the Kepples?"

"Yeah, it's Hank's grandfather, standing in front of the jewelry store on Main Street. There are some great ones of other businesses in Blue Hill in there too, and one of John F. Kennedy."

"What? The president?"

Her father nodded as he rummaged through the box. "Here it is. The mayor from the late 1950s, welcoming Kennedy. I remember my folks saying he swung through Blue Hill on a campaign tour."

"Did you see him then?" Anne asked.

"No, but obviously Aunt Edie did."

Anne stared down at the picture. "Wow, I wonder if this would enlarge well, into an eight-by-ten at least."

"You could ask the photographer at the *Gazette*."

"I'll do that," Anne said. "Let's make a pile of possibilities for the photo exhibit."

Half an hour later, she admitted she was so tired that if she didn't go to bed, she wouldn't be able to concentrate on her work in the morning. She and her father straightened up the boxes, albums, and piles of photographs, and went up the stairs together. On the landing, Anne gave him a hug.

"Good night, Dad!"

He squeezed her. "'Night, honey. Thanks for a fun evening."

She laughed. "You're not hard to entertain."

As she prepared for bed, she thought about the e-mail from Carl H. Summers Jr. She'd found one unknown relative in Heather. Was it possible she would soon discover another? And was he the Carl they were looking for, or was he the son or other close connection to her father's long-lost cousin?

Like Liddie, she fell asleep with Cousin Carl's name on her lips.

Chapter Nine

The next morning, Liddie came to the breakfast table with a plan. As Anne and her mother served oatmeal and fruit, the little girl went into action.

"Grandma, I want you to go to school with me."

"You do?" Anne's mother smiled at Liddie and set a glass of milk at her place. "What would I do there?"

"Play and learn numbers. Things like that."

"I tell you what, I don't think I can stay at school the whole day, but I can walk there with you this morning."

"Okay." Liddie happily spooned oatmeal and fruit into her mouth.

"In fact," Anne's mother said, "if we left a few minutes early, I could go to your classroom with you and meet your teacher. Would you like that?"

Her mouth full, Liddie nodded eagerly. She swallowed and took a large gulp of milk. "I'd like it a lot."

"Use your napkin, Liddie," Anne said, smiling at her daughter's milk mustache. She suspected that having Grandma walk to school with her was what Liddie had wanted in the first place. "I'm sure Miss Reed would like to meet Grandma."

"Ben, is it all right with you if I walk to school with you?" her mother asked.

He looked up at her. "Sure, Grandma. You don't need to go to my class though."

"All right, it's a deal."

"What about you, Grandpa?" Ben asked. "You could meet Mr. Layton."

"I'd like to," Anne's father said, "but I also want to start on the deck this morning. Alex said he could come and help me for a few hours. I'd probably better stay here and work on that."

Ben nodded soberly. "That's more important."

"Well, it needs to be done sooner rather than later. Maybe I can meet Mr. Layton on another day," his grandfather said. "I would like to talk to him about engines."

"He knows a lot about them." Ben seemed content with the arrangement, and a few minutes later he and Liddie left for school with their grandmother walking between them.

Anne was loading the dishwasher, and her father was lingering over his second cup of coffee when the bell to the private entrance rang. Anne went downstairs and opened the door to Alex. He was dressed for work in jeans and a chambray shirt.

"Good morning. I think it's going to rain later, so I thought your dad and I should get right at it. Is he ready to work?"

"Yes, he's just finishing breakfast. Listen, Alex, I want to pay you for your time on the deck. I was serious about that."

He held up a hand in protest. "I know we've kept it professional, Anne, and I appreciate that, but I consider your dad an old friend. I'm doing this as a favor—and *I'm* serious about *that*."

She frowned. "When I first moved in and needed lots of work done in a hurry, I know you rearranged your schedule for me.

That was a big favor from a friend. But to not pay you? No. I can't do that."

Alex sighed. "Your dad ordered all the materials and got the plans. I'm just donating a few hours of my time. Please let me."

She stared up at him for a long moment.

"For your father," Alex said.

She knew it wasn't just for her father's sake, but if she continued to make an issue of it, her dad would probably jump in, and she didn't want them to start the day with a blowup caused by Anne Gibson. She huffed out a breath. "Okay, you win this one, but this is a one-time deal. You got that?"

"Loud and clear."

She smiled. "Come on up."

Anne led the way up to the kitchen.

"Well, hi, Alex," her dad said with a grin. He drained his coffee mug and set it on the table.

"Ready to start in on those joists for the deck?" Alex asked.

"I sure am. Just let me grab my work gloves. I picked up a pair at the hardware store yesterday. I think I left them in the living room."

"There's a hammer and a few other tools in the garage," Anne told him when he returned with gloves in hand.

"I brought my tools," Alex said. "Don't worry about us."

The two men went out, and Anne went downstairs to the library to let Bella in and get her started on her morning's work. A few early birds came in as soon as she opened the front door. Anne helped with the patrons for a while and rearranged the display of new books in the foyer.

"I need to go upstairs and make a phone call," she told Bella when the activity slowed down.

"Sure, go ahead." Bella smiled. Though she was Remi's twin, the two girls looked quite different. Bella was several inches shorter than her sister, and she had blue eyes and light, wavy hair that fell about her shoulders, while Remi's eyes were brown and she usually wore her darker brown hair in a thick braid. Anne wondered if their mother had ever dressed them alike when they were little.

Anne took the stairs up to the family living room so she could call in privacy the number Carl Summers Jr. had sent her. It rang six times and then went to voice mail. Anne was disappointed but left him a message including her cell phone number. She followed up with a return e-mail, giving him a little family background. She ended with, *I look forward to talking with you.*

Another message had come in, and she didn't recognize the sender's address, but the subject line was *Summers family,* so she opened it.

Hi. My name is Thomas O'Brien, and I'm Heather Dailey's uncle. She alerted me to your post in search of members of the Summers family. My mother was a Summers – Olivia Summers, who married Henry O'Brien. I'd be interested in connecting to others in the family.

Anne smiled and opened a reply box. *Mr. O'Brien, I'm glad you contacted me. We're planning a reunion here in Blue Hill, Pennsylvania, a week from Sunday. We'd be very happy to have you come. My dad, Dale Summers, will be here. He's the son of Marvin and the grandson of John Summers.*

She gave a little more information and sent her message. To her surprise, while she glanced through the rest of the messages in her inbox, a reply came back from Thomas.

Thanks so much for inviting me. I live in Wisconsin, and I don't think I'd be able to come that far, but Heather will probably fill me in on the doings. I wish you a happy day for the reunion. Occasionally I travel a bit – not so much as when I was younger. But it's possible that in the fall I might be over that way.

Anne quickly thanked him and assured him that he was welcome to visit anytime.

With no return message from Carl Summers Jr., she decided to check in with Bella and, if she wasn't needed in the library, to work on the exhibit of Aunt Edie's photographs. She had decided to open the exhibit at the library the same weekend as the reunion so that her extended family members could enjoy it. She could leave it up for several weeks for the benefit of the library patrons. Saturday would be the perfect day for the opening, she thought, as the reunion was planned for Sunday afternoon. But that gave her only ten days to compile the exhibit.

She went downstairs to find Bella shelving returned books in the Nonfiction Room.

"How's it going?" Anne asked, looking around. No patrons were in the room, and she hadn't noticed any in the foyer.

"It's been slow this morning," Bella said. "I've got two people in the Fiction Room and one mom in the Children's Room with her little girl. Very quiet. I think it's the weather."

Anne glanced out the window. Dark clouds had moved in, and the new leaves on the trees swayed in gusts of wind.

"You may be right. Alex mentioned it was supposed to rain. The wet forecast may be keeping people home. As long as it's not busy, I'll start working on the new exhibit I plan to put up next week."

Bella smiled. "What is it this time?"

"I'm thinking 'Edie Summers: Views of Blue Hill.' My great-aunt Edie took a lot of pictures, and my dad and I have been going through them. She was really an excellent photographer. I thought I'd have some of the best ones enlarged and framed."

"Sounds great," Bella said.

"I've also been thinking that other people in the community might have some photos that Edie took—ones that are special to them. Maybe we should ask patrons to loan us their best pics."

"Good thinking. We could post a sign in the foyer asking for pictures that Miss Summers took."

Anne nodded. "And Grace Hawkins would probably run the announcement in the paper if I asked her."

She gazed around at the display space available in the foyer. "I'm thinking this one will be bigger than the usual display in the History Room. Maybe I'll feature some of her pictures in each room and in the foyer. And her cameras—they're really interesting. I wonder if my father could help me get the information about them together so we could display them with a group of photos taken with each camera over the years."

"People would find that interesting," Bella said.

"Maybe that's just too complicated. It would probably be time consuming to sort it all out."

"What can I do to help?" Bella asked.

"For right now, how about if you make the sign for the foyer? I'll call Grace and see about getting a news brief. After that, just keep doing what you're doing. That gives me the freedom to work on the display."

Anne sat down at her desk and called Grace. She explained what she wanted.

"Sure, I can do that," Grace said. "We'll run it on page two in a little box in this week's edition." Under Anne's direction, she wrote a paragraph and read it back.

"That's perfect," Anne said. "I hope we get some community participation. Thanks so much."

"What's good for you is good for the *Gazette*," Grace said, a lilt in her voice. "Let's set up an interview to run in next week's paper too. I want to run an advance story two or three days before your event."

Anne set a time for early the next week and briefly told Grace about the puzzling photo in the batch Jay had printed for her.

"Wow, that's really something," Grace said. "You've got to tell me what you find out about that one."

"I will."

After ending her conversation with Grace, Anne turned to the photographs and selected nearly two dozen she felt were worthy of being exhibited. All were views taken within the town of Blue Hill. Reluctantly, she bypassed Aunt Edie's photos from vacations and other trips. Those might be useful at a later exhibit, but for this one, she would focus on the town and its development, as seen through Edie's lens.

She looked carefully over the contact sheet Jay had made. As she had gathered earlier, only the two photos of her house seemed to be Blue Hill shots. The rest were in Washington, DC. The images were so tiny, she couldn't really tell what most of them were, other than one in which the Capitol dome dominated the skyline. She decided it would be worth having the rest of the negatives printed.

A little before noon, she went upstairs to help her mother get lunch ready. Rain began pelting the window as they put the finishing touches on the meal, and Alex and her father came in the back entrance.

Anne met them at the top of the stairs with towels. Rainwater dripped off her father's cap, and their clothes looked decidedly damp.

"Guess you guys got wet!"

"You don't miss a thing, do you?" Alex laughed and took a towel from her and blotted the water on his face.

Her father took the other and wiped his glasses with it. "I'm going to go change my shirt," he said. "Alex, do you want something dry to put on?"

"I think I'll be okay if I just shed this sweatshirt," Alex replied. He headed for the nearest bathroom to clean up.

Over lunch, Anne told them of the contact she'd had with Thomas O'Brien. "So, even though I haven't reached Carl Summers Jr. yet, I have found another long-lost relative."

"That's terrific," her dad said. "Too bad he can't come to the reunion."

Anne then told them of her progress in choosing photos for the exhibit.

Alex smiled. "I remember her posting snapshots on the bulletin board at church after events and letting people take them home. Any time we had a picnic or a celebration, she had her camera with her."

"Maybe some of those will show up after the announcement comes out in the *Gazette*." Anne helped herself to some pickles Mildred had given her. "I was thinking of including other Blue Hill artifacts from the 1970s in the exhibit. Maybe old high school yearbooks, vintage clothing, that sort of thing. What do you think, Dad?"

"Sounds ambitious to me."

"Especially with the reunion the next day," her mother said. "Do you have time to do all that?"

"Maybe not."

"You could ask for volunteers to round up that stuff," Alex suggested. "I'll bet Wendy would help. And Grace would run another brief in the paper, asking for people to bring in the items."

Anne nodded. "I wonder if we'd be overrun with fondue pots and mug trees."

"You might be," her mom said. "And you don't want to offend anyone by not displaying their items. Could get kind of messy."

Anne nodded. "I think I'll listen to the voices of wisdom this time and keep it simple. If I do a good job on the photography exhibit, that will be plenty for this time. But I'll hold on to the thought of doing historical displays by decades for later in the year. It could be a lot of fun, when I have time to do it right."

Her mother brought a plate of cookies to the table. "When we're done here, I think I'll try to call your sisters, Dale. We need to start spreading the word about the reunion, and I'm sure they can help me with some addresses."

Dale turned to Alex. "Are we done for the day?"

"If you don't have something else in mind, we could work in the garage," Alex said. "We could cut a lot of boards to length and be ready to start the decking at our next session."

"Yeah, that would be a big help, if you don't mind."

"I think I'll call Jay at the paper," Anne said.

"Are you going to have him make enlargements for you?" her mother asked.

"If he's willing. I'll pay him, of course. But I'd also like prints of the other frames on that roll of film from Aunt Edie's Pentax. I can't tell if she's in any of them, and…well, you never know what will show up in those photos."

"That's right," her father said. "I should have thought of that earlier. That's the only place we found a picture that we really think is of Carl after his official death date. Let's get a look at the rest of them."

"You know, they might do that for you at the drugstore, since you have the negatives," her mother said.

"I guess they might. I'll keep it in mind if Jay's too busy."

The rain continued throughout the afternoon, and traffic through the library was light. Bella was happy to work on cataloging new books, so Anne took the two boxes of Aunt Edie's photographs down to the Nonfiction Room and curled up before the fireplace in a comfortable armchair. She could hear muffled sounds emanating from the garage, but they weren't loud enough to distract her from her reading.

She went through the pictures slowly this time, beginning with the box her father had started with. Again she set aside several photos that might make good additions to her exhibit. She came across several envelopes of negatives. To her delight, she located some that corresponded to pictures she wanted to use. The photographer would find it much easier to make enlargements from the negatives than from the snapshots.

She pulled out another envelope, this one containing the photos and their negatives from a roll of black-and-white film. As she looked at the first picture, Anne gasped. Here were more snapshots taken in Washington, DC.

She sat up and scrutinized the pictures. Familiar landmarks unfolded before her. The White House, the Jefferson Memorial, the Reflecting Pool, and the Washington Monument. Everywhere, people dressed in colonial garb seemed a part of the scenery. And there it was: a huge display made of flowers—the American flag and the colonial flag. Beneath them, spelled out in floral digits, were the dates 1776–1976.

Anne's pulse thudded. More pictures from Aunt Edie's bicentennial trip. She turned up the next one. Edie and a woman Anne didn't recognize sat on a bench that Anne guessed was on the National Mall. She turned the photo over, but nothing was written on the back. Not for the first time, she wished Aunt Edie had formed the habit of writing names, dates, and locations on the back of every photo, but then she had to smile to herself. It might have been her amazing great-aunt's one and only weakness.

She came to the end of the stack. No pictures of Carl on this roll. With a sigh, she put the photos back in the envelope and set it aside. Perhaps she would find even more in the box. Doubly motivated now, she began to rummage again.

Only a few items were left. Near the bottom of the box, she found a small faux leather folder. Expecting more negatives, Anne pulled it out and opened it. She blinked and stared at the prize she had found. Inside the folder was a diminutive notebook, and the first page said, *Washington Trip, June–July 1976.*

Anne pushed her glasses up on her nose and settled back in the chair. She couldn't help smiling as she opened the little diary.

June 27, Sunday. The services today were magnificent. I'm leaving first thing in the AM for Washington. Can't wait to see all the monuments again and enjoy the festivities. Will stop overnight with Iris Gallagher on the way, in Wellersburg. I hope I can persuade her to go with me.

Anne wished she had a pen and paper to take notes on, but the cozy warmth of the fire lulled her into laziness. If she wanted to find Aunt Edie's friend's name again later, that would be easy, since it was in the first entry. She turned the page and read on.

June 28, 10:00 PM. Arrived at Iris's house about 7:30; she had kept supper for me. We've had a marvelous time catching up. Iris wants to go with me tomorrow, and she'll take the bus home from DC on Thursday, after we visit the Smithsonian. I'm trying to convince her to stay over the weekend with me to see the festivities on the Fourth, but she says no – too many obligations, and she thinks the crowds will be so enormous she wouldn't like it. But we'll enjoy a few days together.

There was no entry for the next day, but late on June 30, Aunt Edie had written quite a lot. Anne squinted over her great-aunt's distinctive handwriting.

Iris and I had a great time yesterday. Traffic was wretched, but we got here about eleven. We checked into the hotel and then ate lunch at the cafeteria in the National Museum of American History. The exhibits are fantastic! I could have stayed there until closing time, but Iris particularly wanted to see the decorations and exhibits on the Mall, so we walked around out there until we were ready to drop. Today we went to several of the monuments and the Hirshhorn Museum and Sculpture Garden. The displays are wonderful – so much to see! I won't be able to take in everything in a week, but I'll try. Iris bought her bus ticket for tomorrow. They are supposed to open the new National Air and Space Museum in the morning, and we plan to be there early. I'll put Iris on the bus at 5:15. I hope the wait isn't too long and that we are able to see everything. I got a ticket to the concert at Constitution Hall, though it was pricey.

Anne caught her breath. Aunt Edie had actually attended a concert at Constitution Hall! Was that when she had run into Carl? Avidly, she read on.

July 1. What a day and what an evening! We did get into the new Air and Space Museum, though we had to wait in line about forty-five minutes. Such a wonderful collection. I wish Iris had stayed. The concert was beyond my expectations.

July 2, Friday. This morning I drove around the Tidal Basin. The cherry blossoms of course were not blooming. I would love to come back some April and see that. There is so much here that I could spend a month exploring. I went to the Capitol and then went back to see some of the special exhibits in the American History Museum. We were a little rushed on Tuesday, and I found today that Iris and I had missed a lot. I may stay in tonight – my feet hurt! But tomorrow I want to see the Arts and Industries Building, and possibly the American Art Museum, if I'm not too tired, and I hope to spend some time at one of the Smithsonian's Research Centers. Perhaps I'll save some of that for Saturday, once I make sure things will be open.

Anne looked up as her mother entered the room.

"There you are! I got hold of Joanna, and I thought you'd want to know. She's planning to come for the reunion."

"Super!" Anne sat up and stretched. "What did you find out?"

"She got Madeline's address for me, and she also gave me her and Faith's ZIP codes—I remembered the rest—and their kids' addresses. I gave her your e-mail and asked her to send you a message, because I thought you might find it easier to reach all the kids by e-mail."

Anne smiled. Most of those "kids" were older than she was.

"That's great, Mom."

"Are you in the middle of something?"

"Wait until you hear!"

"Sounds interesting. How would you like a cup of tea?"

"Oh, I'd love it," Anne said.

Her mother smiled. "I'll fix it in the kitchen down here. Very convenient, having two kitchens in this house. Don't go away—I want to hear all about what you're doing." She headed off toward Aunt Edie's original kitchen on the first floor, which Anne used as a break room and refreshment area for the library.

Anne went back to the little notebook. Aunt Edie's entry for July 3 began with a surprise.

Visiting Washington during the magnificent celebration of our nation's two-hundredth anniversary would be rewarding enough, but finding a lost relative on top of it could only be called the icing on the cake.

Anne stared at the precisely penned words. Whom had Aunt Edie run into in Washington? Or did she mean she'd gone to the research center and found records about an ancestor she hadn't known about before?

Quickly she turned the page and skimmed the rest of the day's entry, but no name jumped out at her. However, Aunt Edie did say, *We went into the exhibit hall together, but I confess my attention was distracted. We had a long lunch and tentatively scheduled another meeting for Sunday.*

Iris had gone home on Thursday. With whom had Aunt Edie lunched and viewed the exhibits on Saturday? Anne felt her excitement mount. Was it possible she'd found proof that Carl had survived his tour in Vietnam?

As her mother entered the room with the tea tray, Anne straightened. "Mom, you've got to see this."

"What is it, dear?"

"Aunt Edie kept a trip diary when she went to Washington, DC. It's all in this little notebook." She held up the leatherette folder.

"How exciting! Where did you find that?"

"In one of those boxes of pictures we were poking through last night. And listen to this: She met someone there. At least, it sure sounds that way."

Anne read the entry for July third aloud as her mother sat down and set their mugs on coasters.

"My goodness!" Her mother said. "That certainly sounds intriguing. But it doesn't say who this person was?"

"Not yet. I haven't read to the end of the diary yet. It's not long though. I think she was only there a week."

"You're not thinking it was—"

"Carl?" Anne asked. "I sure do. He was in that picture!"

"Well, we think he was in the picture. What if it was another nephew or cousin that we haven't considered?"

Anne frowned. She set the folder on the table and picked up her cup. "I suppose it's possible. One of Uncle Fred or Aunt Olivia's descendants, maybe. But she spent some time with this person on at least two days during her trip. And, Mom, she went to a concert at Constitution Hall. That's where the mystery picture was taken."

"Maybe you'll find something else when you read the rest of the journal."

"I hope so. If only she had written his name! Why do you suppose she was so secretive about who she was with?"

"Maybe she didn't realize it," her mother guessed. "Sometimes people write things in journals without thinking how cryptic it would sound to someone else."

Anne shook her head. "I think it's because she was keeping his identity quiet. If it really was Carl and he didn't want anyone else to know he was alive, she might have avoided writing his name so there'd be no chance of anybody else seeing it."

"Oh, Anne, you have such an imagination."

"That's what I would have done," Anne insisted.

They drank their tea and turned the discussion to the reunion invitations.

"Why don't I go ahead and work on the wording for those?" her mother suggested. "You can keep on with the photo exhibit preparations."

"All right. I can't wait to hear what Dad thinks about this diary."

After her mother left her, Anne opened the notebook again. Before long, she came across a few more enigmatic notes. She read them over three times and then closed her eyes to think about them.

I wish C were with me today and I could have seen the Lincoln Memorial with him. Too late now, but I'd love to have a picture of him there, at the monument of his hero.

Was Edie saying she wished Carl had spent another day with her? If the relative she found in Washington was Carl, why hadn't they gone to see the monument together? Edie had taken a picture with him at another location, and it wasn't that far from the Lincoln Memorial. Perhaps they had run out of time. From what Anne could see in Friday's mention, Edie was not able to rendezvous again with the "long-lost relative." Was that what she meant by "too late now"?

The rest of the journal told of Edie's sightseeing and a bit of research, most of which seemed to be focused on her mother's ancestors. Although President Ford had gone to Philadelphia to give his bicentennial address, Edie had completely enjoyed the parades and festivities in the capital. She also noted that Queen Elizabeth and Prince Philip were traveling and would be entertained at the White House a few days later, but she didn't think she would stay over in hopes of a glimpse of the queen. Edie was starting to think of the many projects she had waiting for her at home. She didn't mention the relative she'd met in Washington again before she had headed home on July 5.

But she had mentioned C. That had to be Carl, Anne reasoned, even though her great-aunt hadn't written his full name. If Edie hadn't actually seen the young man, why drop his initial in her diary? What made her think of him? Or was C someone else? It was the same initial she had written on the California postcard she had never mailed.

Anne couldn't think of any other relatives whose names began with C, except for Pauline's husband, Craig. It was true that she didn't know anything about her great-grandmother's family. That was the line Edie had researched most on the trip. It was possible she had met up with a relative from that branch of the family, but none of the names jotted in the diary began with C. Maybe someday Anne would find more detailed genealogy information that Edie had compiled. But that wouldn't help her right now.

Anne decided to focus on what she had in hand and not speculate about the infinite number of other possibilities. The picture was the key. Even if the C in the diary didn't refer to Carl, the picture was evidence that he was there.

To Anne it seemed almost conclusive that Aunt Edie had seen Carl in Washington. She wished she would hear back from the inquiry she had sent on the army's Web site, but so far nothing had come from them. Still, Aunt Edie and Carl had posed for one photo together, and Edie wished they had spent more time together. What else could that paragraph mean? Her dad would probably have another explanation, but to Anne, it was clear. Cousin Carl was alive and well and on good terms with Aunt Edie in 1976.

Chapter Ten

The rain still pelted down when the end of the school day came. Anne left her father and Alex working in the garage and jumped in the car with her mother, heading for the school yard so the children wouldn't have to walk home in the rain.

Liddie and Ben tumbled into the car charged with pent-up energy.

"Grandma, look!" Ben thrust a soggy paper into her hands. "I got an A on my report about jet engines."

Anne's mother smiled. "That's wonderful, honey. I know that took a lot of work."

"It sure did." Ben buckled his seat belt and checked Liddie's.

"Where are we going?" Liddie asked. "Mommy, are you going to surprise us today?"

Anne laughed and looked in the rearview mirror at Liddie's eager face. The moisture in the air had turned the little girl's waves into messy curls. "Grandma and I did discuss the possibility. One of the women who came into the library today told me her family has a batch of new baby chicks. Would you like to see them?"

"What about Hershey?" Ben asked fretfully, thinking of his dog first, as usual.

"Don't worry about him," Anne said. "When we had a lull in the rain, Grandpa and Alex took him for a run in the backyard.

He'll be eager to see you when we get home, but don't let him out for long unless it's stopped raining, all right? We don't want mud all over the library."

"Can he come inside for a while?" Ben asked.

"Yes, if he's clean and dry." That might mean some work on Ben's part, drying the dog and brushing him once he'd had his time outside, but Anne knew Ben would do his best to reach her standard. Since he got the dog, he had tried very hard to keep Hershey from causing work for his mother.

They spent an enjoyable half hour at a farm a mile outside of town. Liddie's eyes glowed as she patted the tiny chicks and a three-day-old calf in the owner's barn. Ben seemed to enjoy the outing but remained slightly impatient to get home.

When they got back to the house, Ryan was in the garage with Alex and Anne's father.

"Hi, Ryan," Anne said. "I wouldn't have kept the kids away if I'd known you were here."

"It's okay," the boy said. "Uncle Alex had left me a note, and he said I could come over after school if I wanted, so I came. Hey, Ben, can we take Hershey outside?"

"Yeah!"

"Change your clothes first," Anne called as the two boys raced for the back door of the house.

When she went into the library, she was pleased to find Mildred inside chatting with Bella.

"Hello, Mildred. I hoped I'd see you soon," Anne said. "I wanted to ask you about something."

"Ask away." Mildred's smile was as sunny as usual.

"Well, remember we were talking a few days ago about Aunt Edie's trip to Washington?" Anne walked toward the Nonfiction Room, and Mildred went with her.

"I remember when she went," Mildred said, "but she never said anything to me afterward about that nephew of hers—the one in the picture."

"I'm still working on that." Anne walked over to the fireplace and waved toward one of the armchairs for Mildred. "I wondered if you knew her friend, Iris Gallagher."

Mildred thought for a moment as she sat down. "Well, yes. Edie mentioned her to me, though I can't remember what the context was. She doesn't live around here, does she?"

"No, but Aunt Edie stayed with her on her way to Washington at the bicentennial."

"That's it." Mildred snapped her fingers. "Edie asked me to go on that trip with her, and I couldn't. I was working at the time, and I couldn't get enough days off. But she did mention this friend she planned to stay overnight with. I don't recall the details—heavens, it was all such a long time ago!"

"I know." The fire in the fireplace had died down, and Anne took the poker from its rack and stirred the embers. "Now I'm curious as to whether Iris is still alive, and if she could tell me anything about that trip. She drove on down to Washington with Aunt Edie and spent a couple of days with her, then took the bus home."

"Wish I could help you," Mildred said. "I don't recall where she lived, and I never met her. Edie's address book is probably your best bet."

"You're probably right." Anne took three sticks of firewood from the woodbox near the hearth and settled them gently on the pile of coals.

"Anything else?" Mildred asked. "I thought I'd go upstairs and spend a few minutes with your mother."

"She'd like that," Anne replied. "If I think of anything else, I'll come find you."

Bella was quite busy at the checkout desk, so Anne took a rolling cart of returned books and went around to the different rooms to replace them on the shelves. While she worked, she kept thinking about Aunt Edie's trip to Washington and her mysterious references to "C" and a long-lost relative. If only she could prove they were one and the same person—her cousin Carl.

She remembered shelving several books about the capital, and when she entered the Nonfiction Room with the cart, she went to the shelves dedicated to United States travel and looked through them. Two were older books about the White House and the Smithsonian Institution. Another was an old travel guide that Anne had nearly discarded. Now she was glad she hadn't.

She opened the book to the front and saw Aunt Edie's name written in her unique hand. Anne flipped through the pages and found several places where Edie had marked items. Anne had bought an up-to-date Washington guide, and it was now shelved next to the old one, but she was glad she hadn't tossed Aunt Edie's copy. Once again, her instincts had served her well. Aunt Edie had probably used this book on her bicentennial trip. And if Aunt Edie saved something, there was usually a reason to hang on to it.

When the library closed, Anne thanked Bella and saw her out. She went upstairs and found her mother starting supper.

"Hi, Anne. Alex and Ryan have gone, and your father's changing his clothes. He just got done cutting Ben's hair."

"Oh, good! It slipped my mind, and I'm glad someone remembered. Ben sure needed it."

Her mother smiled. "I thought I'd throw these dirty towels in the washer before we sit down."

Anne eyed the heap of muddy towels on the linoleum floor. "Let me guess. Ben brought Hershey in and cleaned him up."

Her mother laughed. "I told him a bunch of dirty towels was better than a filthy house. At least he kept all the dirt in the kitchen."

"Right. I'll start the laundry." Anne gathered up the towels. She carried them down to the basement, started the load, and then went up to the living room, where Ben and Liddie were sitting on the rug with a mostly clean Hershey between them, watching a video.

"Nice haircut, Ben," Anne said.

"Thanks." He didn't look up but kept watching the video and absently patting Hershey.

"Time for supper," Anne said.

Liddie jumped up, and Hershey barked and got up too.

"Come on," Ben told him. "You can eat your supper while we eat ours." He clicked off the video and headed for the kitchen.

Over the dinner table, Anne brought her father up to date on her findings.

"I think it would be worthwhile to do a search for Iris Gallagher. Other than that, I'm still stymied about Carl."

Her father examined the little trip diary. "This doesn't prove anything, but it sure looks like she met up with someone she didn't expect to see in Washington."

"Or does it?" Anne's mother asked. "Anne said she mentioned going to one of the Smithsonian Research Centers. Maybe that's where she found this long-lost relative—in an archive and not actually in person."

Anne sighed. "I know—it's just not conclusive. And the one time she does mention *C*—well, what does that mean? If it was Carl, she wished they could have visited the Lincoln Memorial together. Dad, to your knowledge, was Lincoln a particular hero of Carl's?"

He shrugged. "I don't know. We were kids. It's certainly possible that Carl gained an appreciation of Lincoln during the years after I last saw him, but I don't remember him being particularly enamored of history."

"It may not even refer to Carl," her mother said. "Maybe Edie knew someone who was a huge Lincoln fan, and their name started with *C*, and when she saw the memorial, it made her think of them."

"I suppose," Anne said. "I could be reading what I want to see into what she wrote."

"To my way of thinking, it is suspicious," her dad said. "I mean, why not spell his name out, unless she didn't want anyone else to see it? She spelled out other people's names. Like Iris. She never refers to her as *I*."

"True, though that could be a little confusing." She chuckled. "Still, if she did mean Carl in the diary, 'too late' might still have meant either that he was dead, or that he wasn't with her that day."

"Now, Edie always *did* speak highly of Abraham Lincoln," her father mused. "I believe he was one of her historic heroes."

"Yes," Anne said. "She had two biographies of him, one quite recent. They're in the library now. But we really can't say what Carl thought of him."

"At least I have some concrete news," her mother said. "I talked to Joanna today."

"How is my little sister?" Anne's father asked as he passed the plate of biscuits to Ben and Liddie.

"She's fine, and the family's fine. And she gave me Cousin Madeline's full name—it's Culver now—and her addresses, both e-mail and snail mail."

"Hooray," Ben said.

Anne eyed him in surprise. "Why do you say that, Ben?"

"Because you and Grandma have been wanting that address just about ever since Grandma and Grandpa got here. Now you can stop looking for it."

Anne's father chuckled. "You're right, Ben. It's always a relief to find something you've been searching for. It lets you relax and concentrate on other things."

"Like the invitations," her mother said. "I did some work on the wording this afternoon. Anne, if you can look at it this evening, I think we can send out all the invitations tomorrow morning."

"Sounds good."

Liddie, who had been unusually quiet during dinner, looked sleepily up at Anne. "Mommy, can we finish our video after supper?"

"I don't think so, sweet pea. You look really tired. I think a bath and bed are what you need." Anne appraised Ben for a moment. "And you, Ben. You may have gotten Hershey cleaned up, but I think a lot of that mud ended up on you. You'd better have a shower tonight, so you'll be clean for school in the morning."

Ben reached around to the back of his collar and scratched his neck. "Okay. I think I got some hair down my back too."

"The shower will take care of the tickles," Anne's father said.

While Anne took Liddie off to start her bath, her parents went into the living room with their mugs of coffee, and Ben joined them. Anne took a little extra time to wash and comb out Liddie's fine light brown hair.

"Would you like me to read you a story tonight?" She felt a little guilty for not spending as much time with the children lately as she usually did.

But Liddie shook her head. "Grandma."

"You want Grandma to come read to you?"

Liddie nodded emphatically. "She does really cool voices."

Anne laughed. "All right, I'll ask her." She gave Liddie a big hug and a kiss. "You get into bed, and she'll probably be right up."

Anne's mother was only too happy to go up and share a storybook with Liddie.

"Ben, it's your turn in the bathroom," Anne said.

"Good night, Grandpa. I'll see you in the morning." Ben reluctantly left his grandfather's side and headed up to the third floor.

"You're doing a great job with the kids, Anne," her father said.

"Thank you. That means a lot."

As soon as her mother returned, Anne asked her if she planned to call Madeline in California.

"Why don't you call her, dear? Here's the number." Her mother handed her a slip of paper from the notepad on Anne's desk. "You can tell her about the reunion and ask about Carl if you want to. Oh, and Ben's out of the shower, and Liddie wants another hug. I told them both you'd be up in a couple of minutes."

"Ben's all finished? That was fast. I think I'll call Madeline first."

Anne's mother walked over to the sofa and sat down beside her dad. "You know, I've done a lot of thinking about this Washington business too. I've come to the conclusion that the young man in that photo with Aunt Edie isn't really Cousin Carl. I mean, how could it be? It has to be someone else who resembles him strongly."

"You could be right, Mom, but I don't want to discount the possibility."

"Honey," her mother said gently, "we need to accept the fact that Carl was killed in Vietnam."

"Maybe finding this other person who looked so much like him reminded her of Carl," Anne's father suggested, "and that's why she mentioned him in the trip diary."

"I know it's possible, but I still want to be certain," Anne said.

"By all means, go ahead and ask Madeline about it," her mother said. "But you may never find out for sure."

"Do you think she'll mind?" Anne asked.

Her father shook his head. "I don't see why she would. It might make her sad to remember him and the way he died, but I really don't think she was that close to Uncle David's family."

After a moment's thought, Anne punched in the number and waited. The call switched to a voice mail system. Disappointed, Anne left a message, including her home phone number.

As she was speaking, she heard the beeping that indicated an incoming call, but she broke off her connection too late to answer it. After disconnecting her call to California, she checked her messages.

"Hi, Anne! This is Carl Summers Jr. We seem to be playing phone tag. I'm anxious to talk to you, so I'll try again after a while."

"Oh, it was him," Anne said to her parents. "Carl Summers Jr. from Washington." She tried to return the call but only got his voice mail. She sighed and put down the phone. "No luck."

"I guess you're right about Pauline," her father said. "If we really want to find the truth, we need to ask her. I doubt that she knows anything we don't, but I guess it's worth a try."

"I'll go up and say good night to Liddie and Ben," Anne said. "Why don't you call her? You know how to be diplomatic."

"Ha! I guess that's a compliment." As she headed for the stairs, her father said, "I have another question—something to ponder."

Anne paused in the doorway. "What's that?"

"I still keep wondering why Edie never got that film from her Washington trip developed."

"It wasn't like her, was it? But she did have the other roll done."

"Yes, and I'm glad you found that. Likely she forgot the one still in the camera."

Anne went up to the third story and tapped on Ben's door. He was in bed, wearing his pajamas, looking at a book.

"Mom, will you read this to me?"

Anne smiled and took the book from his hand. It was one of his favorites, an old picture book he'd loved for years.

"Sure." She opened to the first page, cherishing the fact that he didn't consider himself too old to let his mother read to him.

When she peeked into Liddie's room, she thought the little girl was fast asleep, but Liddie raised her head and said sleepily, "Mommy, can I wear my new pink dress to the exhibit?"

"Of course you can." Anne stooped to tuck Liddie's sheet in around her shoulders. "We'll go shopping with Grandma and get you some new pink ribbons to wear in your hair that day."

"Who else will be coming?" Liddie asked and then promptly gave a big yawn.

"Lots of people. Mrs. Farley, the Pyles, Reverend Tom—"

"Has Reverend Tom always been the pastor here?"

Anne had the feeling Liddie was stalling, trying to keep her in the room, but she said patiently, "No, there used to be a different pastor here, before we moved to Blue Hill."

"Who was it?"

"I'm not sure. You need to sleep now, honey." Anne kissed Liddie's silky hair and tiptoed out.

As she walked back down the stairs, she wondered if Liddie wasn't onto something. Reverend Tom's predecessor might know something about what happened between Uncle David and Cousin Carl, and he probably held some sort of memorial service for the family when Carl's death was announced.

The idea helped dispel the frustration brought on by her failure to turn up solid information so far. She still had other avenues to explore. She could ask Reverend Tom about the previous pastor, and she had a list of several people she wanted to contact: Cousin Madeline, Carl Summers Jr., and her cousin Carl's sister, Pauline. Her digging was far from done.

Chapter Eleven

The library kept Anne quite busy on Thursday, but when the children arrived home from school, she left Wendy in charge while she and her mother took Liddie shopping for hair ribbons.

Ben was happy to stay home with his grandfather, Hershey, and Ryan, who came over to play.

"I'll put the boys to work for me," her father said. "They can fetch things for me while I work on the deck."

Anne drove to her favorite fabric shop and sauntered through the aisles with her mother and Liddie, until they came to a rack of ribbon spools.

"Look, Mommy! Pink!" Liddie picked out the brightest shade of pink from a rainbow of ribbon colors.

"That looks like an almost perfect match to your dress," Anne said.

Her mother smiled. "Liddie, you'll be the prettiest girl at the exhibit opening."

Liddie raised her chin and smiled up at her grandmother. "Mommy said I can help that day."

Anne gave her a squeeze. "You're always a good helper when we have library events."

"And you're glad I found the camera, aren't you, Mommy?"

With surprise, Anne gazed into Liddie's troubled eyes. "Of course, sweetheart. If you hadn't found it, I probably never would have thought of having this exhibit."

"But you haven't found Carl yet," Liddie said, frowning. "That makes you sad."

Anne hugged Liddie closer. "You know what? We may never find Cousin Carl, but I'm still very glad you found the camera and that it had that picture in it. It's gotten Grandpa and me to dig into the family history a lot, and to get in touch with relatives we haven't talked to for a long time—and some we didn't even know before. So don't you worry about any sadness, okay? There's a lot of happiness too."

Anne paid for the hair ribbons, and her mother bought a craft magazine. After Anne had buckled Liddie into her seat in the car, her mother said softly, "That's a very perceptive child you have there."

"And tenderhearted," Anne agreed. "I have to be careful when I get emotional about something. Liddie picks right up on it."

"Sensitivity can be a good thing." Her mother smiled. "Maybe she'll be a poet. Or a psychologist."

"Or a very good mother," Anne said. She got into the driver's seat and headed her Impala toward Blue Hill Community Church. "I hope you don't mind a quick stop at Reverend Tom's office."

"Not at all," her mother said.

"Thanks. I asked Dad about when Carl died, and he said the family held a memorial service. The former pastor officiated at that, and I'm hoping Reverend Tom can help me locate him."

When Anne knocked on the open door of the office inside the church, Reverend Tom looked up and smiled.

"Ladies! What a nice surprise." He rose and came forward to greet them. "Charlene, it's good to see you again."

After her mother had shaken the pastor's hand, Anne said, "I wondered if you knew anything about my uncle David Summers and his son, Carl."

"Not much," Reverend Tom admitted. "I've only been here since the turn of the century. Didn't Carl Summers die overseas?"

"Yes, Vietnam. I suppose Uncle David had died as well, before you came here."

"I'm afraid so."

Anne nodded. "I assumed as much, but I wondered…do you think the previous pastor might be able to help me?"

"That's possible. Reverend Daniel is very old, but he might remember something about the family. He would probably love to visit with you, even if he can't answer your questions. I believe he's gone into assisted living, but I'm not sure where. Why don't I try to find out for you?"

"That would be very kind," Anne said.

They chatted for a few more minutes and then headed home.

"Disappointed?" her mother asked in the car.

"Not really. At least Reverend Daniel is still alive. I'm learning that these things take time. The Lord has a way of opening doors to the past if I'm patient."

"Are you thinking he might know things about the family that other people don't?"

Anne shrugged. "People do confide things to their pastors. Of course, if it's something confidential, he might not want to share it."

"That's true," her mother said. "I think the family is a more promising source for this particular question."

"You may be right."

When they got home, they stopped to inspect the work on the back deck before going inside.

"Wow, you're coming right along," Anne said to her dad.

He straightened, with one hand on his lower back. "Yes, the boys have been a big help. It should be finished in plenty of time, and Alex is going to try to come by again tomorrow for a few hours if he can. We hope to get the benches and planters done before the reunion."

"That would be fantastic, but I don't want you to wear yourself out," Anne cautioned.

"Thanks. Now that you mention it, I think I'm ready for a break."

"Come on upstairs," her mother said. "As soon as Liddie has changed into play clothes, she'll be having some milk and cookies, and I'm sure she'd love to have you join the party."

"Yeah, Grandpa. You come!" Liddie smiled at him winsomely.

"You don't have to ask me twice, young lady." He patted Liddie's cheek. "You go get changed, and I'll put my tools away. I think I'll leave this until tomorrow." He glanced at Anne. "Say, have you picked out all the pictures for the display yet? I was thinking—we'd better get them to the photo shop."

"You're right," Anne said. "Let's finalize those tonight. Jay McAllister, the photographer at the *Gazette,* called me earlier. He's offered to enlarge the black and whites for a very modest fee, and I'm going to take him up on it."

"Most of the ones we want to use are black and white, aren't they?"

"Yeah, there are only a couple of color ones I have my heart set on. One is of this house with the flowers in full bloom. The other one is of Aunt Edie outside the church with Reverend Tom. It's fairly recent, from the look of it. If we decide for sure which ones we want, I'll get them to Jay tomorrow."

Anne went into the library, where she took over from Wendy. After checking out a patron's books, she peeked into each of the rooms and discovered that she was momentarily alone. Now might be a good time to call Cousin Pauline. Her father had struck out when he'd tried to connect with her the evening before, and he had left it to Anne to make the call today if she had time.

She pressed the digits for the number her dad had given her and waited, hoping she wouldn't get another voice mail message.

"Hello?" A woman said brightly.

"Pauline? This is Anne, Dale Summers's daughter."

"Well, hi, Anne. Good to hear from you."

Anne relaxed in her chair. Maybe this was the break she needed.

"My folks are up from Florida, and we've decided to have a little reunion a week from Sunday. Could you and Craig possibly come?"

"Oh, that sounds like fun! I'll have to check. Dale and Charlene are there now, you say?"

"Yeah. Dad tried to call you last night, but—"

"We went to our granddaughter's recital and then went out for ice cream afterward. We got home pretty late. I'd love to see them both though."

Anne gave her the details about the gathering, and then she took a deep breath. "Could I ask you something about your brother?"

"Carl?" Pauline sounded surprised that Anne had brought him up. "What about him?"

"Dad and I have been looking at the family tree and going through some of Aunt Edie's old albums. We found a picture of her with Carl."

"Oh, that's nice." Pauline's voice softened a little. "I wonder if it's one I have a copy of."

"I don't think so," Anne said carefully. "This was actually on a roll of film still in one of her cameras. We think it was taken when she made a trip to Washington, DC."

"Washington?" Pauline asked. "That's odd. I don't remember Carl ever going to Washington. Do you know when it was taken?"

"That's the problem. It was on a roll with photos taken from the bicentennial. It was in 1976."

For a few seconds, silence hung between them.

"That can't be," Pauline said at last.

"That's exactly what Dad said. We're trying to figure it out, but it's a real puzzle. We found a little trip diary from that jaunt of hers, and she didn't mention Carl's name, but she did say she'd found a long-lost relative, and she referred to someone whose first initial was *C*. But she was doing research on that trip, and we weren't sure if she meant she 'found' someone in an archive, or if she literally bumped into a relative she hadn't seen for a long time."

"And you think it was Carl?"

"Yes," Anne said. "Because of the picture."

"That's just plain impossible."

"That's what we said." Anne waited for Pauline to think about it.

"I've got to see that picture," Pauline said at last. "I will definitely be there next week."

"I'll have a copy made for you," Anne said. "I should probably tell you that my mom doesn't think it's him."

"Who does she think it is?"

"She doesn't know. We know it's not Dad, and nobody can come up with another candidate. This guy has the Summers look, if you know what I mean. And he's in uniform. When Dad saw the picture, he said right away that it was Carl…until he realized that it couldn't be."

"Wow. I don't know what to say."

"So, you've never had any indication that he might not have died in 1970?"

"No," Pauline said. "Nothing like that. It seems bizarre. I'm sorry, Anne, but I wish you hadn't told me."

"You do?"

Pauline let out a ragged sigh. "This has not been easy for me. After Mom died, it was bad enough. I missed her horribly. But then Carl started fighting with Dad all the time. It was awful, being under the same roof with them. There had been a lot of friction between them for quite some time, and it got worse. I loved Carl dearly, but he was being unreasonable. Oh, Dad was too, but somehow they should have been able to find some middle ground."

"About Carl working in the business, you mean?"

"Yeah, mostly that. Carl was afraid it would wreck his life, and he would never get to do anything he wanted. I could understand that, to a point. Dad wanted him to take over the whole company. He was having some health issues. You know Dad died a few years later."

"Yes," Anne said. "I'm so sorry."

"I tried to talk to both of them, but it didn't do any good. Carl got to where he wouldn't set foot in the store, and Dad really needed him."

"Did you work in the store?" Anne asked.

"I had to. Oh, Dad had employees, but he needed someone he could really trust with the financial end of it. I took over the bookkeeping that Mom had done when I was still in high school. I hated it. I couldn't get involved in any after-school activities. At that point, I was furious with Carl too, for not taking the responsibility. And then he left."

"When he enlisted, you mean?"

"Yes. He joined the army, and Dad couldn't do a thing about it. I think Carl wanted to go to college, but Dad wouldn't pay for it because he wanted him in the store full time. I guess Carl thought enlisting was the only way he could truly get free of

Dad and the furniture business. I hoped and prayed that when he came back things would be better between them. But that didn't happen," Pauline. "When we got word that he'd died, I felt so alone. So abandoned. I met Craig around that time. If not for his support, I'd have gone crazy—at least it felt that way."

"I'm so sorry." Anne didn't know what else to say.

Pauline sniffled. "Well, it was a long time ago, but it still hurts. And then I had Dad's illness to deal with. He was still bitter against Carl for leaving when he did. And now you're bringing it all up again."

"I hope there's a happier ending to this story," Anne ventured.

"I don't know how you can think that. The picture you found—there's got to be a mistake. Either you got the date wrong, or it's somebody else who just happens to look like Carl."

"I've put in an inquiry to the army," Anne said. "If I hear anything back, I'll certainly let you know."

"You took it that far?"

"Yes. Dad and I both think that if the army made an error, it's time they admitted it. And if not, maybe they'll send us something more definite than you got in 1970—some hard proof that he's dead."

Pauline was silent for a moment. "Wow. That would be something, wouldn't it? I mean, if he didn't die when they told us he did. But then—"

"What?" Anne asked.

"Never mind. If you knew the answer, you would have told me. I was going to say, if he was alive after that, then why didn't he tell us? I mean, he's my brother! Why would he let me go over forty years thinking he was dead?"

"I don't have an answer for that. And I didn't mean to upset you," Anne said. "In fact, my dad didn't want to tell you until we knew more. He didn't want to raise false hopes. But then we decided, since you were closer to Carl than anyone else, that if it was true, you might know something."

"No. Nothing. Now, I'm actually glad you told me. Thank you, Anne. I'm sorry I got upset."

"It's okay—and you're welcome. I'll see you next week, then."

Anne hung up and sat staring at the phone for several seconds. She wished she hadn't stirred things up with Pauline, and yet she was glad to have made the contact and to know Pauline would attend the reunion.

The front door opened, and a man with a military bearing entered. It was one of her regular patrons, Douglas Pauthen, though his wife usually accompanied his visits to the library.

"Good afternoon, Douglas," she called. "No Marian today?

"Flying solo." He smiled. "She's getting her hair done, so I have some time to kill."

"Can I help you find something in particular?"

"Just thought I'd check to see if any new biographies have come in," he said.

Anne smiled. "You know where we keep them. I've ordered a few new ones, but I don't think they've come in yet. If you can't find a good one, you let me know, and I'll come help you look."

"Okay, thanks." He waved and headed for the elevator and the Nonfiction Room.

Anne looked at her watch and decided to take a minute to check her e-mail. She caught her breath when she saw the most recent message awaiting her. She had received a response from the US Army.

Chapter Twelve

Anne couldn't help feeling a little disappointed at the formal message she received from a Sergeant Amy Potter. Instead of a report on Carl's career, she got a crisply worded e-mail telling her that in order to receive an answer to her questions, she would have to supply more information, such as Carl's Social Security number, his army serial number, or at least his rank and unit.

Anne sighed. She should have realized they would need more to go on, but she'd hoped that giving them Carl's name and his birth date and place, which her dad had supplied, would be enough. She didn't have the details Sergeant Potter asked for, and she wondered who did. If she had read the message first, she could have asked Pauline if she had that information. Surely there must be some records within the family—certificates Carl earned in the army and maybe some letters he wrote home, though judging from what Pauline had told her, he may never have done that. Someone must at least have his Social Security number. Pauline seemed the most likely, but Anne dreaded calling her again.

She pulled a notebook out of her desk drawer. It was time she started keeping records of her efforts. All too easily, she could forget whom she had contacted and what they had said. She could e-mail her father's sisters, Aunt Faith and Aunt Joanna, but she needed a record of the telephone calls she had made and the conversations she'd had with people like Mildred and Pauline.

She went over their conversation in her mind and jotted down the gist of it. After considering the message from Sergeant Potter again, she decided she had to call Pauline back. She didn't want to wait to reply to the sergeant. She pushed the Redial button on the telephone.

"Yes, Anne?" Pauline said a moment later.

Anne gulped. Caller ID had told Pauline who was calling, she supposed. Quickly, Anne explained why she had phoned again so soon.

"Okay," Pauline said slowly. "I have some papers that the army sent to Dad. They're in a folder with the stuff from Dad's estate. Can you hold on?"

"Sure." Anne waited while Pauline went to get out the documents.

She came back to the phone a couple of minutes later. "Anne? I found his Social Security number and his serial number from the army."

"Perfect," Anne said. "Thanks so much. This should help us get something out of them, even if it's only that they don't have any information." She took down the numbers and read them back for accuracy.

"Anne, I'm really sorry I wasn't more gracious earlier," Pauline said. "I do appreciate you and Dale doing this. I mean, if there's the slightest chance…"

"We feel the same way," Anne assured her. "Oh, and Pauline, Craig wasn't ever in the military, was he?"

"No."

"Okay, thanks. Just checking. I found a place where Aunt Edie had mentioned someone whose name began with C, and I wanted to make sure she didn't mean Craig."

When she had hung up, she felt a little easier about the question of other relatives whose names began with C. She opened a new e-mail message box, determined to give all the information now at hand. It took her several minutes to compose her message, and she stopped twice to assist patrons, but at last she completed her narrative. In it she had put Carl's identifying data first in the message, and then she explained the reasons for her own and her father's concerns about Carl, and the hope that he might still be alive. She even put in a line about the upcoming reunion and how exciting it would be to tell the family they had new information. She concluded with her phone number and address.

As she hit Send, Anne felt a little disheartened. She had done what she could. If she didn't get any useful information back, she would feel her efforts were wasted. She hoped the sergeant would try her best to find something. The army was such a large and impersonal organization, Anne feared she might hear nothing further. Even if someone at the Pentagon—or somewhere else—had a file on Carl, and even if it contained information the family longed to know, the army might not agree to share that with her. She knew that sometimes files were sealed for many years, and she hoped that wasn't what had happened in Carl's case.

She still had several other leads to pursue. As she caught up on her library tasks of re-shelving, updating patrons' cards, and adding a new magazine subscription to the periodicals file, she planned her strategy and jotted reminders in her notebook.

The kids came in from playing outside with Hershey, and she took a few minutes to chat with them.

"Can I go to Ryan's?" Ben asked.

"Is Alex at home?"

"He's probably working."

"Then why don't you call Ryan and ask him to come over here? I don't think Alex would want Ryan to have company when he's not there."

"Okay. Thanks, Mom." Ben charged up the stairs.

Anne smiled as Liddie scampered off to find her grandma.

A patron was coming out of the Nonfiction Room with a few books in hand. Anne sent Liddie off toward the staircase and went back to the checkout desk and her duties.

Betty Bultman arrived to volunteer for the rest of the evening shift, since the library was open late on Thursday nights. Anne thanked Betty, gave her a few instructions, and then headed upstairs.

Before supper, she would make one more try. She went to the family living room. Her father sat on the sofa, examining the piles of photographs she had set aside.

"Hi, Dad," Anne said. She told him about her conversation with Pauline and her e-mail exchange with Sergeant Potter. "And now I'm going to try Cousin Madeline again."

He nodded. "I hope you're successful this time."

Anne punched in the California number and held her breath.

The woman who answered sounded elderly and frail.

"Hello, Cousin Madeline?" Anne said. "I'm Dale Summers's daughter, Anne. Anne Gibson."

"Dale Summers? No! It's been ages since I heard from your folks."

Anne smiled. "They're here visiting me. I wanted to tell you about a little reunion we're having with my mom and dad, here in Blue Hill, Pennsylvania, a week from Sunday."

"Blue Hill." Madeline's voice thickened with emotion. "Dear Edie's gone now, but I'd love to see the old place again. It's odd to think of her not being there."

"I know what you mean," Anne said.

"I expect Blue Hill isn't the same without her."

"She left her house to the town for a library, and my children and I live upstairs now."

"So she really did it," Madeline said. "I heard her speak often of doing that very thing. I'm so glad."

"Thank you," Anne said.

"You were a librarian before, weren't you?"

"Yes. At the New York Public Library." Briefly, Anne caught her up on her situation.

"I would love to see Dale and Pauline and any others of the family that I could," Madeline said. "You know, I'm not too old to fly."

"Of course you're not." Anne smiled at her confidence.

"Eighty-one is not too old," Madeline said cheerfully.

Anne looked over at her father. He was watching her with great interest.

"If you should decide to come, do let us know," Anne said. "One of us would pick you up at the airport."

"I think I'll ask my son about it," Madeline said. "Maybe he'd go with me."

"That would be so much fun. I don't think I've ever met your son."

"We'll talk it over and let you know."

Anne gave Madeline her telephone number and asked if she used e-mail.

"Yes, I do, as a matter of fact. I'm not too old for that either."

Anne grinned. Madeline sounded a lot like Aunt Edie. "There's one other thing I wanted to ask you about."

"Yes?" Madeline said.

"Aunt Edie loved to travel."

"Oh, I know it. She came out here to see me...*hmm*, when was it? It must have been a good ten years ago now. No, eleven. I remember she took me out for my seventieth birthday."

"I'm sure you had a good time," Anne said. "Didn't she also visit you in 1977? We have a picture of her at Grauman's Chinese Theater."

"Oh my, yes. I almost forgot about that time. We had the best fun together. Took my two oldest grandchildren to Knott's Berry Farm."

Anne wondered if Madeline's grandchildren might be the cousins Edie referred to on the postcard to "C."

"Did Aunt Edie ever talk to you about her nephew, Carl?"

"That would be David's boy?" Madeline asked.

"Yes."

"Sure, quite a lot. It was such a shame when he was killed."

"You remember the circumstances?"

"He was in the war. As far as I knew, they never got his body back. I know that bothered Edie, and I suppose it upset his father too. I'm sure he wanted some closure, after all that passed between them."

"What do you mean?" Anne asked.

"Well, I..." Madeline hesitated.

"I know that Carl and his father didn't get along well," Anne said quickly, hoping Madeline wouldn't stop talking about it. "A couple of people have told me that Uncle David wanted Carl to take over the store, but Carl had other ideas."

"That's true, I guess. I was never very close to David, but I liked Natalie. She was a sweet thing. After she died, I guess Carl and David had their troubles. Edie told me she thought that was partly why the boy enlisted. Wanted to get away from his father. That's sad, but it happens."

"Yes."

Anne looked over at her dad, and he whispered, "Ask if she's heard anything about him being alive."

"Uh, Madeline," Anne said cautiously, "did Aunt Edie ever talk to you about her trip to Washington, DC, during the bicentennial celebration?"

"I certainly knew about it. She sent me a postcard, I think. And she wrote to me about it afterward."

Anne took hope and pressed on. "That's neat. I was just reading a little trip diary she kept. And we found some pictures she took on that trip too. One is on the Mall with a friend of hers, and another is near DAR Constitution Hall."

"Interesting," Madeline said.

"Yes, very. Because in one of those pictures, she's standing next to a young man, and we're not sure who he is, but he looks very much like Carl."

"Probably it is Carl. No, wait—" Madeline paused, and Anne waited, her heart racing. "That would be after he died, wouldn't it? I was thinking he died around 1970."

"Yes, that's what we were always told, but if it's not Carl, who else could it be?"

"Are you sure it's not your father? Because all of the Summers men have the same nose, you know."

Anne chuckled. "We've noticed the resemblance, but Dad is right here, and it's not him. He wasn't in Washington then, and he has no idea who that is. But when he first saw the picture, he thought it was Carl."

"*Hmm*...I'm sure I can't think who else it would be. Are you certain about the date?"

"Yes. Several of the pictures on that roll of film are of attractions at the bicentennial exposition, and some even have signs that leave no doubt. It was July of 1976. And another thing—this fellow is in uniform. My dad wasn't in the service then."

Madeline sighed. "Well, isn't that odd? Can you send me a copy of the picture?"

"Yes. I'll scan it and e-mail it to you."

"Thank you, dear. Send me the details about that reunion too."

"I will. Good-bye, Cousin Madeline. It was nice talking to you."

Anne hung up and eyed her father bleakly. "She doesn't know any more than we do."

"Well, it sounded as though she knew about Carl and David wrangling before Carl enlisted."

"Yes, but she didn't know anything about his death or whether he could still be alive. You heard, I guess—she thinks it's not him in the picture."

"Go ahead and send her a copy," her father counseled. "Maybe when she sees how striking the resemblance is, she'll change her mind."

Anne's mother came to the doorway. "I've got supper ready. Anybody hungry?"

"Mom, I'm sorry. You didn't come here to be the cook."

"I don't mind. In fact, I don't see how you do it on your own."

"Some days I'm better at multitasking. And then on other days, we eat sandwiches and soup." As they rose and headed for the kitchen, Anne squeezed her father's hand. "I'll send Madeline the picture right after supper."

Determined not to let the lack of new information discourage her, Anne followed through and sent the photo an hour later. She opened her notebook and jotted down the date and time she had talked to Madeline and sent the picture.

She tried the Washington number once again, and this time, Carl Summers Jr. picked up the phone.

"Mrs. Gibson! I'm so glad we finally connected!"

"So am I."

"So, tell me, was your family named Summers before they immigrated?"

"I…so far as I know." What little family research Anne had done led her to believe her father's family traced a straight line back to the British Isles. "Wasn't yours?" she ventured.

His voice fell. "No. My ancestors came here from Russia shortly before the Russian Revolution. Their name was changed from Sumovich."

Anne's elation faded. "Russian? Wow, that's interesting, but it makes me doubt that we're related."

"Yeah, me too. It's too bad. I was hoping to find someone else who came from the same Russian family. So, there's someone in your line named Carl?"

"Yes, my father's cousin. But he was killed in the Vietnam War."

They chatted for a few minutes, and Carl explained to Anne how his family came to leave Russia just as Europe was commencing World War I.

Her mother came into the room as she signed off.

"Any luck?"

Anne shook her head. "Afraid not. That was Carl Summers in Washington, and we're not kin at all. His family is Russian."

Her mother smiled in sympathy. "You're bound to hit a few dead ends. Don't let it get you down."

"I won't. And Dad and I are going to go through those photos again once the kids are in bed. We'll make our final decisions, and I'll take the ones we want to use for the exhibit to Jay tomorrow morning."

"Great. Right now your father's out in the backyard with the kids and Hershey. Do you feel like playing whiffle ball?"

Anne grinned. "Sounds like fun, and I need a little exercise. You playing?"

"In a moment of weakness, I told Liddie I would."

"Let's go, then." Anne linked arms with her mom and drew her toward the private back stairs. "Just think—if we were related to that fellow, we might have names like Anna and Carlena Sumovich."

Chapter Thirteen

"Are you going to work on the deck again today, Grandpa?" Ben asked at breakfast on Friday morning.

Anne's father smiled at him. "Later on, yes. Mr. Alex is coming after lunch, when he's done with another job. We think we can get it mostly finished this afternoon. But I'm free for the morning."

Ben's face looked so hopeful, Anne and her parents chuckled.

"How about if I take you and Liddie to school this morning?" her dad asked. "I could go in and meet Mr. Layton, if we went a few minutes early."

"Yeah! I'm ready." Ben shoved back his chair.

"Hold on," Anne told him. "Finish your milk. I haven't combed Liddie's hair yet."

Ben grimaced. "Hurry up, Mom."

"Relax. You've got plenty of time."

Ten minutes later, her father and the children started out. Anne and her mother enjoyed a second cup of coffee together and then cleaned up the kitchen.

"I told your father I'd pick him up at the school," her mom said as she closed the cupboard on the last clean dish. "We're going to visit some friends this morning, and I want to stop at that craft shop Mildred told me about."

Anne reached for her purse. "Have fun. After I get Remi started today, I'm taking the pictures and negatives to Jay McAllister at the *Gazette*. But I should be back in plenty of time to get lunch started—or will you eat lunch out?"

"I doubt it," her mother said. "I'll be home. And don't forget Alex promised to be here at one o'clock, and he's usually prompt."

Anne went downstairs to open the library. When Remi came in, she gave her three catalogs for children's books.

"When you have time, look these over," Anne said. "We raised more than two hundred dollars at the spring fair, and I want to put most of that into children's books. The kids are always hoping we've got something new."

"Oh, super! I love ordering new books." Remi put away her tote bag and settled behind the checkout desk.

"Make a list, and we'll go over it when I get back," Anne said. "I'm going over to the *Gazette*, but I should be back within the hour."

She gathered her things and went out to the garage, but it was such a bright day that she decided to walk the few blocks to the newspaper office.

She always enjoyed walking along Blue Hill's Main Street, with its charming old buildings greeting her as old friends. She stepped up onto the covered porch of the *Gazette* office and opened the front door. The receptionist looked up and smiled as Anne entered.

"Good morning, Mrs. Gibson. How are things at the library?"

"Fine, thanks. Is Jay in this morning?"

"I think he's in the darkroom. Let me check."

The receptionist left her for a moment, and Anne peeked into Grace's office, but it was empty. Grace must be out covering a news story this morning. Though she served as the newspaper's editor, Grace also did much of the reporting for the weekly.

"He's just finishing something," the young woman said as she returned. "He said to tell you he'll be right out."

A moment later, a tall, athletic-looking young man in his early thirties came from the back of the office. His medium-brown hair hung down over his collar, and he wore jeans and a forest green shirt.

"Hi. You must be Anne Gibson."

"Yes." She shook his hand.

"I'm Jay. Interesting pictures you had on Miss Summers's film."

"Thank you. I brought over the negatives of the ones we want made up for the exhibit next week, and a few other snapshots that I'm hoping you can enlarge for us."

"From what you told me on the phone, there shouldn't be a problem."

Anne opened the envelope she carried and drew out the eight-by-ten contact sheet he had made of Edie's film. "I also wondered if you could print the rest of the photos from this roll."

"Sure," Jay said. "I only picked a few that looked the best the first time, because I wasn't sure what you wanted."

"I'd like to see them all," Anne said. "The ones on this contact sheet are so tiny."

"I know." Jay grinned. "I get used to it, and I use a loupe when I look at them. You certainly will be able to see more detail if I blow them up."

"I found some other pictures of hers from the same trip."

"You did? Color or black and white?"

"The same as these. Maybe you can help me with something. At first, my dad and I wondered why Aunt Edie never had this roll of film developed after her trip."

"It does seem odd that she never used that camera again," Jay said. "Did she get a newer one?"

"Yes, I've come across a newer camera that took film, and two digital cameras. I expect those were purchased over the last thirty years or so."

Jay cocked his head to one side. "You know she took a lot of black and white in the '70s. She probably kept the one camera for that and used her newer ones for color."

"That makes sense to me, but the other pictures I found were probably from the same camera." Anne wished she had brought them so that Jay could give his opinion on that. "Although I don't see how they could be, if she took the house pictures on this roll before the Washington pictures."

"*Hmm*..." Jay flipped through the prints from her envelope.

Anne thought about the films for a moment. "It's just strange. We wondered why she didn't take more, and then I found those others. But it seems she took the photos of the house before she left home. Then she went to Washington and took—what, sixteen? Sixteen pictures on the trip on the film that was still in the camera. I think the others that I found were taken first, because a friend is with her in one picture, and that woman was only there on Aunt Edie's first day in Washington."

Jay frowned. "Maybe she did have another camera with her. Did you find any color snaps from that trip?"

"No, just black and white."

Jay took the contact sheet from her and looked down at it. "Okay, this may be the explanation, or at least part of it. When I took the roll of film out of the canister, I cut it into short strips, with a few frames on each one. That lets me lay them out in rows on the printing paper."

Anne nodded.

"So, it looks like I got sloppy on this one."

"What do you mean?"

Jay smiled apologetically. "I didn't have them in order when I printed this sheet. See the little numbers at the bottom of each frame?"

She looked closely. "Yes. Is that the frame number on the roll?"

"It sure is. Those two pictures of the house weren't the first two on the roll. They were the last two."

Anne eyed him in surprise. "So what does that mean? She took those pictures of the house after she got home from Washington?"

"I'd say so. And the others on this roll were the last ones she took on that trip. She probably took the ones you found later first, took out the film and reloaded, and continued on this one."

Anne nodded slowly. "That makes sense. It's sort of a relief. I was a little surprised we didn't find any color shots though. The flowers must have been beautiful."

"Yeah, it does seem a bit odd, but then, I didn't know your aunt well, but I've heard she was a little...quirky."

Anne smiled. "Yeah, in some ways. But how could she forget about that film? It was from an exciting trip. She even wrote a little diary during the trip, telling what she'd seen and who she'd stayed with. She got one roll processed, but she never took this roll out of the camera."

"I can't say for sure, but maybe she intended at first to have it processed after she finished the roll. But she never went back and finished it."

"I guess so. Just those two of the house, and then she put it aside and forgot. We're interested in the young man with her in this picture." Anne pointed to the thumbnail of the shot with Edie and Carl. "We were hoping he showed up in other pictures. I didn't find any of him in the snapshots I left at home. I'm really hoping he's in one of the others on this roll."

"I'll see what I can do," Jay said. "I'll call you when they're ready."

"Thanks a lot." Anne smiled at what was ahead of her. "I did notice that in Aunt Edie's albums we found, there were some gaps. None of them were from the mid-1970s. Obviously some of the photos in the boxes are from then."

Jay nodded. "Sounds like she took a hiatus from mounting her pictures."

"Well, Dad and I went through the attic, but there could still be more up there. We could easily have missed an album or another box of pictures. There's tons of stuff up there—literally. I think I'll make another foray into the attic, just to be sure."

"Have fun," Jay said. "Oh, and Grace is going to do an advance story on your exhibit at the library. She wants me to go over and take some pictures, so she'll have art to go with it. When would be a good time?"

"I think Grace is planning to interview me on Monday for the advance, but I might not have everything in place by then."

"That's okay. I could take some shots of you putting the exhibit together. Why don't I call you before I come and see if you're ready?"

"Thanks. And I wondered..." Anne hesitated only a second. "I like your work, Jay. Do you ever do private shoots?"

"Sure. I do weddings and senior pictures, that sort of thing."

"How about a family reunion? We're having a Summers family gathering a week from Sunday. Could you come about three o'clock and take some pictures for me?"

"I'd be glad to."

Anne smiled. "Great. And if you can bring me a price list when you come to take the exhibit photos, I'll know how much it will be if family members want to order prints."

"Sounds good."

They talked for a few minutes more, finalizing the arrangements. Anne left the envelope with him and hurried home. She had so much to do before the exhibit and the reunion, she wasn't sure when she would find time to search the attic again, but she knew she would somehow make time.

* * *

Anne found time to do some digging on Saturday for Aunt Edie's old friend, Iris. Her entry in Aunt Edie's well-worn address book appeared to have been crossed out, which Anne suspected did not bode well for finding Iris. But the name of the little town where Iris had lived was mentioned in Edie's trip diary. In an online search, she found three Gallagher family telephone listings in Wellersburg.

"I may as well call them all," she told her mother, who was pinning a patch to the knee of a pair of Ben's jeans. "I'm getting quite brazen about cold-calling people and asking them personal questions."

As it turned out, she only needed to call one, as the woman who answered on her first try revealed that she could help Anne.

"Iris was my mother-in-law," Mrs. Gallagher said. "She's gone now though—almost twenty years."

"I'm sorry," Anne said. "My great-aunt was a friend of hers, and I hoped to make a connection. I recently learned that they took a trip to Washington together in 1976."

"I seem to remember that! It was the year of the bicentennial."

"Yes, and according to Aunt Edie's account, they enjoyed themselves immensely. My great-aunt has passed away, too, but I'm glad she had friends like Iris."

"How sweet of you," Mrs. Gallagher said.

Anne thanked her and hung up.

Her mother gave her a quizzical smile. "Nothing?"

"Afraid not. The woman was very nice, but unfortunately, Iris has been gone for some time. Well, so much for that idea." Anne stood and squared her shoulders. "I've got tons of work to do on the exhibit arrangements."

* * *

After Sunday school, Anne ran into Alex in the foyer of the church.

"Hi, Anne! How's the hunt for the missing cousin going?"

Quickly, she caught him up on her research. "So, I've made a lot of contacts, but I haven't come up with anything solid."

"Sorry," Alex said with a sympathetic smile. "I wish I could help you."

"I didn't get a chance to thank you for all your work on the deck. It looks great! I know we're going to enjoy it all summer long."

"I'm glad you like it. Your dad picked out a nice design, and he's pretty handy with tools." Alex chuckled. "I offered him a part-time job in my business, but he said he likes retirement too much."

"That's true, he does. I think he likes being able to work whenever he wants—and quit whenever he wants."

Alex laughed.

"I sure miss them when they're gone," Anne said, "but he and Mom are able to look out for my grandparents this way, and they really do love Florida. I don't think they want to spend another winter in snow country."

Reverend Tom came out of the sanctuary and walked toward them, smiling at Anne. "Glad I caught you, Anne. I've learned that Reverend Daniel is still living with his daughter and her husband. Last I'd heard, she had mentioned the possibility of assisted living for him, but she says they changed their minds, and he has remained at their house. They're over in Tarryville."

"That's not too far," Anne said.

Reverend Tom opened his Bible and took out a sticky note. "Here you go—that's their address and telephone number."

"Thank you so much," Anne said.

"What's that about?" Alex asked, as Reverend Tom moved on to speak to other parishioners.

"I thought I'd pay Reverend Daniel a visit later this week, just to see if he remembers anything about Carl's death. My dad said he officiated at the memorial service."

"Can I go with you? I'd love to see Revered Daniel again."

She eyed him with mock suspicion. "I'm surprised you'd have time. I've heard your skills are in high demand this time of year."

"They are, but everyone needs a break now and then. I can't go Monday or Tuesday, but later in the week would be all right."

"Fine. I'll set it up and let you know when. And thanks."

They began walking slowly toward the doors of the auditorium. The hum of happy voices inside made Anne smile. Her church family in Blue Hill included many friends, and its gatherings felt much more personal and friendly than the ones at her old church in New York. She loved being part of a congregation small enough for her to know everyone's name.

"You know, I've been thinking some more about that picture," Alex said. "The one with your father's supposedly dead cousin."

Anne nodded. "What about it?"

"Edie seems to have been pretty good at photography. Do you think it's possible she might have superimposed a picture of your cousin over one of her to make it look like they were together? Just as a kind of keepsake or a tribute to him? Or even for the challenge, to see if she could do it?"

"Like some kind of deliberate double exposure, you mean? I don't know. It seems sort of bizarre." Anne frowned. "Besides, the film was still in the camera when we found it, remember."

"So you know it wasn't done during the developing stage," Alex said.

"Yeah. And it wasn't blurry. The lines are crisp."

"A lot of double exposures are kind of fuzzy," he admitted.

Anne tilted her head to one side, thinking about how the negative could have been made. "Nowadays people take pictures with those big cutouts of famous people, but I'm sure she wouldn't have something like that of Carl. And how would she get the image onto the negative like that? Wouldn't she have to have a photo of herself in Washington and another of Carl in his uniform together when she took the picture?"

"I guess you're right," Alex said, pausing outside the auditorium door.

"The other pictures on that roll were taken in Washington, except the two of the house. I'm wondering when she would have had a chance to fiddle with it. I mean, it's not like she came home from the trip, developed her film, and then started playing around with old pictures of Carl."

"True. I guess it's pretty unlikely. It was just a thought."

"It wasn't a bad idea," Anne said. "She might have thought that combining the image of a soldier killed in combat with the celebration of the country he was defending would be a fitting way to honor him. But the way it was left in the camera…" Anne looked up at Alex. "My dad raised the question of why she did that, and I had no explanation."

"Did she have a newer camera?"

Anne smiled. "That's what Jay McAllister, the photographer, asked me. I did find some other photos from the trip, but I think they were made on the same camera, earlier than the roll with the mystery picture. And she did have other cameras. We know there are at least three more, newer ones. There are a couple of digital cameras, but those are too modern for the Washington trip. And there's a Kodak that took regular film. That one's smaller than the Pentax. She might have had a color film going at the same time in the Kodak, and black and white in the Pentax."

"Or even a disposable camera," Alex said. "Those were pretty popular twenty or thirty years ago."

"I think they came out a bit later than her Washington trip, but yeah. I haven't had time to go back upstairs and look for more photos in the attic. I was thinking we'd found them all, but of course there's no way of knowing for sure without doing a more thorough search. And who has time?"

Alex chuckled. "It may take you a very long time to sort out Edie's attic."

"Years. Now we think she just forgot about the film in the Pentax. She put the old camera away, intending to finish the roll, and never did. But something that important…finding a nephew who you thought had been dead for years…"

"Maybe that's another reason to think it wasn't really him," Alex said.

"Now you're starting to sound like Mom." Anne wrinkled her nose, and he laughed.

In the auditorium, the organ's music grew louder and the voices quieted. Anne noticed they were the last two lingerers in the foyer.

"We'd better get inside," she whispered. They ducked in through the doors and separated, Anne to join her family, and Alex to sit with Ryan on the other side.

* * *

Since the exhibit was not yet completed on Monday, Anne went to the *Gazette* office for the interview with Grace. After giving the information for the advance story, Anne told Grace that Jay had called and said she could retrieve her photographs. Grace guided her to the photographer's desk in a small room at the back of the building. Jay was on the phone, and Anne waited until he finished.

"Hey, sorry about that," he said when he had ended the conversation. "Busy today."

"Thanks for taking time out for this."

"No problem." He handed her a folder of prints.

"They're wonderful," she said, leafing through the enlargements. "Thank you so much!"

"The smaller ones are the prints from your roll of film. I did one of each in the four-by-six size. If you want any eight-by-tens, let me know."

Anne started looking through them, and Jay added, "Oh, and I did blow up one of them. This one right here." He reached into the stack and pulled a larger print from the folder. "You said you were interested in the guy wearing the uniform, and I spotted him in this shot, so I enlarged it. That's the same man."

Anne caught her breath and stared down at the photo. The uniformed man in the center of the picture had turned away from the camera and was captured in profile. He was outdoors, perhaps along the Mall, and the pedestrians around him were slightly blurred by their movements. Now they had two images of the man. Would this picture help her prove that Carl had lived beyond his official death date? Or would it reveal that the person with Aunt Edie in Washington was somebody else?

Chapter Fourteen

When Anne left the *Gazette* office, she made a run to Newlands' to restock her kitchen. Blue Hill boasted a larger chain grocer on the highway near the edge of town, but Anne's parents had always shopped at Newlands', and since her return to Blue Hill, Anne had adopted the cozy family-run store for most of her grocery needs. As she shopped the familiar aisles, she kept thinking about the photos Jay had printed for her. Her father would be eager to study them too.

In the dairy section, she was reaching for a container of low-fat milk when a familiar voice called her name.

"Oh, Coraline," she said, turning. "Hello!"

Mildred's neighbor was a personable but talkative elderly woman, and at once Anne determined to keep the encounter short. Coraline loved to discuss anything and anyone at great length, and today was not the day for that.

"I hear you're going to hold an exhibit of Edie Summers's photographs."

"That's right," Anne said. "The opening will be on Saturday. I hope you can make it."

"I'm sure I can. I have a picture she took of me at the Veterans Day parade a few years ago. Would you like me to bring it in?"

"I'd love to see it," Anne said. "We won't have room to display all of her photographs, but we're highlighting ones she took of Blue Hill."

"I'll come by the library with it." Coraline glanced around and then said in a conspiratorial whisper, "I also heard you're asking around about one of your cousins who died mysteriously."

"Goodness, where did you hear that?" Anne scanned the shelves of yogurt, wishing she could get away.

"At the hairdresser's. One of the ladies from the DAR was in there at the same time I was. She said you had a photo of this cousin and that there was something fishy about his death."

Anne blinked. She certainly hadn't told the women from the DAR that part of the story when they visited the library. But she hadn't made a secret of it either. People at the newspaper office knew about it and so did some of her church friends and the library volunteers. She shouldn't be shocked that rumors had gotten around town.

She managed to smile at Coraline. "That's not exactly the way it is. My father and I are trying to determine when this cousin died, that's all. He was in the service, and we seem to have conflicting reports. It's nothing, really."

Coraline nodded, her green eyes glittering behind her glasses. "Was that before I came here?"

"I think it was," Anne said. "It was more than thirty years ago."

Coraline's face fell. "And I've only been here twelve. I guess I didn't know that part of your family."

"I'm afraid not. Well, thank you—"

"I asked Mildred, but she wouldn't say much. She did say they used to own the furniture store downtown."

"Yes, they did. My great-uncle and his wife ran it for many years, but I believe it closed before 1980. If you'll excuse me, Coraline, I really have to get back to the library."

"Oh yes. I expect you do." Coraline grinned. "Who's covering today? Bella or Remi?"

"It's Bella today. Now, I must go. See you later."

Anne rushed to the checkout. Once she was in line, she pulled out her list and scanned it. She had forgotten to get cereal, and the children had finished their favorites. She sighed and pulled her cart out of line and headed for the cereal aisle.

* * *

When Anne reached home, her parents were out back admiring the new deck.

"It looks great," Anne said, juggling several tote bags of groceries.

"Let me help you." Her dad hurried over and took several of the bags. "Alex said he'd help me finish up the planters Wednesday afternoon. I guess you two have an outing planned that morning?"

Anne nodded. "He offered to take me to visit Reverend Daniel. I want to ask him about the memorial service for Carl."

"I guess new information could pop up," her father said doubtfully.

Her mom opened the door to the house for them, and they carried the groceries up to the family kitchen.

"Do you know what you want us to put in the flower boxes when we finish?" her father asked.

"Something nice and colorful. Wave petunias, maybe? And some marigolds?" Anne looked over at him. "Dad, as soon as we put this food away, I want to show you the pictures Jay made up for me."

"Oh yeah. I want to see those."

A few minutes later, the three of them sat down in the living room with steaming mugs of tea and coffee. Anne took out the new photographs and handed them to her father.

"Take a look. And we'll need to decide what frames we want for all the exhibit photos."

Her mother took her tea bag from her cup and squeezed it on her spoon. "Your father and I could go to Thrifty Drugstore this afternoon if you want. They have a lot of frames. Or if you want something older, maybe Mr. Bridges at Midtown Antiques would have something.

"That could get expensive," Anne said. "Unless he had a box of frames for a small price."

"You never know," her father said, eyeing the first picture on the stack. "Is this the one you mentioned?"

"Yes. I think that's Carl, don't you? Jay felt certain it was the same man."

Her dad nodded slowly. "I do. It's not as close as the other one, though it's pretty sharp, and he's turned away."

"Yes, and Edie's not in the picture," Anne noted. "She was probably behind the lens. This one is almost like she took it after they'd separated, without him realizing she took another shot."

The uninformed man had turned partly away from the camera, perhaps studying something in the distance as a throng of people passed him on the sidewalk.

"I suppose that by itself it doesn't prove anything," Anne said. "But the numbers on the frames show that this one was taken next after the one of them together."

"Is he in any more shots?"

"Not that I could see," Anne said wistfully. It would have been so nice to find proof of the young man's identity in the photos.

"The first one may be more helpful," her father said. "At least in that one, his uniform is clear."

The mention of the uniform spurred Anne's hopes. "I was wondering if his insignia would be helpful." She shuffled the prints until she found the one that had started their speculation. "Don't these pins on his chest mean he was in specific battles?"

"Campaign ribbons." Her father held the photo a little closer. "Too bad it's not in color."

"Still, an army expert would be able to tell us what they mean. Maybe I could crop this picture and send a copy to Sergeant Potter. That is, if she ever gets back to me."

Her father pointed to one decoration on the soldier's chest. "I'm pretty sure that's the Vietnam Service Medal."

"Then there must be a record of him receiving that," Anne said.

"Yes. I can't imagine why the family wasn't notified. Now that I think about it, it seems odd that the medal wasn't sent to Uncle David. If Carl was dead, I mean."

Anne nodded. "And very odd that they didn't tell the family that the notification of his death was a mistake."

"Highly exaggerated, as Mark Twain would say." Her dad studied the picture. "There's a campaign star, but I can't tell if it's bronze or silver."

"What would that mean?" Anne asked.

"Bronze for one campaign, silver for five."

"Wow." She couldn't imagine one soldier serving through five battle campaigns in Southeast Asia, but she supposed a great many did. "Who can help us out with this, short of the army liaison?"

"Possibly an antiques dealer who handles military memorabilia.

"I can ask Mr. Bridges."

"He might have some reference books, if nothing else." Her father looked through the rest of the photos. He found one more of Aunt Edie but none in which they could see the tall, handsome soldier.

"Do you think there's another roll of film from the trip somewhere?" Anne asked.

"Maybe. Do you want to take another trip into the attic?"

"Yes, but I'm not sure there's time before the exhibit. I think Jay is right, that she either took another roll first with this camera, or else she had color film in another camera."

"Maybe that little Kodak Instamatic we found," her father said.

"I think there should be another album." Anne reached out to touch the stack of bound photo albums on the coffee table. "There's a gap from about 1974 to 1980. And we know she didn't stop taking pictures then."

"If I get a chance, I'll poke around up there," her father said, "but not today. Too many other things to do."

Anne lifted the stack of new prints and went through them slowly, one more time. When she came to the one of Carl starting to walk away, she paused. "Dad, look at this one again. The angle lets us see the side of his sleeve. Do you see this insignia?" She passed the picture to him.

Her father stared at it and narrowed his eyes. "I can't read it. But maybe I can look it up, based on the shape. May I use your computer?"

"Sure," Anne said. "It's all booted up. I'd better show my face in the library. If you find anything, come tell me, all right?"

She went down the grand staircase and found Bella inundated with patrons at the checkout desk.

"I'm so sorry, Bella. I should have come back sooner. What can I do to help?"

Bella threw her a smile. "Maybe help Mr. Grindell find a book on Mississippi riverboats?"

"Sure." Anne turned and spotted the man surveying last month's exhibit in one of the glass cases. She helped him locate the material he needed and then took a huge pile of returned books off the desk, put them on her book cart, and began to re-shelve them. When Bella's line had dwindled and all of the people had been served, Bella found Anne in the Nonfiction Room.

"Thanks, Mrs. Gibson."

Anne waved away her gratitude. "I was upstairs yakking with my dad when I should have been down here. I do apologize."

"No need. But I did want to tell you that two mothers have asked if we plan to have a summer reading program for the kids."

"Definitely," Anne said. That would be one of her top priorities after the reunion. "Wendy Pyle and I were discussing it recently," she told Bella. "We plan to make up log sheets for the kids, so they can keep track of how many books they read. We'll have a party at the end of summer and give small awards to everyone who met their reading goal."

"Sounds like fun," Bella said. "How can I help?"

"Part of the program will be special story times for the preschoolers. And I've been thinking about possibly doing a puppet show for the finale."

"Oh, I'd love to work on that." Bella's eyes gleamed, and Anne knew she had found the right person to head up that project.

"Great." Anne loved the twins' enthusiasm for their jobs at the library. She smiled at Bella. "In your spare time, maybe you can look through some of our storybooks and folk tale collections for a story to dramatize. Or I suppose we could order a script."

"I like the idea of writing our own," Bella said.

"Then I'll leave that to you. If you don't find something workable within a couple of weeks, we can see what's available online."

"Good." Bella smiled. "As soon as you have the details for the summer program, I'll put it on the Web site."

"Good thinking. Then we can direct the parents there if they have questions. You put Saturday's opening on the site, right?"

Bella nodded. "I used that picture Miss Summers took of the town hall, and I put all the information about the exhibit and the hours for the reception on Saturday."

"Great. I'll look at it later."

By the time they were ready to start mapping out the summer reading program, Anne thought this photography exhibit mania and missing-cousin frenzy would soon be behind her – she hoped. But until she knew for certain what had happened to Cousin Carl, she wouldn't give up on her search.

* * *

Wendy called a few minutes later, and Anne arranged with her to meet the next day to work on the photo exhibit. She had barely hung up the desk phone when she saw Coraline Watson enter the foyer. Anne smiled warmly and walked out to meet her.

"Hello, Coraline."

"Hi, Anne! I've got that picture I told you about right here." Coraline held out a color four-by-six photograph in a small pewter frame.

Anne took it. "That's a lovely picture of you!"

Coraline's cheeks turned a becoming pink. "Thank you. I've always liked it. Edie had a way of capturing everyone's best features."

"Yes." Anne studied the color image. Coraline held a small American flag, and behind her a parade float was passing. Anne recognized the church's youth leader and several of the young people, who were then junior-high age, riding on the flatbed. The float bore an arched trellis decorated with brilliant flowers and a large shield with the legend *Support Our Troops*.

"I'd like to display this on Saturday," Anne said with sudden decision. The colorful photograph was pleasing to the eye, and this would make Coraline very happy.

The older woman glowed. "Of course! Keep it as long as you like."

"I'll put it in the History Room with some others I think will complement it."

Coraline left delighted, no doubt, to tell all her friends that her photo would be featured in the exhibit. Anne turned to the next patron.

* * *

In the middle of the afternoon, Anne's father came into the library and found her working at her desk.

"Busy, kiddo?" he asked.

She smiled. "Not too bad. I'm placing an order for new books." Bella had chosen several picture books for the young children and chapter books for the middle graders, and Anne hoped to complete the order that day.

"Well, your mom and I thought we'd pick up the kids. It looks like it may rain, and it's an excuse to run downtown."

"Oh? You have an ulterior motive?" Anne asked.

He chuckled. "I just thought I'd check out the drugstore for frames."

"Sounds good. Time's getting short."

Her dad held out a sheet of paper. "I also wanted to show you this. I found it online."

Anne took it and gazed down at a printout showing a military shoulder patch. The scroll bore the words *Ranger Airborne*. Each side had some smaller letters: *1st BN* on the left and *75th INF* on the right.

"Oh, you found it!"

"Well, I think so. It's the closest I could get so far. I scanned the picture on your computer and zoomed in on it as far as I could go without it looking like soup. I think that's his outfit—the Airborne Rangers, First Battalion of the 75th Infantry Regiment."

"Is that the outfit Carl was in when he enlisted?"

Her dad shook his head. "I don't remember the Airborne part. And listen to this: That particular regiment, the Rangers, had been disbanded after the Korean War. It was revived during the Vietnam War, but I need to do some more research. I don't think it was formally reactivated until 1974, so that patch probably wasn't around before then."

Anne's pulse leaped. "So that means that if Carl survived after 1970, he was transferred into a different regiment."

Her dad shrugged. "I don't know. I'm just telling you what I found out and what it looks like. Do you have any books on the Vietnam War in the library?"

"Not many," Anne said. "I doubt what we have is that specific, but I'll look."

"Okay." He looked at his watch. I'd better get going, or we won't be there on time to get the kids."

Anne watched him go, more certain than ever that they would find her father's cousin. After all the time they had invested and the progress they had made, they couldn't fail now!

Chapter Fifteen

What do you need me to do this morning?" Wendy asked Anne as she stashed her purse in Anne's desk drawer. "I have two hours free."

Tuesday had dawned bright and sunny. Anne was relieved that the damp weather seemed to be at an end. She wanted clear skies for the events that weekend.

"I'm using a total of forty-two pictures in the exhibit," she told Wendy. "It's more than I planned on at first, but there are just so many great ones! So they all need to be framed, and we also need to make caption cards to stand beside them, explaining what's in the photo and about when it was taken."

"Big job," Wendy said with a grin, "but I'd say we're up to it."

"Good. If patrons come in, you just keep at it, and I'll come back as quickly as I can." Anne pulled a carton of mismatched wooden frames from the closet. "Mom found this at Midtown Antiques. Mr. Bridges let her have the whole box for five dollars."

"Wow! He must have been in a good mood."

"Yeah. Mom said she told him it was for the library. He'd probably had it gathering dust for years. Anyway, I think we can use most of them, but a lot will need mats to make the pictures fit."

"That's a lot of work," Wendy said. "Let's get at it."

"Okay." Anne pushed up her slipping glasses. "And I warned the folks at Thrifty Drugstore that I'll need at least a dozen eleven-by-fourteen frames, with mattes, for the ones we have left over."

"That may not be enough," Wendy said, eyeing the stack of photos and the box of frames critically.

"Then we'll have to get creative. My folks seem to be pretty good at asking for donations, so maybe they can help."

They plunged into the work. After an hour, during which Anne went back and forth between the framing project and waiting on patrons, Jay McAllister called her.

"Ready for some pictures?" he asked. "Grace wants them to go with her story."

"Sure," Anne said. "Can you come at one?" She knew that would give her time to accommodate Jay before the writers' group came in for their monthly meeting. Jay agreed, and she went back to work.

By the time Wendy had to return home, they had framed twenty of the exhibit photos.

"I guess that's it for now," Anne said, putting away her paper cutter and scissors. "Thanks so much!"

Wendy stood and stretched. "I wish we could have done them all today."

"I'll have to get the frames from Thrifty, and then we'll see if we can scare up a few more from the attic."

"I may have a few at home." Wendy opened the drawer to get her purse. "Doesn't the writers' group meet this afternoon? You could ask them. I'll bet they'd come up with some extras for you."

"Brilliant idea—and Mildred might have some too."

Although her afternoon was jam-packed, Anne managed to get all the necessary tasks done and spend twenty minutes with Jay for the photographs. The writers' group was happy to help her out, and two members went home after the meeting and returned immediately with several frames. By the end of the day, Anne had accumulated enough for all of the exhibit photos, and Mildred had offered to come after supper to help Anne and her mother finish the framing and make the needed captions.

The work went quickly, and when they had finished, Ben brought out his shell bag and field guide.

"Miss Farley, would you like to see my shells? Grandpa and Grandma brought them from Florida."

"I would love to see them," Mildred said, adjusting her bifocals. She picked up one of the small brown-and-white fan shapes. "Ah, little cockleshells. This brings back memories, Ben. It's been so long since I visited the coast."

"You're welcome to come stay with us anytime in Florida," Anne's mother said. "We'd love to have you."

"Sure," her father added. "Fly down, and we'll pick you up and take you to our house. You'd get to visit my mom and dad too."

"That sounds like fun. I'll think about it." Mildred picked up a gold-flecked, white, elongated spiral. "And what do you call this one, Ben?"

"My book says that's an auger shell."

"How sensible! It looks like an auger." Mildred and Ben spent a few more minutes sorting through the collection, and he named each one for her.

"We'll have to send you some more shells when we get home, Ben," Anne's mother said.

"Better yet, we need to get you down there to go beachcombing." Her father laughed at Ben's eager expression. "We really should try soon, Anne."

"I know, but with the library and everything...well, as Mildred said, I'll think about it."

Her mother nodded. "I can't wait to get you and the kids onto the beach."

Anne smiled. "I just wish the Summers family was as easy to classify as Ben's shells."

"You've made a lot of progress," her dad said. "And we won't give up until we learn something about Carl, don't you worry about that."

"Right." Anne was glad for her father's support. Finding out what became of his cousin was becoming very important to her, and she had no intention of abandoning her search.

* * *

It wasn't until Wednesday that Anne and Alex set off for Tarryville in Alex's Ford pickup. The children had gone off to school, and Anne's parents had decided to spend the day visiting some of their old friends in Blue Hill.

The glorious day seemed a harbinger of a brilliant summer to Anne. She thoroughly enjoyed driving through the countryside and seeing the farmland under cultivation, cattle grazing in lush pastures, and flowers blooming everywhere she looked.

"Look at all those wildflowers!" she exclaimed. The entire meadow was awash with blooms in every color of the rainbow.

Alex let up on the accelerator, and the truck slowed as he pulled to the side of the road. He looked at her with eyebrows raised. "You want to stop and pick some? We have time. I know the man who owns this property. I'm sure it would be okay."

"No, no, thanks." Anne smiled. "It's enough just to see them in all their finery. Liddie would be over the moon to see them."

Alex nodded and eased the pickup back onto the road.

"I love this time of year," Anne said.

"Me too." Alex smiled at her. "I'm guessing your kids have spring fever. I know Ryan does."

"Yes, Ben especially. He can't wait to be free all day to play with his dog and build things and do experiments. Liddie is more social. She'll miss her friends. Yvette Jacobs has already called me to make sure we can arrange playdates for Liddie with Becca and Cindy this summer."

"I heard Ryan and Ben talking about building a bigger doghouse for Hershey."

"That's a good idea. That old one we have has seen better days."

"I'll help them if they ask me to." Alex turned off the main road at the prompting of his GPS unit. "Looks like we're almost there."

Alex parked in the driveway, and Anne carried an envelope of photos with her as they walked to the front door. Reverend Daniel's daughter, Katherine, greeted them warmly.

"Dad was so pleased when I told him you were coming. Alex, he does remember you—at least he did on Monday. I have to say, he has days when his memory is pretty poor. But sometimes he remembers the funniest things. And, Anne, he was a little hazy on you, but he knew your aunt well. Edie Summers was a great favorite of his."

"Thank you," Anne said. "Everyone loved her."

"He may remember more about your family when he sees you. How are your folks doing? You said they were visiting?"

Anne nodded. "They're great. They live in Florida, and they came up for a couple of weeks."

"I remember them well. Say hello for me." Katherine showed them into her front room, where the elderly Reverend Daniel sat in a recliner with a lap robe over his legs.

"Dad, your guests are here," Katherine said fairly loudly. With a glance at Anne, she said, "Just speak up and he'll hear you. I'll go and get some tea."

"Thank you." Anne stepped forward as Reverend Daniel struggled to work the footrest on his chair.

"Oh, don't get up, Reverend. Alex and I will sit and join you. Stay comfortable." She took his thin hand. "I'm Anne Gibson."

"Gibson, Gibson…do I know you?"

"You might. I lived in Blue Hill as a girl. I was a Summers. Dale Summers is my father, and Edie Summers was my great-aunt."

"Edie Summers." Reverend Daniel's face beamed. "Yes, Edie. Always willing to help with a project, that one. How is she?"

Anne tried not to let her dismay show in her expression. "I'm sorry, sir, but she passed away."

"Oh." His face crumpled. "Did I know that?"

"I don't know," Anne said. "Katherine knew, when I called her a couple of days ago."

"Then likely she told me." Reverend Daniel shrugged. "Sorry. My mind plays tricks on me these days." He gazed past Anne and focused on Alex. "And who are you, young man? Are you a Gibson too?"

"No, sir, I'm Alex Ochs."

Reverend Daniel grinned and extended his hand to Alex. "Sure! I remember you when you were a little tyke."

Alex smiled. "I remember when you were the pastor in Blue Hill."

Reverend Daniel nodded sagely and wagged a finger at him. "And I remember when you brought a frog to Sunday school and made all the girls squeal."

Alex's jaw dropped for a moment, and then he smiled sheepishly. "That's one thing I'd be happy if you forgot."

They all laughed, and Katherine brought in the tea tray. She set it on the coffee table and poured three cups. Anne accepted hers with a smile.

"It's Dad's favorite beverage now," Katherine said.

Alex took his without comment, and Reverend Daniel immediately spooned sugar into his cup and stirred it.

"Now, who are you again?" He gazed at Anne as he stirred, then took the spoon from his cup and laid it on the saucer.

"I'm Anne Gibson, Edie Summers's niece."

"How do you do?"

"I'm fine, thank you," Anne said.

He nodded and looked down at his cup. "Katherine, did I put sugar in my tea?"

"Yes, you did, Dad. Do you want some milk in it?"

"You know I don't like milk in it."

She shrugged, and Anne wondered if Reverend Daniel sometimes forgot exactly what he liked in his tea. He took a sip and set his cup down.

Looking at Alex, he said, "Now, you've got kids in the Bible quiz, don't you?"

"Uh, no," Alex said. "Afraid not."

"Oh." Reverend Daniel looked confused for a moment.

"Alex brought Anne to see you, Dad. They're from Blue Hill."

"Oh, right, right."

Anne decided to jump in and hope for the best, though the dear old man couldn't seem to focus long on anything.

"I'm putting together an exhibit at the library for next week. I'm going to display some of Aunt Edie's best photographs of Blue Hill. There's one of the church that might interest you." Anne opened her envelope and took out one of the pictures. "This was in one of Aunt Edie's old albums, and I had it enlarged for the exhibit."

She held out the eight-by-ten picture, and Reverend Daniel took it, holding it carefully by the edges. He looked down at it, and a smiled wreathed his face.

"It's me and your mother, Katherine, and there you are with Joan. You must be about ten in this." He handed the photo to Katherine.

She smiled and nodded. "Yes, and Joanie's only seven or eight. But look at Pete!"

In the photo, Reverend Daniel and his wife stood on the church steps. He held the youngest girl, and a teenage boy stood next to them. Katherine seemed to be the middle child, and she stood close to her mother.

"He must have been about ready to head for college," Reverend Daniel said.

"*Hmm,* I think not. He was probably in high school though. Fourteen or fifteen, I'd say. He shot up very tall then, remember?" Katherine glanced at the back of the picture and handed it to Anne. "Was there a date on the original?"

"The snapshot said '73.' And I had a copy made for you." She took out the smaller print and handed it to Katherine. "We found the negatives, too, if you'd like more for family members."

"That's very kind of you. I don't remember ever seeing this one. It was after my older sister died, but it's a very nice family portrait."

"That was back around the time the feed mill burned, then," Reverend Daniel said.

"Why, yes." Katherine looked at him in surprise. "I barely remember that."

"Oh, it was terrible," Reverend Daniel said. "One man was killed, and Wesley Lowe's barn caught fire too. That was a big loss for him. We collected an offering to help out him and his family, replacing their livestock."

Anne's heart began to pound. Reverend Daniel seemed to have no trouble recalling events from the distant past. His face was animated as he told of the fire.

"I wondered if you remembered my aunt and uncle, Natalie and David Summers."

"Oh, sure," Reverend Daniel said. "Furniture store. We bought a mattress and box spring from them."

Anne smiled. "Yes, they had the store for a long time."

"It was a good mattress."

Alex chuckled and asked, "What about their son, Reverend? Do you recall Carl Summers?"

"Oh, Carl." Reverend Daniel's face darkened. "He went in the army. Went over to Vietnam. Never came home."

"That's right." Anne's spirits plummeted again. The reverend's bleak pronouncement and sober expression didn't hold much hope of news that Carl had survived his enlistment. She sipped her tea and decided to continue her questioning a little further.

"I hoped you could tell me a little bit about his relationship with his father."

He shook his head slowly. "Can't say as I remember much. He was a nice-looking young man."

"Yes. In fact, I have a picture of him with me. It's one of him and Aunt Edie together." She eased the enlarged photo from the envelope and held it out to the old man. "We believe that's Carl Summers in his uniform."

He gazed at the image but said nothing.

Anne glanced at Alex. She had hoped seeing the picture would stir the old man's memories.

Alex cleared his throat. "Reverend Daniel, this picture has raised some questions in the family. You see the part of a building in the background?"

"Uh-huh."

"Anne has identified that as the DAR Constitution Hall in Washington, DC."

"Aunt Edie mentioned it in her trip diary from that vacation," Anne added. "She visited there and attended a concert in the auditorium during her trip. She also mentioned finding a long-lost relative. But the thing is, Carl Summers was reported dead in 1970. The army informed his father that he was killed in action."

"So sad," Reverend Daniel murmured.

"Yes. But that was in 1970. This picture was taken in 1976."

He frowned and then gazed into her eyes. "I'm sorry. I don't understand what you mean."

"I mean that this photo seems to have been taken several years after the family was told Carl was dead. So I'm trying to find out if it's really Carl."

"It certainly looks like him."

"Yes." Anne glanced at Alex, and he gave her a supportive smile. She went on, "Do you remember anything odd about the memorial service? I'm told they never got his remains home to bury."

"*Hmm*. Yes. His mother had already passed, I think."

"Yes, she had," Anne said, grateful that his memory seemed accurate on at least some points. "Aunt Natalie died before Carl enlisted."

"His father was quite shaken." He looked at her again. "Who was his father again?"

"David Summers," Anne said gently.

"David Summers. No, I don't remember anything about him."

Katherine leaned toward Anne and said softly, "I'm sorry. This is how it is now, unfortunately."

"It's all right," Anne said.

"Maybe we should go and let him rest a bit," Alex suggested.

"You're probably right." Anne stood. "I've enjoyed talking with you, Reverend Daniel." She held out her hand, and he clasped it for a moment. "Thank you for sharing your memories with us."

"Oh, good to see you again...," Reverend Daniel said, gazing up at her questioningly.

"I'm Anne," she told him.

"Yes, Anne." He nodded, but his eyes held a troubled look.

Alex said good-bye to the old man. As they moved toward the door, Katherine said, "This wasn't his best day, but it wasn't his worst either."

"He did remember the family," Anne said. "That's something."

"Wait," Reverend Daniel called. "Edith, wait."

Anne turned and walked back to his side. She smiled and laid her hand on his shoulder. "I'm Anne. Edie's niece."

"You look like her."

"Thank you. People tell me that."

"The funeral...Summers."

Anne stared at him. "Do you mean Carl Summers's service?"

The elderly pastor shook his head. "Not Carl. David. A man called me. Wouldn't give his name."

Katherine walked toward him, frowning. "Dad, what are you talking about?"

"David Summers. I did his funeral."

"That's right," Katherine said. "You led the service. I was there. His daughter had met with you and gone over the arrangements."

The old man nodded. "She gave me the hymns. And someone called me the day before. Wanted to know about the service—what time and where. I asked his name and where he was calling from. I would have given directions, but he hung up. At the time..."

"What?" Katherine asked, leaning close.

"I wondered if it was Carl. But that was crazy, because Carl was dead."

"Yes, Uncle David died in 1977," Anne said. "Are you certain that was when the man called?"

Reverend Daniel nodded adamantly. "He wanted the details, but then he just hung up—*click*. Like that."

"What made you think it might be Carl?" Alex asked.

"Sounded like him. And...I don't know. He called me 'sir,' like a military man would, and the connection was bad, like he was far away. I thought maybe Carl was overseas. Maybe he'd gone AWOL or something, and the report was wrong when they said he'd died."

Katherine's lips parted, and she stared at Anne, as though she didn't know what to say.

"I just had a feeling, when he wouldn't give his name," Reverend Daniel said. "See, Carl and his father had fought a lot before the boy left home. I talked to David about it more than once. He came to me when Carl refused to help him in the business, and I told him, 'David,' I said, 'sons don't always follow their father's bent.' He wasn't too keen on hearing that, I'll tell you. When Carl joined up, David wouldn't come to church for a while. But I went and visited him. I wouldn't let him stew, and finally he made his peace with God and came back regular. But he always grieved that his boy went off to war and died, and he'd never told him that he forgave him."

Anne's eyes filled with tears as she listened. "Thank you for telling me. That means a lot."

"Do you remember anything else about David, Dad?" Katherine pressed. "Or any more about his funeral and that man who called?"

Reverend Daniel swung his head around and looked at his daughter. "What man?"

"The one who called you."

He blinked. "When? Today?"

Katherine sighed. "No, Dad. The day before David Summers's funeral."

"Who?"

Katherine's shoulders slumped.

"It's all right," Anne said quietly. "Thank you. We'd better go now."

Katherine walked them to the door. "I wish he was more coherent. I don't know how much of what he said made sense, or if any of it's true. Not that he would tell a falsehood, but sometimes I don't know if he knows what's real and what's not anymore."

Anne pressed Katherine's hand in hers. "It gave me hope. That's the first hint I've had that the picture might really be Carl and that he survived his time in Vietnam. I don't know if we'll ever find out the truth, but it gives me a little something to work on and pray about."

When they were settled in the truck, Alex reached to start the engine and glanced her way. "Are you okay?"

Anne nodded. "I meant what I said. It was a little disconcerting to see him so addled, but overall, I'm encouraged."

"Yeah," Alex said. "I had the feeling that when he remembered anything, it was rock solid."

"Same here. And my gut feeling is that the anonymous caller was Carl." She snapped the buckle on her seat belt and turned to face Alex. "I think he's still alive."

"That's kind of stretching it, Anne. I mean, even if he was alive in 1977…"

"I know, but you heard what Reverend Daniel said. I hadn't even thought of it. What if Carl did go AWOL and lived in another country all this time? He wouldn't want anyone in the family to know, and he especially wouldn't want the army to know where he was. Maybe he was even afraid to come home for his father's funeral."

"Or too ashamed to show his face," Alex said grimly. He drove out onto the roadway and headed for Blue Hill.

"I'm not going to think about that part," Anne said. "I'm just going to keep on looking for him."

Chapter Sixteen

When they reached Anne's house, her mother and father had returned from their visits and had lunch ready.

"Won't you eat with us, Alex?" her mother said.

"Yeah, since you're planning to work with me all afternoon, you might as well get a meal here too," her father added.

Alex glanced at Anne. "All right, that sounds nice."

They sat down to minestrone, salad, and breadsticks.

"Mom, you've got to give me your minestrone recipe," Anne said. "I've missed this—among other things."

Her mother laughed. "It's very easy. Just take every vegetable you can get your hands on and throw it in a pot."

Anne wrinkled her nose. "Ha, ha. I wish it were that easy."

"It almost is. I made it pretty much from memory, but I'll send you the official version when we get back to Florida."

Anne and Alex told them about their visit to Reverend Daniel and the memories he had revealed.

"He seemed pretty clear on what he could recall from back then," Alex said. "He didn't always put the right name with the right person."

"That's very interesting," Anne's father said.

"Still nothing solid though," Anne pointed out. "But I'm with Reverend Daniel—I think it was Carl who called him."

"But he couldn't have gone AWOL," her father pointed out. "I mean, he was in uniform in the photo with Aunt Edie."

"That's right!" Anne smiled, her spirits higher than they had been in days. "Thanks, Dad. You're absolutely right. He wouldn't have been wearing the uniform if he'd deserted, and he wouldn't have had those medals on his chest if he'd been disciplined."

"That's a good thought," Alex said.

"Well, it's one more thing to be thankful for." Anne dished a generous helping of salad onto her plate.

Her mother passed her the dressing. "We had an interesting morning too."

"Who did you see?" Anne asked.

Her mother named several people in the community who were old acquaintances.

"We also stopped by Marilyn Beckwith's house," her father said.

"Who is she?" Anne couldn't recall hearing the name.

"She was a Turner," her dad said. "Marilyn was a couple of years behind me in school, and her brother Randy was a year ahead. I was fairly good friends with Randy, and I wondered where he was now."

"Oh. What did you find out?"

"He lives in Deshler. Has a service station over there, but he's thinking of retiring and selling the business."

Anne's mind was elsewhere, racing over the information Reverend Daniel had given her, so her attention really wasn't on what her father was telling her, until he spoke again.

"Anne, Randy enlisted in the army at the same time Carl did. They were in boot camp together, and they served in the same unit."

Anne raised her eyebrows. "Wow. Did you talk to him?"

Her dad shook his head. "I'd like to, but I knew you wouldn't want to wait on it. If you like, you can go over this afternoon and see him. Marilyn gave me the address and phone number."

Anne's heart accelerated, but guilt washed over her. "I shouldn't leave Remi alone all afternoon. I already played hooky this morning."

"It's the best time for you to go," her mother said. "The kids are in school. I don't mind going down and helping Remi, if she can show me what to do. I can at least sit at the desk and answer the phone while she helps people, and I could probably shelve books too."

"Thanks, Mom, but I don't know. I feel as though I've neglected the library work lately."

"You've been working on the exhibit," her dad said. "That's part of the library job."

"I suppose so. All right, if you're sure you don't mind, Mom."

"I'll enjoy getting to know Remi better and feeling useful," her mother said.

They finished lunch, and her father gave her the contact information for Carl's old friend. Anne first went downstairs to relieve Remi for her lunch hour. Since Remi was content to have Charlene help her that afternoon, Anne decided to go ahead.

She called the service station from the desk phone, and a man answered. "Hello, Mr. Turner?" she asked.

"This is Randy Turner."

"Hi. I'm Anne Gibson, and my dad is Dale Summers, and—"

"Well, hello! Where's old Dale these days? I don't think I've seen him since high school."

"Actually, he's here in Blue Hill, visiting me. He lives in Florida now though."

"You tell him I'd love to shoot the breeze with him sometime," Randy said. "How can I help you, young lady? Does your car need a tune-up?"

Anne hesitated. Her car probably could stand to be serviced, but this busy week wasn't really the time to do that.

"Well, I might make an appointment for next week, but I really wanted to come and talk to you if I could."

"What about?"

"My dad's cousin, Carl Summers."

"Oh man. Sad story."

"May I come to Deshler and hear it from you in person?"

"Sure, I guess. Not a lot to tell."

"I'd really appreciate it," Anne said.

"Well, I'm pretty busy today, but tomorrow I could spare some time."

"Okay," Anne said. "My dad might be able to come with me then. I'll ask him."

"Great! I'd love to see him. Come by around ten, if you can. We can get a cup of coffee at the diner across the street from my place."

It wasn't what Anne had hoped for, but at least it was progress. She went out to the back deck, where her father and Alex were putting the redwood planters in place.

"I got Mr. Turner," she announced. "He can't see me today, but he said tomorrow morning would work. And, Dad, I told him you might be able to go."

"Sure. I'd be happy to see Randy again."

Anne felt some relief at the idea of having her father along. She would have gone alone, but she knew her dad's presence would ease the conversation with an old acquaintance of his, as Alex's company had with Reverend Daniel.

She looked around at the deck, now nearly complete with three benches and several wooden planters.

"Wow, you guys have done a great job!"

"Thanks," her dad said.

Alex pointed with his hammer to the three steps leading down to the grass in the backyard. "If you decide you want a bigger deck later on, we can add another level where the steps go down. It could even wrap around the far side of the house if you want."

"Pretty fancy. I'll think about it."

"Maybe next year," her dad said.

Alex grinned and set a nail to drive in. "Right. Today we need to put some flowers in these."

"I've got everything we need in the garage," Anne's father said.

Anne went back inside and through to the library. As she entered the foyer, she saw that a woman had come in with her toddler. "Hello! May I help you?"

"I think we'll just go right up to the Children's Room."

Anne nodded. She was about to go to the checkout desk when her mom came down the stairs.

"So, are you heading for Deshler?" her mother asked.

"No, not until tomorrow. Dad and I are going in the morning."

"Oh, in that case, what will I do with myself this afternoon? I guess I could do some baking ahead for the reunion."

Anne laughed. "That would be great, but let me give you pointers on being a library assistant. I'll try to find an experienced volunteer to cover for me in the morning, but if you're still willing, you could help her."

"Sure thing," her mother said.

"Great. Let's start with the computerized catalog. I get a lot of requests for help with that. And when Remi gets back from lunch, maybe we can go make a couple batches of cookies and freeze them."

* * *

The deck was ready to be christened that evening, and Anne cooked hamburgers on the grill for supper. Her father set up a card table outside.

"You need a new picnic table."

Anne held up her spatula. "Please, Dad. No more building this week. We barely have time to get things ready as it is. I'll get by with what I have for chairs and benches for the reunion, and we can mull over the patio furniture concept later."

"Okay, boss," he said with a grin.

When they sat down to eat, Anne brought up her earlier report on what Reverend Daniel had said about the mysterious telephone call he received after David Summers died.

"I sure wish he had told someone in the family about it then."

"Maybe he told Pauline and she shrugged it off." Her father frowned for a moment. "I remember the funeral well. Carl definitely was not there."

"And the reverend said it sounded like a long-distance connection. Could you tell something like that back then?"

"Easier than you can now. There'd be noise on the line, for example. And if he was really far away, there would be a time lag between when the other person spoke and when you heard them. So there would be some delays."

Anne doctored her hamburger patty with ketchup and a dollop of dill relish. "So, it's possible Reverend Daniel wasn't just guessing. He may have had some actual evidence that it was a long-distance call."

"It's possible," her dad said, "but I don't think you can say it was definite, not based on what he told you today."

Anne's mother eyed her sympathetically. "Honey, I know you want to find out what happened to Cousin Carl, but I hate to see you get so worked up over it. You might be wasting your time searching for him."

Anne's father was quick to support her. "I don't see any harm in it, Charlene. Things may not turn out the way we'd like, but I think it's worth something to know the truth." He smiled sheepishly. "All right, I admit, I'm as curious as Anne is. We both know we may be in for more disappointment."

Anne nodded. "Please don't worry, Mom."

Her mother sighed. "All right, I'll try not to. But I can't help feeling you'd be better off putting all that energy into planning the photo exhibit and the family reunion. They'll both take a lot of work, and it's only a few days away."

"I know, but you helped me call all my volunteers this afternoon to make sure they're up to speed with the projects they're doing for the exhibit. Refreshments are all lined up. The photos are framed, and we've started arranging the display cases. Two of the women are going to do a last-minute dusting and vacuuming in all the public rooms. I think we're in good shape for Saturday."

"It does sound like it." Her mom reached for the pitcher of iced tea. "I'll try not to be such a worrywart. And tomorrow after you get back from Deshler, I'd like to start baking for the reunion on Sunday."

Anne knew some of her staples were low. "In that case, we should probably head over to Newlands' Grocery tonight."

"Great," her mother said. "The kids can go along with us if they want to."

Anne's father looked over toward the steps, where Ben and Liddie were eating their burgers. "I think Ben has some homework. I volunteer to stay here with him and see that it's done."

"Thanks, Dad."

"I'll enjoy it. And if he gets his math done, maybe we can look at some doghouse plans. We've got quite a lot of scrap wood in the garage now, and I don't think we'd have to buy much."

"Sounds like an excellent plan to me, but didn't Ryan want to be in on that? Alex mentioned it to me."

"You're right. Would you mind if we go over there for a consultation if we find something we like?"

"Not a bit." Anne reached for the bowl of potato salad and put some on her plate. "Dad, where is Uncle David buried?"

"He's over in the town cemetery in Middle Village. They lived over there when Natalie died, and she was buried there. So when David passed away, Pauline had her father put in the same plot."

"That makes sense," Anne said. "It's not far from here, is it?"

"No, not far. Are you thinking of going there?" her father asked.

"Sort of. Do we have time?"

Liddie got up and carried her plate over to the table. "Mommy, can I have more potato salad?"

"You sure can." Anne scooped a small serving onto Liddie's plate.

"Thank you. I love our new deck," Liddie said.

Anne leaned over and kissed the tip of her nose. "So do I. Wasn't it wonderful of Grandpa and Alex to build it for us?"

Liddie nodded so vigorously that her potato salad was in danger of sliding off her plate. Anne reached out and steadied the dish.

"Can we put flowers all over it for the party?" Liddie asked.

Anne smiled. "I don't know about all over, but it has those pretty petunias in the boxes, and I was going to get a few hanging flower baskets."

"I want to pick flowers," Liddie said. "We could fill the whole backyard with them. Red and yellow and blue and pink, and—and just every color, Mommy. It would be so pretty!"

Anne and her parents laughed.

"That sounds absolutely beautiful," her mother said. "Is there a place we could pick flowers? Other than your front flower beds, I mean?"

"Alex and I passed a field this morning that looked like endless wildflowers." Anne smiled at the memory. "He knows the people who own the field. I could get him to ask if we could pick some."

Liddie clapped her hands and squealed. "Can we go right now?"

"Oh, honey," Anne's mother said, "if you picked the flowers tonight, they would all wilt by the time of the party."

"Maybe Friday after school," Anne suggested. Then they'd be fresh for the exhibit and the reunion."

"You set it up with Alex," her dad said. "Maybe we can combine that with a ride to the cemetery at Middle Village."

Liddie seemed satisfied with that and went back to the steps to tell Ben about the planned expedition.

"More iced tea, Anne?" her mother asked.

Anne shook her head and sat back in her deck chair. This was a perfect moment. She was blessed to have her family here with her in this beautiful place, with so much to enjoy—the new deck, the good food, the promise of good times.

"And we'll pick millions of wildflowers," she heard Liddie tell Ben.

Anne smiled. That would be another precious memory, and perhaps she would also learn something about Carl when she visited the cemetery in which his parents were buried.

Chapter Seventeen

Anne's father parked his car in a corner of the service station's lot on Thursday morning and smiled over at Anne. The compact building had two service bays and a smaller door to the office. She thought it looked old-fashioned, as if time had stopped, but neat and efficient.

"You ready?" her dad asked.

She nodded and released the catch on her seat belt. "I've been praying all the way here that we'll find something…you know, something conclusive, one way or the other."

"I hope so too," her dad said, "but if not, you need to keep your chin up. This could be one of those things we'll never understand this side of heaven."

"I know. It *has* gotten me down a little." She eyed him earnestly, looking for understanding. "I really thought I'd hear back from the army by now. It doesn't give me a very good feeling that Sergeant Potter hasn't gotten back to me."

"How *does* it make you feel?"

She shrugged, uncomfortable with the question. "I'm not sure. I want to trust our government. You know I love our country, Dad."

"You're as patriotic as they come." He smiled and reached over to squeeze her hand. "I've been praying too that if we don't get the answers we're looking for, we'll be able to accept that. Come on. Let's go see what Randy can tell us."

Anne followed him into the office of the station. A man about her father's age stood behind the counter, ringing up a customer's transaction. His brown hair was peppered with gray, and she could see his sixty-odd years in his face. He wore a short-sleeved uniform shirt, with *Randy* embroidered on the pocket in a jaunty script. His face and muscular arms were tanned, but the skin on his hands looked reddened and rough.

"There you go," he said to the customer. "Let me know if you have any problems." He glanced at Anne and her father and broke out in a grin as the customer went out the door. "Dale Summers! Look at you!" Randy came over and pumped her father's hand.

"Hi, Randy! Good to see you. This is my daughter, Anne Gibson."

Anne held out her hand, and Randy grasped it, looking her over in quick appraisal. "Glad to meet you."

"Thanks," Anne said.

"Let me just tell my mechanics I'm taking a break." Randy went to a door that connected to the service area and opened it. A metallic whirring sound grew louder, and the smells of oil and exhaust wafted in. "Hey, Ronnie," Randy yelled. "I'll be at the diner."

He shut the door. "There. They'll be on the lookout for customers. Let's step across the street, where it's quieter."

They walked out to the curb and waited for traffic to pass, then crossed over the street. A small restaurant sat on the opposite corner, its bright sign proclaiming, *Kay's Koffee.*

Randy laughed as he opened the door and held it for Anne and her father. "Kay has been in business here for longer than I have. I keep telling her it's about time both of us retired."

As they entered, a woman behind the counter waved and called, "Mornin', Randy." Anne guessed she was Kay. Her hair was an even chestnut, her face bore some wrinkles, and she wore bifocals. Anne smiled and followed Randy.

About half the booths were empty, and they took one at the end of the row, with a window that allowed Randy to observe his station across the street.

A woman of about twenty-five came over to take their orders. She smiled at Randy. "Hi, how are you today?"

"I'm good," Randy said. "Brought some company today. I'm paying."

"Oh, you don't—" Anne's father began, but Randy already had put a five-dollar bill in the girl's hand.

"None of that," he said. "My treat. The usual for me, Ali."

"Gotcha." The waitress smiled at Anne. "You don't argue with Randy. What can I get you?"

"I'll have a black coffee."

"Same here," her father said.

Ali nodded. "Be right back."

She walked away, and Randy turned to Anne's father. "So, tell me about yourself, Dale. Are you retired?"

"Yes, five years ago. Charlene and I live in Florida, near my parents."

"Oh, they retired down there too?"

Her dad grinned. "It's hard to beat the Sunshine State."

"My kids want me to move to Texas."

"Oh, how many kids do you have?" Anne's dad asked.

"Two boys. Jordan moved out there first, and he liked it so much he talked his brother into going. They're both in the Fort Worth area." Randy glanced over at Anne and then back at her father. "What's this about Carl? Are you just reminiscing, or what?"

Anne said, "We got to looking at some of Aunt Edie's old pictures, and that's what got us thinking about him."

"Edie! I sure remember her. She lived in the big old house on Bluebell Lane, right?"

"That's right," Anne said. "It's now the Blue Hill Library."

Randy shook his head. "Things change. But that's good. The town needed a library."

Anne's father sipped his coffee and set his cup down. "Randy, I don't want to make you uncomfortable, but we want to know what happened to Carl over in 'Nam. Did you two stay in the same outfit over there?"

Randy nodded. "We were together four or five months. Right up until he was wounded." He looked down at his cup. "Crazy thing, that."

"What do you mean?"

"We had a little skirmish with the Cong. It wasn't much, really, as things went out there, but Carl got hit. It was all over pretty quick, but there was Carl with a bullet in his leg. We were in a remote location, and on foot. They called in a chopper to lift him out. I stayed with him while we waited." Randy sat in silence for a moment, frowning down at his coffee.

"I'm sorry you had to go through that," Anne said softly.

Randy shrugged. "I didn't mind going. I volunteered. So did Carl. It sure was different from what I expected…but then, I guess war always is."

Anne's father nodded. "It sounds as though Carl's wound wasn't life threatening."

"We sure didn't think so. He was conscious the whole time. I mean, he bled quite a bit, but we got that under control. I don't think it had hit an artery or anything like that. He looked like he was in pain, and he couldn't stand up, but I didn't think he was about to die."

"So what happened?" Anne prompted.

"I wish I knew." Randy shook his head slowly and then gazed at her. "I thought he was going to be okay. He was the only one hurt, and our lieutenant called for the chopper to take him. Before the chopper got there, he told me he guessed he'd be going home sooner than me. He pulled out a picture of Blue Hill. I think it was a snapshot someone in the family took, and they made it into a postcard."

"Sounds like Aunt Edie," Anne's father said with a smile.

"You know, I think it was from her. But Carl said, 'Here. You can have this. Anytime you want to see home, just look at that. I won't need it now.' I kept that thing the whole rest of my tour, and wouldn't you know it? Once I got home, my mom washed my uniform with that in the pocket. It was ruined, and I threw it away."

Anne chuckled. "I guess it served its purpose."

"It sure did. I'd look at that thing whenever we'd stop to rest in the field, or when we were in camp and had some free time. I could see the town hall in it and the old high school and that house of your aunt's up on the hill. Lots of familiar places. When I finally got home, I wanted to thank Carl and see how he was doing, so I called their house. Pauline answered. That's when I found out he'd died." Randy looked keenly at Anne's father. "Did they tell you how it happened?"

Her dad shifted in his seat. "We just heard he'd been killed in action."

"That's pretty much what Pauline said. I asked her, 'Was the chopper shot down, or what?' She said he'd died in battle. That's what they were told. But that didn't sound right to me. And then she told me they didn't get his remains. I asked again later, years after the war ended. They never got his body home."

"That's right," Anne's father said.

"But how can that be? They had him. I saw them put him in the chopper—a Huey, it was. And his wound wasn't that bad. Even if he died on the way to medical care, they still had him, you know what I'm saying?"

"It does seem weird," Anne said.

The waitress came over with the coffeepot. "More coffee?" she asked.

Anne held her hand over her cup. "None for me, thanks."

The men nodded, and the waitress filled their cups. When she had left, Anne's father cleared his throat. "Randy, we've wondered for the last week or two if perhaps the army made a mistake about Carl."

"What kind of mistake?"

"The kind that maybe mixed him up with another soldier who died in action. I don't know how that might happen—maybe a similar name, or someone wrote down his serial number wrong. Something like that maybe, but…" Her father nodded at Anne.

She brought out a copy of the picture of Carl and Aunt Edie together and laid it on the table in front of Randy.

"We found this among Aunt Edie's things."

Randy smiled as he picked up the photo. "That's a good picture of Carl. Was this taken after—" He broke off and frowned. "Wait a sec. He's got the medal. And what's this patch?"

Anne passed him another photo. "This is an enlargement of another snapshot taken the same day—one of Carl from a different angle. I zoomed in on his sleeve patch."

"Rangers! Carl wasn't in the Rangers." Randy lifted his chin and stared at Anne. "When were these taken?"

"It was 1976, the bicentennial in Washington, DC."

"Then he made it." Relief and wonder cleared Randy's baffled expression. "He was okay. But why…?"

"That's the big question," Anne's father said. "No one in the family ever heard that Carl was alive—except Aunt Edie, apparently. When we first found the picture, we wondered if it was someone else, maybe someone in the family who looked like Carl."

Randy studied him for a moment. "*You* kind of looked like him, Dale."

"Yes, but not that much. I could show you a photo of myself in 1976. If you put them side by side, you'd know this wasn't me.

And I certainly wasn't in Washington that year. The first time I ever saw the capital was in 1995."

"Okay." Randy looked down at the pictures again. "Did you have any brothers or any other cousins?"

"Carl was the closest thing I ever had to a brother. No other cousins the right age for this photo, and not any in the military at that time."

"Man." Randy swiped a hand across his forehead. "I can't believe this. I mean, if Carl made it okay, why didn't Pauline know?"

"That's a good question," Anne's father said. "And why didn't Aunt Edie tell us all that he was alive? Charlene and I lived in Blue Hill in 1976. Why didn't she come home and tell us she'd seen him?"

"It's a big mystery we're trying to solve," Anne said. "I've put in an inquiry to the army. So far, we haven't learned anything."

"You may not," Randy said darkly.

"We'd like to think they'll give us an explanation," Anne's dad said. "It's been difficult all these years, thinking he was gone but not being able to bury him. That hurt his father a lot. And now, to find evidence that he survived—well, I think the Summers family deserves to know what really happened."

"You got that right." Randy picked up his cup and took a long swallow. "Let me know if you find out anything, okay?"

"We'll do that," Anne said. She put the pictures back in an envelope and slid it into her purse. "And I'm having an exhibit of Aunt Edie's photos of Blue Hill at the new library. The opening is Saturday. You're welcome to come."

"I might just do that. And thanks for coming over here. Carl was a good buddy, and I'd sure like to know what happened to him."

Before Randy could take out money for a tip, Anne's father laid a dollar bill on the table.

"Say, you might want to talk to Linda Wright," Randy said.

"Linda Wright," Anne's father mused, his forehead wrinkling. "Haven't seen her since high school."

"She and Carl were pretty tight their senior year, I think," Randy said. "I know he got at least one letter from her after we enlisted. More than one, if I remember right. I razzed him a little about her."

"*Hmm.* Does she still live in the area?" Anne asked.

"I'm not sure, but my sister might know."

They filed outside and walked over to the service station in silence. When they reached Randy's parking area, Anne and her dad called their good-byes and got into the car. Randy stood near the curb, waving as they pulled away.

"Nothing new, really," her father said, "except that we've found a person who was close to him and thinks the official account of Carl's demise isn't right."

"Randy feels strongly it isn't right. We can't give up on this, Dad. If we can find this Linda Wright, maybe she can tell us something. I mean, if Carl was in love with her, maybe she heard from him—you know—after…"

"We can try."

Anne stared out the window as her father drove, her mind on the young man who had vanished so many years ago. What had happened after the medics placed Carl in the helicopter? She hoped they'd be able to uncover more of the story, but at the moment, she had no idea what else she could do to figure it out.

Chapter Eighteen

Anne felt good about her preparations on Friday. While she'd tended the library the previous afternoon, two women from the writers' group had come in to help clean the public rooms. Between patrons, Anne had put the final touches on her displays. Meanwhile, her parents had pitched in to clean the family quarters and get the decorations and some of the food ready for the reunion. The guest list for the Sunday event was shaping up, with both her father's sisters coming, as well as Madeline, Heather, Pauline, and a few others.

After lunch, she left Bella on duty at the checkout desk and went upstairs to try to locate Linda Wright. A call to Randy Turner's sister Marilyn was her first step.

"Linda went to college," Marilyn told her. "I think she got married after she graduated." Marilyn didn't know Linda's married name, but she did supply Anne with a telephone number for the woman's parents. "They still live at their old place."

When Anne called the Wrights' number, an older woman answered. "Yes, I'm Linda's mother," she said.

Anne explained that she was Dale Summers's daughter and that they were trying to locate people who had known his cousin Carl.

"Oh my, it's been a long time since I've thought about Carl Summers," Mrs. Wright said. "Linda was heartbroken, you know."

"I'd heard they were close." Anne felt bad that she was bringing up sad memories for people.

"Yes, they were. I think Linda planned on marrying that young man. They weren't officially engaged or anything, but she wrote to him constantly after he went overseas. And then we heard he'd been killed. So very sad. She was off at school, at State College, and we had to call and tell her."

"Do you think she'd mind talking about it now?" Anne asked.

"Probably not. It was a long time ago. She's been married almost thirty years and has three grown children."

Anne was glad to hear that Linda, at least, had moved on and accepted Carl's death.

"She only lives about a half hour away," Mrs. Wright went on. "I'll give you her number. You could call and maybe get together with her."

"Thank you very much." Anne took the number and phoned Linda. She wasn't sure whether or not to tell her about the photo they believed was of Carl and Aunt Edie, but after talking to her for a few minutes, she decided to do it.

"You think you have a photo of him taken later?" Linda said. "I don't know what to say."

"That's exactly how my dad and I felt when we saw it," Anne told her. "We're trying to establish that it couldn't have been anyone else, and I've inquired with the army about his record."

"I'd like to know what you find out," Linda said. "And I'd like to see the picture, if you wouldn't mind."

Anne told her about the photo exhibit to be held the next day. "I could show it to you then, if you want to come to Blue Hill."

"I'll be there," Linda said firmly.

* * *

Anne and her parents drove to the school in Anne's Impala at the time when classes let out for the weekend. Children streamed out the front doors of the brick building. Ben and Liddie separated from the crowd and dashed over to join them. Anne's father climbed out and held the back door open for them.

"Flowers, Mommy!" Liddie called out as she settled into her seat.

"Yes, honey. This is the time." Anne grinned at her in the rearview mirror.

Ben got in more slowly, and he carefully stowed his backpack before fastening his seat belt.

"How are you doing, Ben?" his grandmother asked.

"Fine. We set off a rocket in science today. We all went out to the ball field to do it."

"That's exciting," Anne's dad said. "How big was it?"

As Ben unfolded the story to his grandparents, Anne drove along the rural roads, thankful for another balmy day and a good forecast for the weekend.

"Madeline's plane doesn't land until nine this evening," her mother said, once Ben's tale had ended.

"Are you sure you and Dad want to pick her up?" Anne asked. "You'll be late getting home."

"It's fine," her father said. He was buckled in back with the kids and enjoying pointing out farm equipment, animals, and other sights to them. "We'll get her settled at the inn and be home by eleven or so. If there's any holdup, we'll call you."

"Thanks so much," Anne said. "I would have offered her a room at the house, but—"

"But your guestroom is taken," her mother said wryly. "Anne, don't feel guilty. Madeline was happy to stay at the inn, and now that you've given up more than half the house to the library, you can't be expected to open up to many guests."

"Yeah, but we're special," her father said with a chuckle.

"You sure are."

"Mommy, look! There are the flowers!" Liddie's voice rose in excitement as she tapped on her windowpane.

"Sure enough."

Anne pulled in to a farm lane that gave access to the field. She gazed out over the array of waving grasses and weeds. Buttercups and sundrops grew in dazzling abundance, and she spotted a few daisies, as well as yarrow and, at the wooded edge of the field, forget-me-nots. Near the road, a bank of feral lupine was beginning to open its blooms.

"Mommy, look at the purple flowers! I want those," Liddie said, fumbling with the buckle on her seat belt.

"The owners said we can pick all the flowers we want," Anne told her. "While I go to the cemetery, you and Grandma and Grandpa are going to pick a gazillion flowers."

"And let's be careful, kids," her father added. "The farmer said it's okay for us to pick here, and he doesn't have anything planted in this field, but he does plan to cut it for hay later, so try not to trample down more grass than you need to."

While Anne had hoped her father would go with her to the graveyard, she and her parents had decided it might be best not to take the children, but to stay with them to gather flowers while Anne drove the few extra miles and viewed the headstones. That way, they would get home in time to eat supper before her parents needed to leave for the airport to pick up Madeline.

Her father had brought some gloves and gardening shears in case they needed them, plus several large plastic buckets to hold the flowers on the way home.

"Sure are a lot of yellow ones," Ben said, surveying the field.

"Buttercups and dandelions," her mother said. "Sundrops too."

"Yes, but look around. There are lots of white and some red and bluish-purple flowers too," Anne said. "We can add lilacs and lilies at home without totally depleting the flower beds, I think."

"Your irises are coming on too," her mother said. "Come on, Liddie. Let's get a good bucketful of lupines first."

Anne watched for a minute as they started into the field, stopping to pick handfuls of blooms and exclaiming over each new discovery. Smiling, she got back into the car and put the transmission in gear. Five minutes later, she found the cemetery on the outskirts of Middle Village.

Her father had told her that the Summers plot was to the right of the mausoleum, but he couldn't remember exactly where. Anne wandered the rows of headstones slowly, reading the names and a few of the inscriptions. After ten minutes she hadn't found the names she sought, and she knew she needed some help.

Across several rows, she spotted a gray-haired groundskeeper trimming grass around one of the larger monuments. She strolled toward him and waved when she was a few yards away. He shut off his string trimmer.

"Can I help you, ma'am?"

"Yes. I'm looking for the Summers plot. David and Natalie Summers."

"Let's see…" He turned around slowly, as though finding his bearings, and then pointed. "Yonder, about four rows over and maybe two down."

"Thank you. I'll head over there." Anne noticed several lovely plants growing at the foot of the monument where he was working. "How lovely."

"Are you the one who puts flowers on the Summers lot?" he asked.

"No, not me."

He nodded. "Guess you wouldn't have had to ask where it was if you were."

"Does someone come to the grave regularly?" Anne thought of Pauline.

"Regular as clockwork, on Memorial Day or a day or two before. I thought it was the daughter at first."

Anne arched her eyebrows. "It's not? Pauline is my cousin, or rather, my father's cousin."

The groundskeeper shook his head. "I asked her. I saw her out here putting in some creeping phlox one spring, and so I mentioned the bouquets. Cut flowers, they are. She didn't know anything about them. But she comes once or twice a year and keeps the plantings nice. Last year, she put in a couple of begonias. Real pretty, they were."

"Has she been here this spring?"

"I don't know. I'm working my way over there. She may have brought a few plants, or maybe not yet. Right before Memorial Day—that's when most folks like to spruce up their family plots."

"These flower bouquets—what do they look like?" Anne asked. "Are they wildflowers or garden flowers or what?"

"White roses. No box or anything, just a bouquet of roses on each grave—Mr. Summers's and his wife's both. A dozen, I guess. I probably wouldn't have noticed except I have to clean up after Memorial Day. A lot of people leave flowers and don't come back. If there are vases or ribbons or anything like that, I have to move them so we can mow without running over things."

Anne's pulse quickened. Memorial Day was only three days away. "Do these roses have vases?"

He shook his head no. "Usually they're plain, with some kind of ribbon tying them together. They look store-bought, though, not from somebody's garden. Nice, long-stemmed white roses. They're laid on the graves, between the big headstone and the flat foot markers. It's a mystery."

"What about Pauline's plants?"

"Those are right up next to the big stone. I leave those alone, and we don't mow them. I trim around her plantings. But the roses, they die after a few days, and I throw them out. Pity. They're nice flowers."

"Thank you."

Anne supposed she was too early to see the mysterious annual bouquets, since it was only Friday and the groundskeeper had specified that they were left on or close to Memorial Day, but she was more eager than ever to view the gravesite. Walking more quickly now, she headed for the area he had indicated.

Within a couple of minutes, she found the solid granite monument. The rectangular headstone stood about three feet high and had the Summers name engraved deeply on the front. As she drew nearer, Anne caught her breath.

On the short-clipped grass before it lay two green-and-white bundles. She stepped closer and stared down at the two perfect bouquets of white roses. They were so fresh, fragrant, and lovely that she thought they must have been left today, perhaps within the last hour.

Beneath the large stone grew the creeping phlox the groundskeeper had described, with lavender flowers blooming. Pauline must not have been here yet this year, Anne decided, as no new annuals had been planted.

She located the flat markers, side by side, with David and Natalie's names on them and their birth and death dates. The entire plot looked well manicured, and the flowers—both lavender and white—spoke of loved ones who had come to pay their respects.

"Thank You, Lord," Anne breathed. She accepted the delicate rose bouquets as a sign of hope. This was not absolute proof, but in her heart she was certain Carl was the one who had left the roses. And that meant it really was him in the picture with Aunt Edie, not a look-alike relative or some trick of photography.

She took out her phone and clicked a picture of the headstone. Then she walked closer to one of the rose bouquets and took a close-up of it. She turned back toward her car smiling. If she kept searching, she was sure she would get to the truth, and her belief that she would find Carl was stronger than ever.

Chapter Nineteen

When the family arrived home, Anne and the children put the flower buckets on the back porch. Remi was just closing the library when Anne went into the foyer. The twins had swapped days, as Bella was taking a one-day seminar on Web site building.

"Mrs. Gibson, Miss Farley called about the refreshments for tomorrow," Remi said, "and I told her you'd be back around six. She'll try then."

"Thank you, Remi. How did things go here this afternoon?" Anne helped her straighten the checkout area as they talked.

"Very well. I checked out almost a hundred books."

"That's impressive," Anne said.

Remi grinned. "Yes, two homeschooling families came in, and they took a lot. You said there's no limit for them, right?"

"Absolutely."

"A member of the Tea and Book Club left a list of their selections for the next three months." Remi handed her a sticky note with the titles on it.

"Great. Some of the women like to buy their own books, but I'll order three copies of each of these." Anne smiled as she read the selections. "It's a good variety—and I haven't read any of these myself."

"Are you going to their meeting?" Remi opened the bottom desk drawer and retrieved her purse.

"Not today." Anne took out the business checkbook. "Let me give you your pay and Bella's. I couldn't have managed without you girls this week, with my company and everything that's going on."

"Thank you. We'll both be here tomorrow during the exhibit opening."

Anne gave Remi both their checks and walked with her to the door.

"I'll see you tomorrow," Remi said, and she set off homeward with a quick stride.

Anne put away the checkbook and locked the desk drawers. She was about to head for the stairs when the phone rang. She picked up the receiver. Probably Mildred, but she couldn't be sure, so she cleared her throat and put on her librarian voice.

"Blue Hill Library, Anne Gibson speaking."

"Ms. Gibson, so glad I reached you. This is Sergeant Amy Potter, Army Liaison."

It took a moment for Anne to register that the sergeant had actually telephoned her and that she must have news about Carl's case.

"Oh, hello! Thank you so much for calling."

"You're welcome," Sergeant Potter said. "In light of your relationship to Private Summers and the short time left before your family reunion—I believe you said it's this weekend, isn't it?"

"Yes. Sunday afternoon." Anne brushed back her hair, still scarcely able to believe she was having this conversation.

"I thought that under the circumstances, it would be best to telephone and make sure you got the message on time, so you can share it with your family."

"Thank you!"

"You're welcome, Ms. Gibson. I admit your message touched me. It seemed so genuine and heartfelt. I hope that I'll be able to encourage you and your father, as well as the rest of your family."

"You have good news, then?" Anne's chest tightened, and she plunked down into the desk chair.

"It took a while," Sergeant Potter admitted, "but I was so moved by your e-mail that I spent hours poring over old records, searching for Carl Summers's complete records."

"That was most generous of you," Anne said. "What did you learn?"

"It appears that you were right on at least one score."

"Oh?" Anne's heart raced.

"Your cousin wasn't killed in Vietnam. He came up for honorable discharge in 1972."

Relief flooded Anne, and she slumped back in the chair. "Thank you so much! You don't know how much this means to me." She caught her breath. "But—"

"Yes?" the sergeant asked.

"If that's true, why was his family told he was killed in action two years earlier? And why weren't they informed of the mistake, if it *was* a mistake?" Her hand clenched around the telephone receiver.

"I don't have all the answers for you yet, but I'll keep digging. I *can* tell you that Carl Summers received a wound in the line of duty in 1970. This may be where the report of his death originated."

"What sort of wound was it, and how bad?" Anne asked. "We heard it was a leg wound."

"I don't have details. The mistake seems to have occurred about the time he was wounded. I believe it was a clerical error and that portion of his records may have been placed in the wrong file. I haven't gotten to the bottom of that yet. But it seems he did recover, though he appears to have spent several weeks at a military hospital in Germany, and later was treated in Washington."

"Washington!" Anne's mind flashed to the photograph taken in 1976. "Please, can you tell me if he's still alive?"

"I don't know for certain. Ms. Gibson, I'd like to do some more searching and get back to you. As you know, Monday's a holiday, so it may be well into next week before I have anything more for you."

"Of course. I understand. But we found a picture of him. I think I mentioned it in my message—it was taken in 1976. And he was in uniform."

"*Hmm.* I'll check to see if he reenlisted. I was assuming that he separated from the army when his initial enlistment expired. It's possible he re-upped then, though I would think the records I saw would have noted that."

"If it helps," Anne said quickly, "we've identified a shoulder patch in the photo as one for the Airborne Rangers, First Battalion. That wasn't his unit when he was wounded."

"Rangers. That would be Special Forces. I suppose it's possible he was transferred to a different regiment, and the records for some reason are not linked to earlier ones that I found. I'll certainly look into the possibility. And I'll write up an e-mail outlining the things we've just discussed, so that you have a record of our conversation," Sergeant Potter said. "In the meantime, I hope you and your family enjoy your reunion."

"Thank you," Anne said. The connection ended, and the phone hummed softly. She hung up, realizing that any other questions she had would need to wait.

She sat at the desk for a long moment, thinking over what she had just learned. Closing her eyes, she drew in a deep breath. "Thank You, Lord! Thank You for this much. It's more than I expected. Please let us find Carl. And soon!"

She opened her eyes, having come to a decision. She would wait a bit to share this news with her parents. If she told them that Carl had survived his stint in Vietnam, her father would be ecstatic and want to tell the world. But then, if Sergeant Potter told them that Carl had died later on, her dad would be crushed. And how badly would Pauline take that? She was already against poking around and stirring up painful memories.

It would be nice to tell everyone the good news at the reunion, she thought. But wouldn't it be better to wait until she knew the whole truth? She didn't want to raise false hopes, only to dash them a few days later.

Even if Sergeant Potter didn't come through for her with more information soon, Anne knew she would stay on the trail. One way or another, she would track down Carl Summers.

Chapter Twenty

Anne's pride swelled as she gazed over the crowded rooms of the library. It was two o'clock on Saturday afternoon, and the foyer and reading rooms were full of guests. She had laid out the guest book on the center table in the foyer, and more than fifty people had already signed it.

She sidled up to Wendy and leaned toward her. "I have to admit I didn't really expect the turnout to be this good today."

"People have been wonderful about supporting the library, haven't they?" Wendy smiled at Anne and patted her arm.

"They sure have. It tells me how much they loved Aunt Edie. Seeing them all here to view her pictures says a lot about our community, and about her."

"And about you, Anne. The people of Blue Hill have taken you into their hearts."

She couldn't keep her lips from twitching. "I feel as though I should get all modest and say it isn't true, but you know what? It feels good to agree with you on that. Everyone's been wonderful to me and the kids."

Wendy gazed across the room at Anne's parents. "Your cousin Madeline kind of looks like Edie."

"Some," Anne agreed. "We're tickled that she flew all the way from California for our reunion. Dad hadn't seen her in ages, and I barely remembered what she looked like. The last time I'd seen her, I think I was in junior high."

"It's great to reconnect," Wendy said.

"It sure is. This morning Dad took her on a drive around town to show her all the things that have changed in Blue Hill since she was last here."

Anne noticed that one of the refreshment trays on the center table was nearly empty. "Looks like we need more mini-muffins and cookies. Excuse me."

She picked up the tray and carried it to the downstairs kitchen, greeting people along the way. The couple who owned the Keystone Café stopped her for a moment to tell her how much they had enjoyed Edie's photographs.

"Aren't they wonderful?" Anne said. She started once more toward the kitchen.

"Hello, Anne," said Mayor Bob Bultman. "This is a lovely gathering, and the pictures are superb. I especially like the ones of the town hall and the train depot."

"Thank you," Anne said. "Aunt Edie certainly had an eye for composition."

"My mother used to tell me about the day President Kennedy came through town," Betty Bultman added. "And to think your Aunt Edie was there with her camera!"

"She caught some amazing moments." Anne noticed that her mom and dad stood nearby, talking to Madeline, Mildred Farley, and Coraline Watson. "Oh, have you met my parents?"

"I don't think I have," the mayor said.

"Let me introduce you." Anne took the mayor and his wife over to the little group and made the introductions. "And this is my father's cousin, Madeline Culver, who is visiting us from California."

Anne excused herself and left the group, happily chatting. She entered the kitchen to find Remi, Bella, and their mother arranging more plates of finger food.

"Those look great," Anne told them. "Thanks for doing this, Mrs. Miller. I was afraid I wouldn't get my mom out of the kitchen, and I really wanted her and Dad to have a chance to reconnect with old acquaintances and meet new people."

"We're happy to do it," Mrs. Miller said.

"You all need a chance to mingle too." Anne frowned and glanced over her shoulder. "You don't need to do much more, do you?"

"Don't you worry," Bella said with a laugh. "We're popping in and out and seeing everyone."

Anne left the empty tray and picked up one filled with dessert squares and gingersnaps. "So many people contributed food!"

"It's a wonderful spread," Remi said. "If there are any leftovers, you can serve them at your reunion tomorrow."

Anne chuckled and carried her tray out to the foyer. At the rate the refreshments were disappearing, even with all the extras her friends and the book club had brought, there wouldn't be much left. But she had nothing to fear—her mother had baked all week for the reunion, and her father's sisters had promised to bring several dishes with them on Sunday.

After depositing the tray, she noticed a woman coming in the door. She looked about Anne's mother's age, dressed in a navy pantsuit and striped top, with gold dangle earrings and a cuff bracelet. She stopped and looked around as though seeking someone. Anne hurried toward her.

"Hello, I'm Anne Gibson." She extended her hand.

The woman smiled in relief. "Linda Wright. I'm so glad to meet you."

"Thanks for coming, Linda. I know you want to see that photograph we talked about. Would you like to come into the checkout desk?"

On the way, Anne flagged her father down, and he joined her and Linda at the front desk. Anne introduced them and then took out the picture of Carl and Aunt Edie.

"I'm stunned," Linda said, gazing at the photograph. "That has to be Carl."

"Since I spoke to you, I heard from the army's liaison," Anne said. "She told me there was some sort of glitch, and Carl's records were mixed up. He was alive at least until 1972. I think this picture proves he lived longer."

Linda's face paled. "But why—?" She swayed slightly, and Anne's father reached out to steady her.

"Maybe you should sit down for a minute, Mrs. Wright."

"Thank you." Linda sank into the chair behind the desk. "I'm sorry, I just don't understand. Why didn't Carl write to me?"

"That's what we've been asking," Anne's dad said gently. "None of us knew either."

"We think he had a long recovery after he was wounded and then went into another unit," Anne told her, leaning over the desk. "It may have been some sort of secret unit."

"Clandestine," her father added. "That's the best explanation I can think of."

Linda nodded soberly. "It hurts, you know? I thought he loved me."

"I do know," Anne's father said. "We all loved him."

"He never proposed or anything," Linda said. "In fact, I didn't think he was that serious about me. But in his letters he sounded like he really missed me, and that when he came home he wanted to spend time with me. I had hopes, I guess you might say."

"It doesn't make a lot of sense to us that he might be alive and didn't let anyone know," Anne said, her heart aching for the young woman who had waited so eagerly for Carl's letters.

"But your aunt knew." Linda picked up the photograph.

"Apparently she did, but for whatever reason, she didn't tell anyone else in the family."

"Thanks for telling me and for letting me see this." Linda took a deep breath and rose. "I'm happily married, you know, and I wouldn't trade my family for the world, but I would like to know what happened to Carl. You will keep me informed?"

"We will," Anne said. "Would you like to see the exhibit?"

"I think I'll just go home, but thank you."

Anne watched her father walk with Linda across the foyer to the front door.

She heard a booming voice call her name and turned to see Randy Turner. He approached her with an attractive woman his age who had short, layered hair and wore dark blue slacks and a knit ivory top. Randy grinned and came toward her.

"Anne! This is my wife, Dolly."

The woman laughed and held out her hand. "Dorothy Turner, but everyone calls me Dolly, so you may as well too."

"I'm so pleased that you and Randy came," Anne said. "Did you know my great-aunt?"

"No, I'm afraid not," Dolly said.

"Dolly's from upstate New York," Randy explained. "After we got married, we moved over to Deshler, and I don't think she ever met Miss Summers. But I'd told her about the postcard Carl gave me, and she wanted to come."

"Please enjoy looking around at the photographs," Anne told them. "There are some here in the foyer and some in each of the reading rooms. A couple of the rooms are upstairs. And do help yourselves to refreshments."

Anne decided to make a round of all the reading rooms to see if she had missed greeting any of their guests. When she reached the Children's Room, she found Liddie cuddled up beside Hannah Pyle, who was reading a story to her three youngest brothers, Liddie, and Liddie's friends Becca and Cindy Jacobs.

"Mommy!" Liddie jumped up and ran to her, with her pink dress shimmering around her. She hugged Anne around the waist. "Can we have some cookies?"

"You sure can," Anne said, straightening one of Liddie's pink hair ribbons, "but you'll need to go downstairs for that. Remember we don't bring food up here to the Children's Room."

"Right." Liddie gazed up at her knowingly. "'Cause we don't want to spill on the books."

Anne smiled. "After Hannah finishes the story, you may come down and get your refreshments."

Liddie happily returned to Hannah's side. Anne went on to the Nonfiction Room, where she discovered several people commenting on the display case there.

"Anne," Reverend Tom called to her. "Maggie and I were just saying how extraordinary these photographs are. Did Edie leave them to you in this form, or did you have them made up special for the exhibit?"

"Most of them were snapshots," she said. "The ones from the really old cameras were pretty faded, but my dad sorted through the old negatives and found some good ones. That's how we got this photo." She picked up a framed view of Blue Hill from the top of Main Street, taken in about 1950.

"I can see this all took a lot of work," Jessica Myer, the attorney, said. "You didn't run across any old shots of the building where my office is now, did you?"

Anne thought about it. "There may be one or two. My father is downstairs. You could ask him if he remembers any. He went through tons of pictures and negatives. I do know that most of the buildings on Main Street show up more than once."

"Let me know if you find any," Jessica said.

"I will. Dad also fixed the camera displays and looked up the information for the placards on those."

"Sounds like he may be able to help me," Jessica said. "I'll go find him." She headed out toward the stairway.

"Beautiful event, Anne," Maggie Sloan said quietly, patting her arm. Anne chatted with her and Reverend Tom for a few minutes before moving on.

She looked into the Fiction Room and greeted several guests there, then went down to the History Room, where she exchanged pleasantries with several library patrons. Next, she drifted out into the foyer. Grace and Jay were just coming through the door.

"Anne! Great turnout! I'm going to do a write-up for Monday's paper," said Grace.

"Terrific," Anne said. "You know I'm happy for any publicity you can give the library."

"Jay's going to take some pictures." Grace nodded to the photographer. "Make sure you get a nice one of Anne with the vintage cameras."

"You know what?" Anne asked. "I think it would be better to put my dad in the photo. He helped me do all this, and it's been a long time since his picture ran in the *Gazette*."

"You could both be in it," Jay said.

Grace grinned. "That sounds like a keeper. And I'll want to get a few quotes from you before I leave, Anne."

"No problem." Anne pointed out her father, and Jay and Grace headed in his direction.

Poor Dad, Anne thought. *He's the go-to man today.* But he seemed to be happy and handling all the attention well.

After Jay took his photos and she had answered a few questions for Grace's article, Anne noticed Randy and his wife were standing in front of one of the displays. Randy beckoned to her, and Anne walked over to them.

"This is the picture," Randy said eagerly.

At a loss, Anne gazed at the print he indicated. Recognition dawned on her. The panoramic view of the town showed Blue Hill laid out before them, as it had been in the late 1960s. In the distance, she could see the very house they were standing in, the church steeple, and the cupola on the town hall. Many other landmark structures were visible if one looked closely.

"This is the one that was on the postcard Carl gave me," Randy said. "I think it's exactly the same. Only better, of course, because it's bigger, and it's not all creased and ragged like the little one."

Anne grinned. "I'm glad. We found the original in one of Aunt Edie's albums, and my dad found the negative. If you'd like, Randy, I can have a print made for you."

"He'd love that," Dolly said.

Anne nodded. "I'm going to go write it down this minute, so I don't forget. I'll be having some other pictures made up anyway, since we're having a family reunion tomorrow."

"That'd be great," Randy said. "Thanks a lot, Anne. It means a lot to see this picture. I can't wait to see the rest."

"Have you been in the Nonfiction Room yet?" she asked. There's a good one of the high school in there."

When Randy and Dolly left her, Anne hurried to the desk in the next room and wrote herself a note to get them a print of Edie's photo.

"Mrs. Gibson!" Bella came into the room carrying an empty tray. "Mr. Kepple just asked me if it's possible for him to get a print of that picture of his family's store."

Anne laughed. "Sounds like I'd better make a sign-up sheet for people who want prints."

"I'll do it if you like," Bella said.

"Would you? Thanks—and make columns for their names and phone numbers and the prints they want. We can call them next week, after I talk to Jay about costs and make sure he wants to do the prints. If he doesn't, I'll have to set it up with someone else, but I think Jay will do it. He seems to enjoy doing extra jobs like this on the side."

"Just make sure he charges enough to make a profit," Bella said, taking a clipboard from a nearby shelf.

"Oh, Anne, I was looking for you." She whirled to find Alex at her elbow.

"What's up?" she asked.

"Aside from another wonderful event, there's a deliveryman at the front door."

"Oh dear. Bad timing. Is it books?"

"I don't think so." Alex walked with her between clusters of people to the door and opened it.

A man who had been gazing at the flowerbeds turned to face them. He had a long, pale blue box in his arms. Beyond him, Anne could see a florist's truck double-parked in the street at the end of the crowded driveway.

"Flowers?" she asked, rapidly reviewing the list of things she had ordered for the weekend's two events. The one floral piece she had purchased for the main display had been delivered the day before.

"Yes, for Anne Gibson. I believe that's you." The man smiled, and Anne realized he had been to her house with deliveries on other occasions.

"It is, but I can't imagine..."

Alex grinned. "Just say thank you and sign."

"Right." She did, and Alex carried the box inside for her.

"Where do you want it?" he asked.

"On the distribution desk, I guess. I'll open it there and see who it's from. It may be for the reunion."

Alex walked across the foyer and laid the box on top of the desk. Anne quickly lifted the lid of the blue box. She gasped.

"They're nice," Alex said, eyeing her cautiously.

"Yes. But white roses!" Anne fingered one of the gorgeous blooms. "And so many."

"There must be at least three dozen," Alex said. "You'll need a big vase."

She stared at him. "I didn't have a chance to tell you about the cemetery, did I?"

"Cemetery?"

Anne felt a little lightheaded. She reached out and grabbed Alex's arm. "I think I'd better sit down. Pull up a chair, and I'll tell you a story."

It took her only a minute to relate the call from the army sergeant and tell Alex what the cemetery groundskeeper had told her the day before.

"And they were lying there on the graves," she finished. "Two bouquets of beautiful white roses—just like these." She nodded at the florist's box. "I'm sure Carl is the one who is sending them."

Alex cocked his head to one side, frowning. "Maybe you should open the card."

"Good idea." She felt steadier now, and she stood. The green tissue nestled around the flower stems partially hid the small white envelope. Anne took it out and opened it. The card had only two words written on it: *Thank you*.

Anne stared bleakly at Alex. "He didn't sign it."

"Maybe it's not him."

She plopped down into her chair. "That's why I haven't told Mom and Dad about the flowers yet. I don't want them to be disappointed if I'm wrong. But it has to be him. Don't you think so?" She gazed up at him, hoping he would assure her that she was right.

His lips pressed together in a thin line as he considered her question. "Anne, I don't know. It seems to me that it could be anyone related to the family."

"But Pauline told the cemetery groundskeeper that it wasn't her. Who else is there?"

Alex sighed. "I think you should talk to her personally. The man at the cemetery told you she said that, but maybe she just didn't want him to know her private business."

"No, I'm sure it's not her. Why would she set out plants *and* leave cut flowers? That doesn't make sense to me."

"Okay, then someone else."

"There's nobody."

"Not true. There's your mom and dad and Cousin Madeline, whom I just met today—and, by the way, she's charming. There are probably other cousins, aren't there? And I believe you told me your grandparents are still alive."

"Yes, but they can't come for the reunion. Do you think they'd send flowers every year? They are Carl and Pauline's aunt and uncle."

"There you go. It might be them. Maybe they call the florist from Florida every year and order them sent to the cemetery. And they know you're having your party tomorrow too."

"I doubt it's them."

"But you don't know," Alex said. "In fact, if she hadn't died recently, I'd have said Edie was a strong possibility. We know she didn't send these flowers, but it could be someone in the town who wanted to thank you for mounting this exhibit. The mayor, for instance—or the library volunteers."

Anne slumped down in the chair. "I suppose you're right, but I still think any of them would have signed the card. And besides—they're just like the ones at the cemetery. They have to be sent by the same person, and I'm sure the mayor didn't send those."

"Here's a thought," Alex said, laying his hand gently on her shoulder. "Tomorrow, when you have all the family together, you can show them these lovely roses and ask if anyone knows anything about them. But I was serious about Carl's sister too. I think you ought to speak to her privately before you tell anyone else. Because she seems the most likely candidate to me. Make sure she doesn't know anything about it."

Anne nodded slowly. "And then, if I haven't found out anything, tomorrow I'll tell everyone and see if anyone can add to the clues. But I hate to disappoint so many people, Alex."

He smiled. "I know. You were always like that. You want everyone to be happy, and I can understand that. But I don't think it's right to keep this to yourself. If there's any chance someone else can shed a little light on things, you should tell them."

"I guess you're right. And if none of them admits to knowing anything, at least I'll know that much." Her spirits rose a notch, and she smiled at Alex. "Thanks. I'm ninety-nine percent sure it was Carl, and until I learn otherwise, I'm going to keep believing that, even if it's only for one more day."

He reached out a hand, and she took it.

"Come on," he said. "Let's find you a vase, and you can arrange these. Would you like me to carry them upstairs for you?"

Anne let him pull her to her feet. "Yes, thanks. I'll leave them up there until the reunion."

"Your folks will see them."

"That's right." She frowned, thinking of her options. "I guess I won't try to hide them, but I'll just tell them someone sent them anonymously, and I won't tell them about the cemetery flowers yet. Tonight, when the library's closed, I'll call Pauline. You're right about that."

She replaced the lid on the box. She would have to answer a lot of questions tonight and tomorrow. She hoped that somehow she'd have more information by the time of the family gathering. Wouldn't it be fantastic if she could share more than just the beautiful flowers, and give her father and Pauline and the rest of the family a wonderful surprise?

Chapter Twenty-One

Saturday evening, when all was quiet in the lower rooms of the library, the extra food was put away, and the serving dishes were clean, Anne's father suggested they all pile into his and Anne's cars, including Cousin Madeline, and go out for supper.

"Go out?" Anne stared at him. "We've got so much food here! And I'm not even hungry. I sampled several of the goodies this afternoon."

"You need to get away from all this for a little while," her dad insisted.

Anne looked to her mother and Madeline for support, and Madeline was smiling. "I think that's a great idea. The kids would enjoy it, wouldn't they?"

"Yeah!" Ben said.

Liddie only yawned.

Her mother said doubtfully, "Personally, I'm a little tired, Dale. Anne may be right, and we need a quiet evening at home."

Her father looked disappointed, but Madeline was still cheerful. "What if Dale and Ben and I run out and get some fried chicken takeout and bring it back here? We can munch on that and leftovers from the exhibit, and if Anne wants to, she can put the children to bed early."

"I'm not tired," Ben said.

"Me either." Liddie yawned broadly.

"All right," Anne said. "I think that would work best for me. I don't want to squelch your fun, Dad—"

"No, it's okay," he said. "Do you want soft drinks?"

"None for me and the kids," Anne said. "I think we've all had enough sugar for one day."

Liddie didn't even fuss when they left without her, and Anne took her by the hand. "Come on, let's get you in the tub."

"Am I going to eat in my pajamas?" Liddie asked.

"Yes, if you still want to eat when they get home." Anne led her up to the third floor.

When Liddie was scrubbed clean and decked out in her pink sleepwear, they went to the family living room and discovered Anne's mother leafing through a magazine.

"They're still not back," she told them. "Liddie, want to read a story with Grandma?"

Liddie nodded and wriggled onto the couch beside her.

Anne realized this was the perfect time to call Pauline. She had promised Alex she would do it, but she hadn't had a chance to make the call when the others would not overhear her asking about the mystery flowers. "If you don't mind, Mom, I'm going to go make a phone call."

"Sure, go ahead," her mother said.

Anne went up to her room and called. Pauline answered on the third ring.

"Well, hi, Anne. I just finished making my taco salad for tomorrow. I can't wait to see everyone."

"We're excited about it too." Anne sat down on her bed and stretched her legs out in front of her. "Pauline, I wanted to ask you something. I went to the cemetery yesterday, and the groundskeeper told me about the white roses that are put on your parents' graves every year."

After a moment's silence, Pauline said, "He told me about that two or three years ago. I've only seen it once."

"I saw them Friday," Anne said. "They were lying on the graves. Beautiful roses."

"I haven't been to the cemetery yet myself," Pauline said. "I thought I'd wait until Monday morning, since I'll be driving to Blue Hill tomorrow."

"Do you know who puts the flowers there?" Anne asked.

"No. It isn't me. I thought maybe it was someone in my mother's family, but I've asked around, and nobody admits to it."

Anne took a deep breath. "This afternoon, I got a delivery at the library—well, at my house."

Pauline didn't say anything, so Anne plunged on. "It was three dozen white roses, Pauline. Just like the ones at the cemetery."

Pauline gasped. "That's kind of creepy."

"I didn't think so," Anne said. "There was a card that said, 'Thank you,' but it wasn't signed."

"Do you think it's from someone who wanted to thank you for holding the reunion?"

"I don't know for certain, but I had a feeling it was more in response to the inquiries Dad and I have made."

"Well, I certainly didn't send them to you."

"No, I didn't think you did."

"What are you suggesting, Anne?"

She straightened her shoulders. "My dad and I have been trying to find out more about Carl's military service."

"Yes. You know I've had mixed feelings about that."

"It was never my intention to upset anyone," Anne said. "Tomorrow at the reunion, I'll share with everyone what we've learned so far. But I wondered if it ever entered your mind that Carl might be the one sending those flowers to the cemetery every year."

"I've thought of it," Pauline admitted, "but I didn't see how it could be true. And I've tried not to think about it for quite a while now. It ties me up in knots, Anne. I just can't keep hoping. Carl is dead. Someone else is sending the roses."

Anne sighed. "I suppose it could be a coincidence that the bouquet is the same as the cemetery flowers. Well, maybe tomorrow we'll learn who is sending those."

"I hope so. If it's someone's idea of a joke, it's ghoulish."

"I'm sorry I brought up a touchy subject," Anne said, "but you're the only other person who knows about the flowers at the cemetery. I haven't even told Mom and Dad about those. I didn't want to get Dad's hopes up until I had more to go on. They saw the bouquet I got today, of course, but I didn't tell them about the others yet. I will tomorrow though. I'd like everyone to know, so that maybe together we can puzzle out what this means."

"Good luck," Pauline said. "I doubt you'll find out any more than you already know."

"Don't you want to know what really happened to him back then?"

Pauline let out a sharp sigh. "Of course I do. What I don't want is another round of fruitless speculation. It makes me…I almost don't want to come tomorrow."

"Oh, please don't say that! We all want very much for you to be here."

After a moment, Pauline said, "All right. I'll be there."

Anne decided it was best to leave it at that, and she heard her dad, Madeline, and Ben returning with the food.

"Great. We'll see you tomorrow then." She hung up and exhaled slowly.

"Mommy!" Liddie shouted up the stairs, "They brought chicken and biscuits and ice cream."

Anne let out a little moan and headed for the stairs.

* * *

After church on Sunday, Anne rushed home to make sure everything was ready for the reunion.

"Ben, you take Hershey over to Alex's house first thing," she said as they walked into the house.

"Okay," Ben said, heading to the kitchen to get Hershey's leash.

"And don't get dirty. There isn't time to change into play clothes and back again."

"Why does Hershey have to go over there?" Liddie asked.

"He's going to stay with Ryan for the afternoon," Anne told her. "I don't want to take any chances of his upsetting any of our older guests or causing anyone's allergies to act up."

Ben clipped the leash to Hershey's collar and disappeared down the path toward Alex and Ryan's house.

"I'll start making the punch," Anne's mother said, "unless there's something more urgent."

"Just tell us what you want us to do," her dad agreed.

"Me too," Madeline chimed in.

"I don't expect anyone else for at least forty-five minutes," Anne said with a glance at the clock. "Dad, you hung the family tree chart, right?"

"Yes, over the fireplace in the Nonfiction Room, where you asked me to."

"Good. Are the photo albums all ready?"

"Everything's set out the way you wanted it."

"Thanks." Anne reached for a bib apron. All of the mounted photographs were still in place from the exhibit, but they had grouped the more personal family pictures in albums the guests could browse.

Madeline smiled. "Between the albums and the displays you made for the library, we'll have lots to look at."

"We know for sure that it's not going to rain," Anne's father said. "Shall I take out the small library table and set up the patio chairs?"

"I think it's safe to do that now, and these can go out there, on the picnic table." Anne handed him a package of nametags and several felt markers.

"Let me lay the tablecloth first!" Her mother grabbed a large plastic cloth from the counter.

"I can help Dale with that while you make the punch," Madeline offered. She took the tablecloth and smiled at Anne's father. "Lead the way."

"What do I do, Mommy?" Liddie asked, with just a hint of pout to her voice.

"Have you forgotten?" Anne smiled and bent down close to Liddie. "The wildflowers."

Liddie gasped and clapped her hands together. "It's time to do the flowers!"

"Yes," Anne said, "but you need to put on a big apron first, like I did. Then we'll put them in the pretty vases and pots."

Soon she and Liddie were in the garage, where they arranged the wildflowers in ten assorted containers, ranging from Aunt Edie's porcelain vases to a rustic wooden bucket her father had found in a cluttered corner of the garage.

Her father came to help them, and they carried the containers to various points around the backyard. The flowers had held up well, and they complemented the perennials Aunt Edie had planted over the years. When they finished, the whole yard looked like a garden. Liddie spun slowly, getting the full effect of their efforts.

"It's perfect!"

"It sure is," Madeline called from near the picnic table, where she was making nametags for all of them.

Ben came whistling up the path from Alex's house.

"Oh, Ben, you need to go put on your emergency shirt," Anne said. "It looks as if Hershey got a little demonstrative when he said good-bye."

Ben grimaced. "Yeah, he jumped up and put his paws on my shirt."

"Well, hurry." Anne sighed, glad she had followed her mother's advice and laid out one extra outfit for each child and even a clean blouse for herself, in case an accident happened during their preparations.

Anne dashed inside and up to the private living room. The large vase of white roses sat on an end table, where Alex had placed it last night, and she picked it up carefully. This item would have pride of place in the foyer. She had brushed off her parents' inquiries as to where they came from. Her mother had the impression that someone in town sent them because of the exhibit opening, and Anne hadn't disillusioned her.

She went to the elevator and rode smoothly down to the ground floor. The centerpiece from yesterday's exhibit could move to the oak table where she usually displayed new books. The stand in the center of the foyer would show off the roses for this one day.

She positioned the vase and went to the front door to check the view guests would see as they entered. The fragrant roses were beautiful. She went back to the stand and turned the bouquet just a little, for the best effect, then went to the library kitchen to get a little extra water for the vase.

Her mother was entering from the back door as Anne returned to the foyer. "Anne, someone just drove in. We heard a car door."

"Coming!" Anne put the small pitcher of water into her mother's hands and groped to untie her apron strings. "Top off that vase, would you, please?"

She took a deep breath and strode toward the front door. As she hurried across the foyer, the scent of the white roses reminded her of Carl, and her hope that he was still alive and aware of her. Did he know the family would be gathering today? Her guests were arriving, and she was no nearer to the truth about her cousin or the mysterious roses than she had been the day before. She remembered Alex's encouragement and raised her chin as she opened the big door.

Aunt Joanna and her husband, Uncle Philip, were getting out of their car.

"Hello," Anne called as she went down the steps.

"Anne! How wonderful you look." Aunt Joanna hugged her and kissed her cheek.

"Thank you." Anne smiled at her uncle. "Welcome, Uncle Philip. And whom do you have here?" She looked at the two children getting out of the backseat.

"My daughter's two, Jacob and Aria."

"Hello," Anne said. "I do believe I'm your first cousin, once removed."

Jacob, who looked about Ben's age, blinked at her. "Okay."

His sister smiled and held out her hand. "May I just call you Cousin Anne?"

"Of course. And we have nametags on the deck out back." Anne shook Aria's hand. "How old are you?"

"Eleven."

"I'm so pleased that you came," Anne said. "My children are inside—Ben and Liddie. So far, it looks like you're the oldest of that generation."

"I don't mind," Aria told her.

"She means she doesn't mind bossing people around," her brother said.

"Jacob," Joanna said with a mild warning in her tone.

Anne smiled. "Come on in. I'm sure Ben will enjoy showing you two around."

Her father and Cousin Madeline were descending the grand staircase when they entered the foyer, to join Anne's mother at the bottom. Joanna and Philip greeted everyone.

"This house looks fantastic," Joanna said. "You've done a lot of work, Anne."

"Yes, well, I've had lots of help." She smiled.

"Well, you've got to give us a tour of the library."

"Your aunt would have loved this," Philip said, looking appreciatively around the foyer and all the way up to the cathedral ceiling high above. "Did you do any remodeling?"

"Yes, some, to make the rooms more accessible to the library patrons, and we put in a family kitchen upstairs. There were some repairs too." Anne preferred not to remember the day a huge chunk of the ceiling had crashed to the floor in the foyer. "The house was structurally sound, and I had a great contractor. We're in good shape now."

"I'd be happy to show Joanna and Philip around," Anne's mother offered.

Anne decided to take her up on it, as she thought she heard another car pulling in.

"Maybe we can start with the kitchen." Joanna held out a covered dish.

"Right this way." Anne's mother led them toward the library kitchen, where her dish could go temporarily into the refrigerator, and Anne hurried back outside.

Sure enough, another car was easing into a parking spot next to Philip's. Anne sent up a quick prayer of gratitude for the beautiful weather—a perfect late-May day. The lilies and irises in the flower beds stirred as a light breeze caressed them.

A woman with graying short hair got out of the newly arrived vehicle. At once, Anne knew she was a Summers. She had the same pleasing features she had noted before in her dad, Aunt Edie, and other members of the family.

"Pauline?" she guessed. She hadn't seen this cousin for many years.

The woman smiled. "Yes. You must be Anne." She took Anne's hand and looked into Anne's eyes. "I didn't want you to think I don't appreciate what you've done. About Carl, I mean. Of course I want to know what happened to him. If the army knows anything, they owe us an explanation."

"I think so too," Anne said softly.

"My husband couldn't come," Pauline said, "but I knew I couldn't miss this get-together. Is Dale here?"

"Yes, and Cousin Madeline too."

"You told me she might, but I'm surprised she came all the way from California." Pauline's blue eyes went wide behind her gold-rimmed glasses.

"She flew out to visit for a few days. She'll be tickled to see you."

"I can't wait." Pauline reached back into her car for a covered dish and a tote bag. "I brought a taco salad and some of the famous

Summers Family Ginger Chews cookies. You can never have enough cookies, right? That's my theory, anyway."

Anne laughed and accepted the plastic box she offered. "Right! I haven't had a Ginger Chew cookie in years and years. I can't wait! Thanks very much. Come on inside. Joanna and Philip got here a few minutes ago, and they brought two of their grandchildren."

"What about Uncle Marvin? I think you said he and Arlene couldn't make it?"

"Afraid not. Grandpa and Grandma are happily ensconced down in Florida, but they send their love." Anne knew she'd be answering the same questions all day, but she didn't mind. She led Pauline inside.

Her guest stopped and stared at the vase of roses that dominated the foyer. "That must be the mystery bouquet."

"Yes." Anne darted a glance about, to be sure her parents weren't within earshot. "Mom and Dad don't know yet—about the 'mystery' part, I mean."

Pauline nodded and looked about her. "Wow! You really did it! This looks like an official library."

"It is," Anne said, smiling with pride. "The Blue Hill Library. Aunt Edie's gift to the town."

Her parents, Uncle Philip, and Aunt Joanna were just emerging from the History Room.

"Oh, Pauline's here," her dad said, coming forward to greet his cousin and give her a kiss on the cheek.

"Pauline, how wonderful." Anne's mother stepped up to embrace her. "We were just showing the others what Anne's done to the house. Why don't you join our little tour?"

"I'd love to."

Within half an hour, all of the guests had arrived. Aunt Faith and Uncle Mike brought their son and daughter-in-law. Anne's cousin Kevin and his wife, Julie, were about Anne's age. Her father seemed very happy to have both his sisters, Faith and Joanna, in the same room with him.

Last to drive in was Heather Dailey, with her husband, Jack. They had brought along a granddaughter, Emily, who carried a baby doll in her arms. Liddie quickly accepted the little girl and invited her to join her and Aria in playing with her dolls in the family living room.

"Thank you so much for making the long drive," Anne said to Heather and Jack.

"It wasn't that bad," Jack said.

Heather smiled and held up a small photo album. "I brought pictures of my parents and grandparents, so everyone can see what our part of the clan looks like."

"Wonderful," Anne said. "My dad remembers Aunt Olivia and Uncle Henry, but I sure don't."

When all of the adults were gathered in the backyard and the introductions had been made and nametags distributed, Anne called all the children down for refreshments. Ben and Jacob were talking animatedly about race car engines, but they stopped long enough to listen as Anne's father asked a blessing on the refreshments.

Liddie was determined to help serve, so Anne gave her and Emily small paper plates and napkins to hand out, and she let Aria follow them with a tray of cut vegetables. The rest of the food she left spread out on the picnic table, and she encouraged the guests to help themselves.

An hour of talk followed, about every aspect of the Summers family's heritage and activities. Anne jotted some notes so that she would be able to remember the names of Heather's siblings and children, and Madeline's children and grandchildren. The cousins and aunts helped her fill in several blanks on the large family tree chart.

Finally Madeline said to Anne, "Thank you so much for doing this. I wish your grandparents could have been here, but this has been terrific."

Anne nodded. "You're welcome. Actually, Dad talked to them last night, and they're expecting to Skype with us at three." She glanced at her watch. "That's only a few minutes away! I'd better set up the laptop."

Her father helped her make sure everything was ready, and Anne let him make the connection with his parents.

"Hey, you're looking good," Grandpa Marvin Summers said with a laugh when he saw his son on his screen.

"So do you, Dad. We've got lots of folks here who want to say hi to you."

They took turns sitting down before the computer and chatting with Anne's grandparents. Anne took the last turn.

"Thanks for doing this, Gram and Grandpa," she said. "It's wonderful to talk to you."

"It's a treat to see everyone," her grandmother replied. "We miss you all. Come see us, Anne! And bring those children."

"I hope to sometime," she said.

When they had signed off and Anne had closed the connection, Pauline came to stand beside her.

"That was so nice. Definitely worth coming over for. I wish Craig and our kids had come."

"There are several people I know we all miss and wish could be here," Anne said. She thought once more of Carl. Was it time to bring out the photo of him with Aunt Edie and her cryptic travel diary? She looked toward her father. He met her gaze and raised his eyebrows. Anne nodded in reply.

She stood and walked over near the door to the house, where everyone seated around the deck could see her.

"Could I have everyone's attention, please?"

The guests all stopped talking and gazed at her.

Anne smiled. "I have a few announcements to make. First of all, I have a special gift for the person who traveled farthest for this reunion. Cousin Madeline, I believe that's you!" She picked up a small wrapped gift and carried it to Madeline.

"Oh my, how nice!" Madeline removed the wrapping paper and smiled. "One of Edie's pictures."

"Yes, it's one of her in front of this house, with the flowers in full bloom. Her friend Mildred took that." Anne was pleased that Madeline seemed touched by the gift.

"And now, I'd like to tell you about the lovely bouquet of roses in the foyer. Several of you commented on them. They arrived yesterday, and there is a story behind them. I believe it's a story that will affect us—" She broke off as the muffled sound of the doorbell ringing reached her.

"Someone's at the door," her mother said. "Shall I go?"

"I'll get it," Anne said. "It's probably Jay." She smiled at all the guests. "I've hired a photographer to take some pictures for us, and you'll each receive them in the mail or by e-mail in a few days—your preference. Excuse me just a minute, while I let him in."

She hurried inside as the guests exclaimed over Anne's thoughtfulness. Her timing hadn't turned out to be so great. She wished she had brought up Carl earlier and told the story of their search, beginning with the photo of him with Aunt Edie and ending with the bouquet's connection to the flowers in the cemetery. But now she would have to wait until after their photo session with Jay, and the afternoon would be waning.

The bell rang again as she reached the foyer, and she dashed across the hardwood floor and flung the door open.

Instead of Jay, a tall, light-haired man in his early sixties faced her. He wore gray slacks and a short-sleeved cotton shirt. He pulled off sunglasses, and Anne caught a quick breath. His resemblance to her father was uncanny. His skin was tanned, and his blue eyes gazed keenly into hers.

He smiled. "Hello. You must be Anne Gibson."

Chapter Twenty-Two

Anne caught a quick breath and her mouth fell open. "Hello...Cousin Carl?"

He laughed. "That's me."

"Oh my goodness! You *are* alive—and you're *here!* I'm so glad you came."

"I wouldn't want to spoil your party."

"I don't think you need to worry about that." She couldn't hold back a grin. "Forgive me for staring. You're so obviously a Summers." A small laugh bubbled out unbidden and she put a hand to her mouth. "You've certainly come to the right place."

He held out his hand, and Anne clasped it. "I'm in time for the reunion, then?"

"Perfect timing. Everyone's in the backyard. Come on, I'll take you through."

He stepped inside, and his gaze went immediately to the vase of roses.

"They came yesterday," Anne said. "Thank you so much—they're beautiful, as you can see."

"You're welcome." He looked up and then slowly around at the foyer. "It's the same, only different."

"It's the town library now. That was Aunt Edie's wish."

"She spoke to me about it more than once. She also told me about your training, and that she'd chosen you as the best possible librarian and owner of this house."

Anne felt her face flush. "You have the advantage over me. I'm afraid she never mentioned you at all."

"She couldn't. I asked her not to. I didn't mean to cause anyone distress, but once I was 'dead,' it seemed better that I stayed that way."

"Well, there are twenty or so people in the backyard who will be very glad to see that you're alive."

"I'm ready," he said.

Anne's smile stayed on her face as she led him to the back door and out onto the deck. The joy she had felt when her parents arrived had been eclipsed by her anxiety, but that had lifted now. She felt happier than she had in weeks.

All heads turned in her direction as she stepped forward.

"Dear ones, I have a surprise for you all—a wonderful surprise."

The newcomer stepped up beside her. Anne's father shot up out of his chair.

Cousin Madeline gasped. "David!"

The newcomer smiled. "No, David was my father. I'm Carl."

Pauline rose slowly from the bench where she'd been sitting with Aunt Faith and walked toward him across the deck, staring at his face. Carl turned toward her. Stress lines wrinkled the corners of his eyes, but they gradually relaxed, and his lips curved in a smile.

"Polly!"

She hastened her steps and threw herself into his arms. Laughing and crying at the same time, she clung to him. "Carl! Carl! Why didn't you let us know?"

Anne was standing close enough to hear his quiet reply. "I'm sorry, Polly. I didn't mean to put you through a bad time or cause you grief."

Anne's father had come over, and he was the next to welcome Carl back into the family circle.

"Glad you're back." He gave his cousin a bear hug. "I expect you've got quite a story to tell."

"I know," Carl said. "I guess it's time."

"Let us introduce you to everyone first, and you can get something to eat," Anne's father said. "Then we want to know everything. That is, everything you can tell us."

While he guided Carl around the deck to meet and renew acquaintances with his family, Pauline stepped over to Anne. Tears misted her eyes.

"Thank you so much, Anne. And I'm sorry I was angry with you earlier. I didn't—" She paused for a moment and cleared her throat. "I didn't believe this could happen…I couldn't allow myself such a wild hope…and I thought it would only hurt worse to relive what happened more than forty years ago. But I was wrong. Can you forgive me?"

"Of course. But there's nothing to forgive." Anne gathered her into a warm embrace.

Pauline hugged her for a moment and then drew back, her gaze pulled once more to her brother. "How long is he here for? And where does he live?"

"I don't know. I expect he'll enlighten us."

Anne saw that her father was nearly to where Liddie was sitting with Emily and Aria. The little girl wriggled with pent-up excitement. Anne walked over quickly.

"Did you understand, Liddie? We found Cousin Carl—or rather, he found us."

"I'm so happy!" Liddie squeezed Anne tight.

"Come on, honey. I want you to meet him."

As Anne straightened, her father brought Carl closer. "And that's my granddaughter, Lydia," he said to Carl.

"I prayed for you," Liddie blurted.

Carl's eyes widened. He bent down next to her and smiled. "Thank you for doing that. I'm pleased to meet you, Lydia."

She shook his hand solemnly. "How do you do, Cousin Carl? You may call me Liddie."

He chuckled. "Thanks. It's an honor."

He moved on to meet the rest of the cousins.

A few minutes later, Carl sat on one of the new padded redwood benches with Pauline. Anne's mother made sure he had a tall glass of punch and a laden plate of food. They gave him a short time to eat some of it, and then Aunt Faith leaned forward. "Carl, we're all dying of suspense. Please tell us where you've been all these years."

"Most recently, I've been in Montana. I decided to retire there about fifteen years ago, and I love it. If any of you want to visit a remote, somewhat primitive ranch, let me know."

"I do," Jacob said, and the adults laughed.

"Come anytime, buddy," Carl said, "but you'll need a sponsor over twenty-one."

"It sounds great, Carl," Anne's father said. "I'm glad you're doing something you love. But we'd also like to know about the in-between time, if you care to tell us."

Pauline grasped Carl's wrist. "Yes, please do tell us. We thought you were dead. Why did the army tell us that if it wasn't true, and why didn't you let us know all this time?"

Carl's chin sank for a moment, then he looked up and smiled ruefully. "I was a rash and foolish young man, I'm afraid. At first it seemed like a stroke of luck. I was wounded – not all that badly, but bad enough. My leg needed skilled care, and I was flown to Germany. Once I'd been there a week or so, I realized they had me confused with someone else, and the name on my chart wasn't mine. The medical staff was quite upset when I told them, and they promised they would take care of it. Two days later, a colonel came to see me in the hospital. He talked to me for a long time. He told me the army had made a clerical error somewhere along the line and that my family had already been informed that I had been killed in action. Of course, my first impulse was to set that straight and make sure you all knew it wasn't true."

"Why didn't you?" Pauline's eyes were filled with tears. "That would have been the decent thing to do."

"Yes." Carl covered her hand with his. "I *am* sorry. But the colonel presented me with another option. He promised to clean up the mistake on my record, but he'd also taken note of my communications skills. They were opening a new division of the Signal Corps, and he asked if I would consider transferring into it.

That was a top-secret project, and he explained that this clerical error could work in my favor. I could transfer in there with nobody outside the new division knowing I was still alive. I could be a genuine 'spook' for the army—for my country."

"You mean, the army asked you not to tell your family you were alive?" Joanna asked, frowning at him. "That was cruel."

"I suppose it was. But, as I said, I was young and not the most thoughtful person at that time. I'd had a big falling out with Dad over the business. I expect you all know about that."

Pauline grimaced and nodded.

"When I left home, I honestly didn't ever want to talk to Dad again," Carl said. "I know that was wrong, and that I was a pigheaded, selfish kid. But it's what happened. When the colonel came to me with his proposition, it looked to me like a way to go on living in a new and exciting life, without the baggage from the past."

"Baggage?" Pauline said.

"Polly," he said, "you know I didn't mean you. I meant the ongoing friction between me and Dad. I always felt I couldn't please him, no matter what I did. When I worked at the store, he always criticized the way I did things, and I hated it. But when I told him I didn't want to run the business, he got mad. I felt trapped. That's why I enlisted—to get away from it."

"I admit, I wasn't exactly supportive of you at the time," Pauline said. "When you and Dad were fighting a lot, I tried to talk to him about it, but he was too emotionally tied to the store. I think I understood at least a little bit about how you felt, but I couldn't do anything about it. And you and Dad were both so angry all the time." She shuddered. "It did upset me, and I came down on Dad's side because...well, because I thought it was the right thing to do and that maybe it would sway you to try a little harder to please him. I'm sorry about that. If I'd tried harder to keep a good relationship with you before you enlisted, instead of being angry with you all the time, maybe you wouldn't have been so mad at me and contacted me. Even after Dad died." Her voice cracked.

Carl patted her arm. "I wasn't really mad at you though, Polly. I should have taken your feelings into consideration. I know Dad was grieving for Mom, and you were only trying to help. But at the time I was recovering from my wound, I felt as though no one would care if I didn't show up again. You already thought I was dead, so I wouldn't be hurting you any worse if I didn't tell you I was alive. But I see now that wasn't true."

Anne's father cleared his throat. "We all missed you, Carl. I'm sorry you let that get in the way of our knowing you all these years."

"You and Dad could have worked it out," Pauline said.

Carl sighed. "You may be right. I can see that now. And Aunt Edie told me that very thing when I ran into her accidentally in Washington."

"The picture," Anne said. Several of her guests had blank looks on their faces, so she stood and spoke to them all. "A couple of weeks ago, Liddie found a camera in one of Aunt Edie's old trunks. It's the Pentax on display in the History Room inside. It had exposed film in it, so I had it developed."

All of the guests were silent, listening to her, even the children.

"There was a man in one of the pictures with Aunt Edie," Anne continued. "Dad and other people have identified him as Carl. But the photo was taken after Carl had officially died, and his uniform wasn't right for the unit he was in originally, so we were puzzled. We've spent the last couple of weeks trying to get to the truth."

"Once she showed me that picture," Anne's father said to Carl, "we just couldn't believe you were dead. She's put a lot of hard work in on this. We even called up a long list of people named Summers, trying to get wind of you."

Carl laughed. "Sorry I made it so difficult."

Anne swung around and looked at him. "So how did you know? Obviously, somewhere along the line, you heard we were looking for you."

"Once again, the army contacted me. I've been retired a long time, but a Sergeant Potter tracked me down and told me I had a bunch of relatives who wanted to know if I was still alive. As she put it, you never got the memo." He looked around at the faces watching him so joyfully. "When she told me how hard Anne was working to find me, and that she had planned a big family reunion for today, well, I decided it was time to reappear in Blue Hill."

"I'm so glad you did," Anne said.

"We all are," Cousin Madeline added. "This is the nicest gift I've had in some time."

Anne's mother smiled. "I agree. And tomorrow is Memorial Day, so it's very fitting."

Anne whirled toward Carl. "You put the flowers on your parents' graves."

He nodded sheepishly. "About ten years ago, I decided it was time I forgave Dad and started honoring him and Mom. So every year since, I've had roses sent to the cemetery on Memorial Day."

"You didn't bring them yourself?" Anne asked, a little disappointed. She had imagined him walking stealthily among the tombstones at the crack of dawn with his arms full of flowers, looking about furtively to make sure no one saw him.

"Actually I did, on one occasion. That was about five years ago, and Polly nearly caught me in the act."

"Why didn't you show yourself to me?" Pauline cried.

Carl shrugged. "It had been so long. I thought…I guess I thought you'd be angry."

"I'm angry, all right. I'm furious that you didn't tell us!" Pauline smiled. "But I'm so glad you're here now."

"Thanks. That was the first and only time I'd been back to Blue Hill—until today."

"Did you see Aunt Edie then?" Anne asked.

He ducked his head and sheepishly smiled. "Yes, I did. We drove around town together, but I wouldn't go into any of the shops or the diner with her. I was afraid someone would recognize me. She tried to talk me into seeing Polly, but…I guess I just wasn't ready. I was afraid it would be too much of a shock. I did see a few other people I knew, but I didn't speak to them."

"Like who?" Pauline demanded.

He shrugged. "Linda, for one."

"Linda Wright?"

"Yeah. She had a couple of kids with her, and they were going into the drugstore. I could see that she had a full life now. It wouldn't have made much sense to go over and say hi, especially since most of my own family thought I was long gone."

Anne decided to tell him later about Linda's family and offer to give him her telephone number, since she had asked to be kept informed. She looked around at all her guests.

"Carl not only put the flowers in the cemetery, he sent the lovely white roses in our foyer," she said.

He turned his smile on her. "I wanted to thank you for your persistence. I thought I couldn't face an occasion like this, even after I stopped being angry at my father. But now…now I'm glad you didn't give up, and I'm glad that I came."

"We're glad too," Anne's father said. "I hope you're here for several days, at least."

"I left it open ended," Carl said. "I wasn't sure what sort of reaction I'd get. But thank you all for being so kind. I hope you'll forgive me for my actions, especially you, Polly." He turned to his sister and took her hand. "I could have told you a long time ago. After the war ended and I was no longer doing secret work—that would have been the logical time, I guess. Or after I saw Edie in Washington. I certainly should have told you five years ago, when I came here."

"Tell us about the time in Washington," Anne said, settling back into her seat. "That photo from the bicentennial is the thing that started all of this, and we want to know how it came about. Did you know Aunt Edie would be in DC?"

He shook his head. "It was purely coincidental. After our troops were out of Vietnam, I was assigned for a short time to special duty in Washington. I was in charge of a unit detailed to guard the exhibits and make sure security was tight, while allowing the people visiting them plenty of freedom. That's tricky sometimes. When I finished my duties one day, I was walking down the street, and someone called my name. I turned to see who it was and got a blast from the past. Aunt Edie at her finest! She had just come out of the DAR Constitution Hall, and she said she'd been doing some genealogy research there. But she told me that later. She was so shocked at first, I had to find a bench and have her sit down while I went and got her a cold drink. I was afraid she would faint on me!"

"Hold on a second," Anne said. "I want everyone to see the picture we're talking about." She went over to an envelope she had earlier placed on the table with the old photo albums. "Dad and I had several copies made up so that each family here could take one home. We felt it might be the last picture of you alive. We were pretty sure that it was you in 1976, but we had no proof you'd survived after that."

She took out a stack of the prints. Her mother came over and held out her hand. "Let me help you pass them out, dear."

Soon everyone was staring at the photographs and exclaiming over the good likeness of Aunt Edie and the handsome young man in uniform.

"I'd forgotten all about that," Carl said, smiling as he looked at it. "She asked a tourist to snap that for her. In all the excitement, I posed for the picture but then I asked her not to show anyone."

"I can't believe Aunt Edie kept this a secret for more than thirty years," Aunt Joanna said. "Why didn't she tell us?"

"When we met that day, my father was still living," Carl said. "I begged her not to tell him. She didn't want to give her word, but she finally did. She wanted me to reconcile with Dad, but I refused." He shook his head. "I should have listened to her."

"She was a wise woman," Uncle Philip said.

"Yes, she was. But I wasn't ready. She wrote to me after that, and we spoke on the phone a few times. She also sent me postcards, mostly of Blue Hill, but from a few other trips she took too. Several times she hinted that she still wanted me to make up with Dad. He was sick at the time, but even so, I refused. I told you I was stubborn."

"You did," Anne's father said, "but Edie was stubborn too."

Carl smiled. "Yeah, she might have won if she'd had time to keep after me about it. But Dad died in early 1977, and after that, it was too late."

"You called about your father's funeral, didn't you?" Anne asked.

Carl stared at her. "I phoned the pastor listed as officiating at the service. How did you know?"

"I visited Reverend Daniel, and he told me he got an anonymous call. A man was asking about the time of the service."

"It was me. I was stationed in Libya at the time, and Aunt Edie sent me a telegram. I was deployed when it came in. I didn't talk to her directly, but I did get the message that my father had died. I wondered if I could possibly get back here in time. I tried to phone Aunt Edie, but I couldn't get through to her. Finally I called the pastor. It seemed impossible to make the service, so I dashed off a message to Edie and let it go. I told myself it wouldn't have mattered, anyway."

"I think it would have," Anne's father said. "I don't want to make you feel guilty or anything, Carl, but your dad was pretty torn up after he heard you were dead. It would have meant a lot to all of us if you had come forward at that time. But that's water under the bridge—you're here now, and that's what matters."

"Thanks, Dale."

"There are other people you'll want to touch base with," Anne said. "Randy Turner, for one."

"Old Randy?" Carl laughed. "I'd get a kick out of seeing him."

"He'd love to see you too," Anne said. "He lives in Deshler. In fact, he was here yesterday."

"Where are you staying?" Cousin Madeline asked.

"I don't know yet," Carl said.

"I'm sure the inn, where I'm staying, can find a room for you." Madeline pulled her phone from her pocket. "In fact, I'll call right now and book it for you if you want."

Carl hesitated only a second. "Thanks. I think I'd like that."

Anne's mind raced with plans for the next few days, places to show Carl, and people she wanted him to reconnect with.

She turned to her parents. "We'll have to call Grandpa and Grandma again this evening and tell them the good news."

"Maybe Carl can talk to them this time," her mother said. "What a joy that would bring them."

"Absolutely," her father said. "They'll be so sorry they missed this."

Carl came over to stand beside them. "Polly has agreed to try to get Craig to fly to Montana later this summer to visit me. I wish you two would consider doing the same. Anne, you're welcome too."

"I couldn't leave the library for long," Anne said, "but thank you. Maybe next year. But, Mom and Dad, you two should go."

"I'd love to," Anne's mother said. "Do you have horses?"

"I do—and a big old hound dog. I've got a neighbor looking after things while I'm away."

"It sounds great," Anne's dad said. "We'll have to see when we can arrange it. My parents live near us, but they're in a senior citizens' home. They have the care they need, but we won't want to take another extensive trip for a few months."

"Your folks are still living?" Carl's face lit. "Uncle Marvin and Aunt Arlene were two of my favorite people—in my old life, that is."

"You should fly down and visit us all in Florida," Anne's mother said. "But do it soon."

"I just might," Carl said.

"Did the army require you to cut off contact with your family?" Anne asked. That aspect still bothered her, as family was extremely important to her.

"They didn't demand it at first, when I changed units, but they let me understand how expedient it would be. And once I got into intelligence, it was pretty much required that I didn't have outside contacts in the civilian world."

"That's a hard life." Anne's mother's brow wrinkled as she studied Carl's face. "Are you all right?"

"I'm fine," he said. "I experienced some tight spots, but I'm doing okay."

"You don't have a family of your own," Anne's father said, though it was a question.

"No. It seemed foolish to even think about it for a good twenty years. And then, when I stepped back a little and started thinking about retiring, I realized I didn't know anyone anymore. Not outside the military intel community." Carl smiled suddenly. "There's a nice woman in Montana though. She's a widow, and she's got a small ranch a few miles from mine. Her husband died a couple of years ago, but she's stayed on the place, and she's making a go of it. I ride over once in a while to see if she needs any help."

"Sounds like a friendship," Anne said.

Carl nodded. "For now, that's it. But I like her. You never know what the future will bring, do you?"

Anne's father chuckled. "Better not wait too long. We're not getting any younger, in case you haven't noticed."

Pauline came over to join them and slipped her hand through the crook of her brother's arm. "Carl, I wondered if you might come over to our place when you leave here. Craig and I could come and get you in a few days."

"That sounds nice, but I was just telling Dale and Charlene, I can't leave my place for too long. The man tending my stock would get tired of it. Couldn't you get Craig to run over here and stay at the inn for a night or two?"

"I don't know. I can ask him," Pauline said a bit doubtfully. "He does have tomorrow off, for Memorial Day."

"Get him to come," Anne said. "You can all hang out here tomorrow if you want. The library is closed for the holiday."

"I'll call Craig," Pauline said.

Anne's mother touched Pauline's sleeve. "If he can't come, maybe you could stay anyway. Anne and I could lend you some overnight things."

"Let me go inside where it's quiet and give him a ring." Pauline looked up at Carl for a moment, her eyes shining. "Are you sure you want me to?"

"Of course! I'd love to meet my brother-in-law. I've been family starved for the last forty years or so. Get him over here!"

Pauline laughed and hurried in through the back door.

"I hope it works out," Carl said. "I have felt some guilt whenever I thought of Polly. I found her on Facebook, so I knew she was all right and that she had a nice family."

"You're on Facebook?" Anne asked, eyeing him sharply. "That's one of the first places I looked for you."

Carl smiled and gave a little shrug. "I'm afraid I was so used to living covertly that I set my security settings ultra-tight so people couldn't search for me by name and find me. But federal intel agencies have used social media since their infancy. It was my one connection with the family, aside from Aunt Edie—of course, but it's all been one sided. I really don't spend all that much time on the computer, now that I have the ranch."

"You're probably better off in the saddle," Anne's father said.

"I intend to stay fit as long as possible. I don't bust broncos or anything like that, but I do enjoy riding on a well-mannered horse."

The sound of the doorbell echoed through the walls of the old house.

"Now, *that* is probably Jay," Anne said, looking at her watch.

"Let me show him in," her mother said. "You can alert people, so they'll be ready for some group pictures. I want a photo of this whole gang together. They might want some smaller groupings as well."

"I know I'd like a nice shot of me and Pauline," Carl said.

"Oh, are we doing pictures now?" Aunt Faith called. "Let me go get my camera. I want to get some too."

An hour and a half later, when all of the pictures were taken and Carl had spent a few minutes with each of the adults in the group, the guests began to gather their dishes and children and say good-bye.

Anne went out onto the front steps to see them off. Liddie came tearing around the corner of the house and charged up the steps, her skirt flying, to stand beside Anne.

"Good-bye, Aria! Good-bye, Emily!" Liddie shouted, waving frantically.

The two girls waved to her and got into their grandparents' vehicles.

"Did you have a good time with the girls?" Anne asked.

Liddie nodded. "I like having cousins."

"Me too." Anne smiled and gave Liddie a little hug.

Madeline, Carl, Pauline, and Anne's parents came out of the house.

"Carl and Pauline and I are going over to the inn to get them settled," Madeline said.

"Craig is going to drive over in the morning," Pauline told her. "He said he was too tired to come tonight, but he wants to meet my long-lost brother."

Carl gave her shoulders a squeeze. "I'm glad you're staying."

"These three are coming back here later, so we can have dinner together," Anne's mother said.

"Are you sure you don't want us to help you clean up?" Pauline asked.

"It's nearly all done," her mom said. "Dale will take out the trash bags, and Anne and I will put away a few things. There's not much to do, really."

Anne knew her mother was minimizing the work so that Pauline and Carl could get away guilt free, but that was all right. It wouldn't take too long for them to put away the deck chairs, photo albums, and other things in the backyard.

As the last of the guests drove away, Ben came out the door.

"Mom, can I go get Hershey now?"

"Let's help Grandpa put away the chairs and folding tables first. Then you can go."

"Mommy," Liddie said, looking up at her with wide blue eyes, "I think the best thing about the party was the wildflowers, don't you? Well, and the people."

Anne smiled. "The flowers are beautiful, but I do think the best part was being with the people I love most in the world."

"Like Cousin Carl?" Liddie asked.

"Yes, like him, and Grandpa and Grandma—but especially you and Ben."

About the Author

Emily Thomas is the pen name for a team of writers who have come together to creat the series Secrets of the Blue Hill Library. *Gone in a Flash* was written by Susan Page Davis. Susan is the author of more than forty novels in the romance, mystery, suspense, and historical romance genres. A Maine native, she now lives in western Kentucky. The move has taken some getting used to. She swapped hurricanes for tornado warnings and mosquitoes for poisonous snakes. Overall, she enjoys the milder winters and being closer to her grandchildren. Susan is a past winner of the Carol Award, the Will Rogers Medallion for Western Fiction, and the Inspirational Readers' Choice Award. Visit her Web site at susanpagedavis.com.

A Conversation with the Author

Q. *Describe your writing process.*

A. For a Secrets of Blue Hill Library book, it all starts with the idea that my wonderful editors come up with. From there, I write an outline to fill in the details of the story. At the same time, I create a timeline to help me keep the days and events in the story straight. Once the outline is approved, I'm off and writing in earnest. I often go back and revise as I write. When the rough draft is complete, I go over it several times, looking for errors and ways to make the book better. With this series, it's been enjoyable at every step.

Q. *What are the challenges of collaborating with other authors on a series? How does it compare to writing a stand-alone novel?*

A. There's less pressure for deadlines, since my books are spaced several months apart. It is sometimes hard to know that what I've written agrees with what authors of previous books have done. We have several people helping us make sure we get it right, and a series guide listing all of the previously introduced characters, their descriptions, and other important facts about them. That helps a lot!

Q. *Name the top three entries/things on your bucket list, and why did you choose them?*

A. One of my daughters lives in England, and I want to get over there to visit soon. She's been able to visit home, but we have not been able to go there. I would also like to spend more time with my grandchildren on an individual basis. I never get enough of them! And I've always wanted to see some of continental Europe, especially sites of medieval history interest.

Q. *What is the most memorable photograph you have on your wall?*

A. It's one my grandfather took from the days before they had snowplow trucks. It shows three pairs of draft horses hitched to a giant roller, packing down the snow in the road in front of my great-grandfather's house, so they could drive to town in a sleigh.

Q. *Which scene in this story was your favorite to write? Which was the most challenging for you?*

A. The reunion at the end was the hardest, because it had so many people in it. I had to create most of those people and come up with names too. The phone book can come in handy at times like that. I liked best the scenes where Anne and her dad discover various things.

Recipes from the Library Guild

Summers Family Reunion Ginger Chews

½ cup butter, softened
½ cup shortening
1¼ cup light brown sugar
½ cup molasses
1 teaspoon vanilla
1 egg
2½ cups flour
½ teaspoon salt
2 teaspoons ginger
1 teaspoon cinnamon
½ teaspoon cloves
1 teaspoon baking soda
1 cup white-chocolate chips

Cream first six ingredients together until fluffy. In a separate bowl, sift dry ingredients together. Fold into creamed mixture until blended.

Shape into one-inch balls. Roll in sugar (equal parts brown and white). Bake at 350 degrees for ten minutes.

Let sit on baking sheet for a minute or two before moving to cooling racks. Melt white-chocolate chips and drizzle over cookies when they are cooled. Makes three or four dozen cookies, depending on size.

From the Guideposts Archives

"The Big Taco Reunion" by Karen Hessen originally appeared in Guideposts *magazine.*

I was preschool age when my older sister, Amy, and I first followed Mother to the kitchen, huddling close while she made her specialty—tacos. Instead of browning the meat first, she'd use her hands to spread some over each tortilla. Then she'd fry each one meat-side up, fold it in half, and fry it again on each side.

Nearly all of our extended family lived in the same county, and there was no better way to celebrate birthdays and special occasions than over Mother's tacos. One of my cousins, Lee, liked them as much as I did. He and I really bonded over the years. Actually, those family meals kept all of us—cousins, aunts and uncles—connected. For a time, at least.

We kids grew up and left San Diego—I moved to Oregon. Amy moved to Oregon too, but several hours away, and Lee to northern California. We stopped having those big family get-togethers. You can probably guess what became a staple on our menu when my husband, Douglas, and I married. Tacos, Mother's way. "These are as tasty as your mother's," Douglas said. But to me, nothing could compare to hers.

Through the years, it wasn't just physical distance that separated Amy and me. I'm not sure how it started, but we argued over everything. Those misunderstandings got between me and family members who were close with Amy—even Lee. "You're sisters; why can't you forgive each other?" Mother would say. "And you're not talking to your cousins either?" I know our estrangement hurt her. Truth be told, I felt like I was letting God down too. Lord, I prayed, help me make things right with my family. I daydreamed about somehow getting together a family reunion and sharing one of Mother's taco dinners, just like old times. But I didn't get a chance before Mother died.

My grief was compounded by guilt. Why hadn't I tried harder to mend fences with my sister and cousins? I could have given Mother the joy of one last family reunion! Now that wouldn't happen. Still, slowly, Amy and I reached out to each other. Life was too fleeting, we agreed, for spats. Time for me to patch things up with the rest of my family.

The first person I needed to see was Lee. I called him. Our conversation was awkward, but he said he was up for company. Douglas and I drove to his home in California. "I'm sorry we drifted apart," I said, hugging Lee. Soon it was like we were kids again. We talked all afternoon.

"I'm heading over to my son's for dinner. Why don't you join me?" Lee said. I hadn't seen Matt since he was three. Matt's wife led us into their kitchen. I couldn't believe it. There were tacos lined up on the counter, waiting to be fried. Not just any tacos. The meat was flattened on each tortilla and spread out to the edges. These were Mother's tacos!

"How did you learn to make tacos this way?" I asked Matt.

"I just know that's the way tacos are made in our family," he said. Our family. Those words never meant more to me. I knew Mother would be proud. It was as if we'd had our family reunion after all.

Read on for a sneak peek of another exciting book
in *Secrets of the Blue Hill Library*!

All Sewn Up

Anne Gibson lit a fire in the Nonfiction Room fireplace to take the chill off the room. She hated starting up the furnace to heat the large Victorian home and library so early in the fall, but she might have to if the cold weather persisted. As she looked up, she pushed her large-framed glasses back up to the bridge of her nose. A glance at the clock told her she had a few minutes before the members of the Biography Club arrived for their meeting.

The fire caught in several spots, then erupted in a *poof* of flame. She closed the screen as her son's chocolate Labrador retriever began to bark from the back hall, a signal that her children were home from school. She moved to the hallway where she could see Wendy Pyle's car through the front door.

Anne watched Ben and Liddie climb out of Wendy's car and run toward the back staircase that led to their personal quarters. Where was Liddie's coat? She'd left it either in Wendy's car or at the school, which would mean the entire weekend without it, and the weather reports predicted a week of unseasonably low temperatures. Anne reached the front door in time to see Wendy wave as she pulled away.

Anne directed a patron to the Nonfiction Room, then looked in on the other rooms on her way up to their living quarters. A man sat reading in one corner of the History Room. On the second floor, a young mother browsed the shelves with her preschooler in the Children's Room, and Remi, one of her part-time assistants, was shelving returned books in the Fiction Room. Satisfied that everything was under control, Anne went to the back stairs and sprinted up the staircase to the third floor.

"Ben? Liddie?" She knocked on their bedroom doors. Both doors opened.

"Hi, Mommy! Tomorrow's Saturday, so I get to play all today!" Liddie gave her mother a hug. Anne leaned over and kissed her. Liddie loved school, but she also loved unfettered time to play with her dolls.

"Hey, Mom. Can I go outside and play? Please?" Ben asked. Hershey sat beside him, wagging his tail, looking up at her with a me-too expression.

"May I," Anne corrected with a smile. "Do you have homework?"

"A little, but can I do it later? Please?"

"All right, after you change you can go out. But come in if it starts raining. Do you want a snack?"

"Later, thanks." Ben shut his door.

"Mommy, can I have a snack?" Liddie said.

"Sure. Liddie, where is your coat? Did you leave it in Mrs. Pyle's car?"

"No, Mommy." Liddie shook her head. "I gave it to a girl at school. It was cold outside on the playground and she didn't have a coat or sweater or anything. I felt sorry for her. Besides, I had my sweater, so I wasn't cold."

"Did she forget her coat, honey? Is she going to bring it back to you on Monday?"

Liddie shook her head again, sending her light brown hair swinging over her shoulders. "She didn't have one."

"Oh. I see. Well, that was very nice of you, honey." *Except now you don't have a coat either.* "Let's get that snack."

As they went downstairs to their personal kitchen at the back of the second floor, Anne considered what to say to Liddie. Nothing came to mind. Her five-year-old daughter had a soft heart and wanted to help everyone. She tried to encourage that, but Liddie also needed to learn the value of things. How could Anne get that message across without discouraging Liddie's compassion?

Oh, Eric, what do I say? How she missed her husband. And never more than when she needed wisdom to guide their children. Eric was one of the most compassionate people she knew. And one of the wisest. What would he tell their little girl? Anne would have to replace Liddie's coat, and soon. Winter was coming on faster than usual. Anne sighed as she got out the hot chocolate mix. Liddie watched as she put on a kettle of water to heat and got out two mugs and the graham crackers. September seemed too early to switch from cold milk to hot chocolate.

"Mommy, may I have marshmallows? Please?"

"Sure, sweetie." Anne added the cocoa then stirred in the hot water, adding mini-marshmallows to Liddie's cup. She sat across from her daughter and looked into her big brown eyes that reminded her so much of Eric. "Now tell me about your day. How was school?"

Liddie took a bite of graham cracker and washed it down with the cocoa, leaving a chocolate-marshmallow mustache on her upper lip. She licked it off. "Good." As she told about her day, Liddie's legs swung back and forth under the table. She never stayed still for long.

"I'm going to play in my room now," Liddie announced, wiping her mouth on a napkin and getting up from the table.

"All right. I'll be downstairs for a little while." Anne felt relief that her daughter had chosen to stay inside.

Liddie started toward her room, then darted back to give Anne a hug. "Thank you for the hot chocolate." Anne smiled as she made her way downstairs to the library.

* * *

The wind howled all night, making the Queen Anne Victorian house creak and groan eerily, which sent Liddie and Ben to Anne's bedroom, seeking comfort. It hadn't rained, but the wind whistled through the trees and howled around the eaves, keeping them all awake. At midnight they went to the kitchen, and Anne warmed milk and got out vanilla wafers, which they dipped into the milk.

After the warm snack, they'd all settled down and they'd been able to sleep through the rest of the night, but Anne felt bleary-eyed in the morning. The hardwood floor chilled her bare feet as she got out of bed. She would have to use the library fireplaces this morning and see if that warmed the rooms enough to delay using the furnace. Thankfully, Alex and the boys were gathering wood today. She hoped they got enough for the season. Starting this early, it could be a long, cold winter.

Alex Ochs and his nephew, Ryan, came by after breakfast to pick up Ben for their woodcutting expedition.

"Be careful and do as Alex says," Anne told Ben.

"I will, Mom."

"He'll be fine," Alex said, accepting a cup of coffee while the boys went to Ben's room to get his boots and some extra clothes, just in case he got muddy. Alex had on jeans, a plaid flannel shirt, work boots, and a stocking hat. With a day's growth of beard, he looked rugged, like a logger. He smiled at her and his blue eyes sparkled. "I'll take good care of the boys, Anne. Don't worry."

* * *

On Sunday morning, Anne bundled Liddie up in several layers against the cold, and the family headed out to church. As Anne pulled into the church parking lot, she noticed a flash of color that she recognized. Liddie's coat. The young girl wearing it walked toward the church entrance with her mother, who wore a tattered flannel shirt for warmth. The fuzzy white kittens on the girl's pink jacket were confirmation that the girl had on the coat Anne had bought for Liddie from a department store catalog. In that moment, Anne's heart swelled with pride and gratitude for her daughter's tender heart.

They found their favorite pew and sat down just as the organ played the introduction to one of Anne's favorite hymns. "Great is Thy faithfulness, Lord unto me!" the congregation sang with great enthusiasm. Next to Anne, Liddie held onto one side of the hymnal, although she couldn't read most of the words. The sunlight shining through the stained-glass windows cast a rainbow glow over them like a sweet reminder of God's presence.

"Please be seated," Reverend Tom said, then called the children up front for the weekly children's sermon. Ben and Liddie went to sit on the steps going up to the platform with the other children. Reverend Tom sat on the top step and told them that the hymn they just sang was about God's compassion that never fails. He asked them what *compassion* meant. Several children spoke up with answers about being nice to other people. Ben suggested it meant feeling sorry for people.

Reverend Tom explained that compassion included recognizing people's suffering and helping them. He told a story about a school bully who picked on one small, shy boy. The boy had a new video game, and the bully stopped him on the way home from school and demanded his video game. When the boy resisted, the bully punched him in the nose, making it bleed, then he took the boy's backpack with the game and turned to the other kids and laughed, daring them to try to stop him. The other kids ran off, except for a small boy named Sammy, who went to help the injured boy. He took him to his house and his mother helped stop the nosebleed and cleaned off the blood. She gave the boys milk and cookies, and then took the injured boy home. "Why did the other kids run away?" Reverend Tom asked, looking at the children.

"Because they were afraid," a child answered.

"Yes, but Sammy showed compassion when he stopped to help, even though it could have caused him trouble. Just like the story Jesus tells about the Good Samaritan in the Bible. The

Samaritan, who helped a stranger, was a true neighbor to that man because he showed mercy and kindness. Jesus said, 'Go and do likewise.'"

Anne couldn't help thinking about Liddie's kindness to the little girl she had just seen coming to church. She glanced around the room and spotted the fuzzy pink coat in the back corner. She heard Reverend Tom challenge the children to look for ways to help others.

"For instance," he said. "We have a donation box in the foyer for winter coats and other warm clothing. Have you seen it? Look on your way out this morning. I believe the new stove in the church kitchen came in it. Some of our ladies covered it in bright red, yellow, and blue striped wallpaper. It's beautiful. But it's empty. With winter arriving early, it is sadly in need of warm items."

He invited the children to go downstairs for Junior Church. Liddie retrieved the new coat that they'd bought the day before after the library closed, and then she followed her brother and Ryan and the other children downstairs.

On the way home, Liddie squirmed in her car seat. "I'm going to look through my room for things I can give to the poor," she announced.

"We can all do that," Anne said. "But, remember, we gave away lots of things you'd outgrown when we moved from New York, so we may not find a lot."

"I want to give too, but I can't think of anything I have that I don't need," Ben said, looking thoughtful.

"I'll help you look," Anne said. "Right after lunch."

* * *

Anne stared at the stack of clothing on the kitchen table, amazed at how much they'd accumulated. Sweaters and warm pants the children had already outgrown since last season. Clothing pieces she hadn't worn in several years. Ben had found an extra jacket and gloves. Even considering the clothes they'd given away before their move, they still had more than they needed.

"I'm going to ask my friends for clothes too," Liddie said, her eyes shining "I'm going to fill up the box at church all by myself! Mommy, can we go shopping and buy some more coats?"

"Sweetheart, having me buy coats for the clothing box wouldn't be the same as you collecting coats to give. Reverend Tom didn't mean we have to go out and buy a lot of clothing, although we will watch for sales and pick up a few things. I imagine some of our friends have gently used clothing they can donate if you ask them. And what about Mrs. Farley? You could call her and ask."

"Oh." Liddie's animated expression disappeared. She looked up at her mother. "But I want to fill the box by myself."

"You both helped children in New York when we donated your outgrown and extra clothing before we moved."

"Oh yeah. I forgot about that!" Ben said, smiling.

"That's good, isn't it, Mommy?" Liddie asked, perking up.

"Yes, sweetheart. It's very good. But it means we don't have that many extra coats left. This pile is it. When you involve other people, it gives them a chance to be generous, and you can collect a lot more."

"I'm going to ask my friends at school," Liddie declared.

"Now you're getting the idea," Ben said.

Just then, Anne's cell phone rang. It was Wendy.

"Hi."

"Hey, Anne, I have a great idea."

Anne wasn't sure whether to smile or grimace. Wendy did have great ideas with enthusiasm to match, but her great ideas often meant extra work for Anne. "What's that?"

"Reverend Tom said we need to fill the clothing box, right? I thought about crocheting scarves, but it would take time to make enough to help. Then I thought, what if we held a crochet class at the library and taught everyone how to make a scarf, and we donated them to the box. It would teach people a skill, give the library an activity, and fill the box, all at the same time. What do you think?"

"I…think I like it. Aunt Edie loved to crochet and knit and she left lots of supplies. We can even use her yarn."

"Super! Then we don't have to buy any. I can come over tomorrow so we can go through it. We can put up signs and flyers and start next week."

"So soon?"

"It's already getting cold. The sooner, the better, I say."

"I suppose you're right." Anne could barely think as fast as Wendy could act. At the moment, though, she couldn't think of any reason not to start right away. The clothing box needed the warm items.

After she ended the call, Anne thought about all the supplies and old clothing of Aunt Edie's in the attic. She might not have time to go through it tomorrow with the library open, but she could look now.

"I'm going to the attic to look for yarn. Anyone want to come with me?" she asked Ben and Liddie.

"Cool!" Ben yelped. "I love going up there," Ben said.

"Not me. It's dark." Liddie shook her head.

"You can stay down here," Anne said.

Liddie frowned. "All by myself?" Her voice quavered. "I guess I'll come with you."

"All right. Put on your jackets. It'll be chilly up there."

After they bundled up, Anne unlocked the attic door and turned on the light. The light that came through the small windows was muted and gray, and the overhead bulb barely illuminated the large room, filled with Aunt Edie's possessions and Anne's extra furniture and belongings.

"Let's look for yarn first. Then we'll see if we can find any coats or sweaters in Aunt Edie's boxes. I put the crochet and knitting supplies back in the corner." She led the way along aisles between stacks of boxes and unused furniture. She intended to sort and catalogue the attic's contents, but there hadn't been time. Taking care of the library and the children filled her days.

They reached the back corner. Anne found the stack of clear plastic bins. "Here they are." She opened the top one.

"Wow, look at all that yarn," Liddie said. "Can I have some for Cleopatra? Maybe I can make something."

"Sure, honey." Cleopatra was Liddie favorite doll. Anne pulled out a thick pink yarn. There was only one skein. "How about this one?"

"Oh yes. She'll love it!" Liddie took it and held it against her face to feel its softness.

Anne pulled out several knitting and crochet pattern books. "Ben, would you hold these? Wendy might want them."

"Okay."

Anne handed him the stack, then looked through the contents of the bin. "This has a lot of sewing supplies." She sorted the contents of the second bin, leaving yarn and crochet hooks in it. Anne removed the lid on the last bin. *Eureka!* Skeins of yarn in every possible color filled the container.

"Wow," Ben said. "I bet that could make lots of sweaters."

"Wendy is going to teach a class on how to make winter scarves. You can take the class if you'd like. Aunt Edie loved to make things to give away. She'd be pleased that we're using her yarn for scarves."

"Isn't that a girl thing?" he asked.

"Not necessarily. Some men like to knit and crochet."

The doubtful look on his face made Anne chuckle.

"I want to make a scarf," Liddie said. "Can I take the class, Mommy?"

"Yes, dear. I'd like to take it too."

She took out several multicolored skeins. Below them, she found fine yarn suitable for babies. "Maybe we can do some other winter project too, later on. There's plenty of yarn."

Anne pulled out a shiny trifold brochure. She started to set it aside, but it felt thick and had a staple in the top. Curious, she held it up. It showed a picture of a sewing machine with the word *Bernina* across the top. Anne opened the brochure. Inside, a receipt was stapled to the top. She held it up to the light so she could read it.

"What's that?" Ben asked.

"It's a receipt for…" Anne gasped. "It looks like twenty-four sewing machines. It must be a mistake."

"Wow. That's a lot of sewing machines," Ben said.

"Yes, it is. It has Aunt Edie's name on it."

"There's a sewing machine in the craft room," Liddie pointed out.

"That belonged to Aunt Edie. But this can't be right. Aunt Edie only had one sewing machine, and it isn't a Bernina."

A Note from the Editors

We hope you enjoy Secrets of the Blue Hill Library, created by the Books and Inspirational Media Division of Guideposts, a nonprofit organization that touches millions of lives every day through products and services that inspire, encourage, help you grow in your faith, and celebrate God's love in every aspect of your daily life.

Thank you for making a difference with your purchase of this book, which helps fund our many outreach programs to military personnel, prisons, hospitals, nursing homes, and educational institutions. To learn more, visit GuidepostsFoundation.org.

We also maintain many useful and uplifting online resources. Visit Guideposts.org to read true stories of hope and inspiration, access OurPrayer network, sign up for free newsletters, download free e-books, join our Facebook community, and follow our stimulating blogs.

To learn about other Guideposts publications, including the best-selling devotional *Daily Guideposts*, go to ShopGuideposts.org, call (800) 932-2145, or write to Guideposts, PO Box 5815, Harlan, Iowa 51593.